A DC KENDRA MARCH CRIME THRILLER

JUSTICE

Book 6 of the 'Summary Justice' series

Theo Harris

ALEMAR PUBLICATIONS

Justice
Book 6 of the 'Summary Justice' series

ISBN: 979-8-865525-20-2 paperback

Second Edition, © 2024

PRAISE FOR THEO HARRIS

'Couldn't put the book down. Loved it.'

'The pacing of the book was impeccable, with each chapter leaving me hungry for more.'

'WOW! I was not expecting much but totally surprised.'

'One of my favourite reads of the year, waiting for the rest of the series!'

'Really gripping storytelling that is clearly well researched and engaging.'

Cool gritty romp... Excellent lead character and plot - really enjoyed the story.'

Before AN EYE FROM AN EYE...
There was

TRIAL RUN

An exclusive Prequel to the **'Summary Justice'** series, free to anyone who subscribes to the Theo Harris monthly newsletter.

Find out what brought the team together and the reasons behind what they do... and why.

Go to **theoharris.co.uk**
or join at:
https://dl.bookfunnel.com/7oh5ceuxyw

ALEMAR
PUBLICATIONS

Also by Theo Harris

DC Kendra March - 'Summary Justice' series

Book 1 - An Eye for an Eye

Book 2 - Fagin's Folly

Book 3 - Road Trip

Book 4 - London's Burning

Book 5 - Nothing to Lose

Book 6 - Justice

Book 7 - Born to Kill

Boxset 1 - Books 1 to 3

Boxset 2 - Books 4 to 6

Think you've gotten away with it? Think again!

PROLOGUE

Thirty years ago, London

'Goodnight, princess.' Amy March leaned down into the cot and kissed her baby on the cheek.

She stroked Kendra's warm face and pulled the woollen blanket over her, leaving just her chubby face exposed. The baby yawned and smiled, struggling to keep her eyes open as her mother looked down at her.

'I can't believe you're already nine months old, you'll be running around in no time,' Amy said, imagining her daughter as a tiny toddler, running around at full speed and wreaking havoc.

Talking to the baby always made her settle faster, and tonight was no exception.

Amy smiled as the baby finally stopped resisting and closed her eyes, continuing to smile ever so slightly as she slept. Amy stroked her little face once more and then left the small room, turning the light off on the way out and keeping the door slightly ajar.

Thank God for giving me a baby who loves to sleep through the night, she thought as she went downstairs.

In the kitchen, she made herself a cup of chamomile tea, a nightly ritual that helped her rest well during the night, before relaxing on the sofa in the lounge. The three-bedroomed end-terrace was less than ten years old and had been theirs for just twelve months. The minute she and Trevor had stepped foot inside to view it, Amy had smiled and turned to her beloved husband, nodding enthusiastically.

'This is the one, love,' she had whispered.

'Then this one it shall be,' he had replied, kissing her gently on the lips and holding her hands against her slightly swollen tummy.

Their offer had been accepted and they'd moved in ten weeks later. Trevor, a soldier in the British Army, worked tirelessly during the few occasions he was on leave, making sure that all the work was done in time for the baby's arrival. The house was ready with a week to spare, so when they arrived back from the hospital with baby Kendra it was a fresh new home for them, one to enjoy and cherish for many years to come.

Amy smiled at the memory, taking a sip of her tea as she thought fondly of her husband. Their attraction had been instantaneous; they'd met at an outdoor concert. He was with a group of squaddie friends and she with her cousin Tracey. They'd started dating and had known within weeks that they wanted to be together. It was a whirlwind, intensely romantic courtship, leading to disapproval from her father, and suggested restraint from Trevor's parents. They neither listened nor cared.

Only one thing bothered her, and that was the amount of

time Trevor was spending away from home, and the worrying effect it had been having on him. He rarely spoke about his work, and she knew better than to ask too many questions. The last few times they had spoken had been a little strange; tense, almost, as if something were playing on his mind. Amy hoped that whatever it was that was distracting him so much would pass and they could go away for a much-needed holiday. She closed her eyes and dozed off, dreaming of a sandy beach and imagining the sound of waves.

Her dream then changed from the sandy beach to a darker moment from a week earlier when she had heard someone trying to get into the house. She had quietly taken the baby and hidden in the loft, but only after calling the police and a nearby friend. She wanted someone, whoever it may be, to come quickly. The police sirens had alerted the supposed intruders and they had fled in a car. Luckily, the friend, Charlie, had arrived in time to see the car speeding away. He had taken the registration number down and given it to the police. Unfortunately, the number had either been written down incorrectly or was a fake plate, so it wasn't traceable. The police did not investigate further, and as there was no sign of attempted or forced entry, the matter was quickly closed. The police told Amy and Charlie that they suspected a group of local teenagers whose MO was to post fireworks through people's letterboxes or play other pranks they found amusing.

It was the sound of the squeaky back door opening, the door from the kitchen to the garden, that woke her with a start. As she sat up and turned towards the sound, her dreams of the perfect holiday were shattered by the appearance of two intruders, one male and one female, who rushed her before she could do anything. The former, a tall but stockily built black man dressed in jeans and an unusually bright orange t-shirt, grabbed her by one of the arms. The latter, a tall, athletic white woman with dark-brown wavy hair and striking blue eyes, wearing a blue vest and brown shorts, grabbed the other.

'Let go!' Amy shouted, trying to wrestle free. Her immediate concern was for her sleeping baby; she prayed Kendra would do her usual thing and sleep through everything.

'She's a feisty one,' the woman said with a laugh.

'Yes, she is. Her man is gonna be happy that we found her safe and well, eh?' The man's gruff West Indian accent was a stark contrast to the woman's American tones. For a split second, Amy thought them an odd couple to be here in northeast London.

'Please... take whatever you want, just leave me alone,' she pleaded.

'Now why would we do that, pretty lady? We want to take you to your man, make sure he knows you're safe and well with us,' the man replied.

'My man? What are you talking about?' she said, 'my husband is away working.'

'You mean Tony? No, missy, he's been with us all this time. He's been a bad boy, you know, lots and lots of lies, so we found out who he really is and where he really lives and now, here we are!' He laughed.

'Tony? No, no, my partner's name isn't Tony, it's Trevor,' she pleaded again, praying they'd made a mistake.

'We know, dear, we know,' the woman said, smiling malevolently.

'Time to go,' the man said, pulling her towards the door.

'No!' Amy cried, wrenching her arm free from the

woman. She lashed out and caught the man across the face with her fingernails, slashing the skin and drawing blood.

He held onto her arm with a vice-like grip and used his free hand to wipe the blood from his cheek. His eyes turned cold and angry, and as swift as a snake striking its victim, he backhanded her across the cheek.

Amy barely held onto consciousness as the vicious blow forced her back into the arms of the woman, who grabbed her again, this time holding on tighter.

'Do that again, bitch, and he'll rip your head off,' she hissed.

They dragged her from the lounge to the adjoining kitchen and dining area and out of the back door that led to the garden. The man covered her mouth as they made their way down the garden path running along the side of the house and towards the front, rivulets of blood running down his cheek. Amy could see the gate had been left ajar and her heart sank when she saw a white van parked on her drive, blocking any view her neighbours may have had of her abduction. As they approached, the side door slid open and she was jostled into the back of the van where another man grabbed her and pinned her down while the woman taped her wrists behind her and stuffed a tea towel into her mouth, almost choking her.

'There you go, that wasn't too bad, was it?' the first man said, 'now let's go and find Trevor, shall we?'

'Boss, haven't you heard?' the other, younger man said.

'Heard what?'

'He had a fight earlier with Banjo and ran off. I thought you knew. They can't find him now and Banjo thinks he's the police.'

'Shit, that bastard. We need to phone the club and see if they've found him yet, let's go.'

The younger man jumped into the driver's seat while Amy's captors stayed with her. The van moved off and was soon heading towards Hackney. They stopped by a telephone box soon after leaving the estate and the leader went to make a phone call. He was gone for a few minutes and returned angrier than ever.

'That bastard boyfriend of yours is a policeman, a damned fifth-columnist, isn't he?' he shouted, removing the tea towel from her mouth. 'They just raided my club and took three of my men away!' He lashed out with a foot, kicking Amy viciously in the side.

She screamed in pain, confused about what Trevor had gotten himself involved in.

'Go screw yourself,' she yelled. 'He's not a policeman but he is a real man—one who doesn't beat women up.'

'Is he, now? Well, let's see how much of a man he'll be when he finds out we have his woman, shall we?' The man laughed.

The van drove off again and the boss whispered instructions to the driver. After just a couple of minutes they stopped, and the engine was switched off. It was dark outside and there was no passing traffic. When they opened the sliding door, Amy could see they were in a remote area with no housing and very little street lighting. When they yanked her out of the back of the van, she realised they were on a bridge that had recently been opened and which was part of a large construction project close to the M11.

'I'm gonna ask you one more time,' the man said, glaring into her eyes, 'is your man a policeman?'

Amy knew she was in deep trouble and looked around for

an escape. There was none. Her only option was to tell the man what she knew and hope that she'd be spared.

'No,' she whispered, 'he's not a policeman. He's a soldier.'

The man looked at her and knew she was telling the truth.

'A soldier, eh? Then what is he doing working for me in my club?'

'I don't know. He doesn't tell me about his work, I thought he was posted up north somewhere,' she replied truthfully. ' I think you've made a mistake. Please, just let me go. My man hasn't done anything to you, I'm sure.'

The man nodded and his expression softened. He took out a penknife and for a moment Amy thought she was done for. She stepped back instinctively but the man grabbed her hands and cut through the tape tying them together, peeling it away from her wrists. She rubbed the skin to help the circulation.

'Thank you,' she said.

The man glared at her with his deep, cold eyes.

'I don't make mistakes,' he said.

He suddenly picked Amy up by the waist and threw her over the side of the bridge. The forty-foot drop to the concrete below was fatal but didn't kill Amy instantly. She struggled for breath and tried to move, to no avail. Her back was broken, and she couldn't see out of one eye, so severe was the injury to her head. She lived for a few minutes, struggling the entire time to try to get up so she could get back to her sleeping baby daughter. She hoped Trevor would be back home soon to take her away. Away to the sandy beach she'd dreamed of.

A passing motorist found her lifeless body.

The inquest took place six weeks later, and the police

investigation found no evidence of foul play. There was no sign of forced entry into the house, no sign of any struggle, just a couple of drops of blood on the carpet that could have been there for some while. The report suggested that the pressures of being a mum whose partner was not present to assist with the baby had brought on a mental breakdown that led to suicide. Trevor and Amy's parents argued that this was not something she would have even considered; she was a strong-willed woman who wanted nothing more than to bring up their daughter.

What the report didn't cover was the corrupt pathologist who was paid by the corrupt police detective covering up critical evidence such as the bruising on her side from the kick, which was reported incorrectly as an injury from the fall, and the evidence under Amy's fingernails that would have linked her directly to the blood on the carpet, a small but significant detail which was omitted completely.

The inquest gave an open verdict, as there was insufficient evidence for any other. The coroner explained that despite the report, there was no evidence that Amy had had any mental health issues, nor were there any previous records of self-harm. He also said that despite Trevor's insistence that there was foul play involved, there was no evidence to prove him right.

Amy March's death was reported in the local papers as a suspected suicide, despite the open verdict. Very few people sent sympathy cards or gave support to Trevor or Amy's parents, such was the stigma attached to mental health issues at that time. Trevor, distraught as he was, took Kendra to his parents, who gladly took her in and raised her. He sold their dream house and moved farther away, initially plunging into his work as an undercover operative in the British Army, which placed him in many dark, dangerous, and uncertain situations, before realising that his life had changed immeasurably, and that the army life was no longer for him. He resigned soon after.

The killers were never brought to justice.

1

POPS AND NANA

It had been some time since Kendra had visited her beloved grandparents. Clive and Martha Giddings had brought her up after the death of her mother, a mother she could not remember. She was just nine months old when her father had turned up at their doorstep, tears streaming down his face, holding Kendra in one arm and a holdall filled with baby clothes in the other.

Kendra had nothing but the deepest love for them, they had been there for every important moment in her life, unlike Trevor. Since reuniting with him and finding out some of the reasons behind his absence, she now understood how much he had sacrificed to keep her safe. Clive and Martha were the best possible option for raising her while he still served as a soldier. Despite his resigning just a few months later, it was an easy decision to keep Kendra with his parents as he sought to make changes to his life. Sadly, his parents weren't privy to the reasons for his absence from Kendra's life, resulting in a strained relationship, particularly with Clive.

Martha opened the door and her eyes lit up when she saw her granddaughter.

'Kendra, what a wonderful surprise! It's been so long, darling, come in, come in,' she said, her voice heightened in excitement. 'Clive, you'll never guess who's here,' she shouted.

'Is it that damned courier again?' came the response from the lounge. 'Dammit, woman, how much more is there for you to order on that tablet of yours? Can't you leave something for the rest of the country?'

'Stop cursing, you miserable old man, and come and say hello to your granddaughter,' Martha said, smiling at Kendra as she let her into the house. The hallway was, as always, spotlessly clean. The pale cream carpet was mostly covered by a Turkish rug, with a large ornate mirror on one wall and several framed pictures of the couple in their youth on the other, including one featuring a much younger, fresher-looking Trevor with Amy, holding their baby.

'Did I hear correctly?' Clive said as he came into the hallway still holding his newspaper, 'did you say *granddaughter*?'

He swept Kendra up in a bear hug and lifted her off the ground, laughing. Kendra squealed in delight, remembering this having been their thing when she was a child.

'Put me down, Pops, I'm not a kid anymore. You'll do yourself some damage!'

'Oh, sod that, it'd be worth it. How are you, my darling? It's been way too long.' Clive stroked her cheek fondly.

'I know, and I'm sorry to you both. It's been a very strange year, and I can't tell you how busy it's been. I know that's not much of an excuse, and I'm very sorry. I'll try and do better, I promise,' she replied.

'Never mind that, love, have you recovered fully?' Martha asked, looking down at her granddaughter's now-healed legs. Kendra remembered the shock on both their faces when she had been hospitalised with her broken legs, courtesy of the Qupi gang. She had vowed never to put them through such a harrowing experience again, and so had not visited as often whilst the team were engaged with their recent... *adventures*.

'They're much better, Nana, thank you for asking. Dad has helped a lot with some training,' she replied.

Clive's face darkened at the mention of his son. Martha placed a restraining hand on his arm.

'That's good, love,' she said. 'Now, come on through, and you can tell us all about it in the kitchen. I'll make us a nice pot of tea.' Martha looked back at her husband, who stood unmoving in the hallway.

'I'll bring one out to you, love,' she said, knowing he wouldn't want to discuss his son with them.

They sat at the oak dining table that Kendra remembered doing her homework on, as Martha poured tea from the porcelain teapot she loved so much. Before sitting to join her, she took her husband a cup, returning quickly.

'Don't mind your grandad, love. He's still angry with your dad, he's not the most forgiving man, is your pops,' she said, laying a hand on Kendra's arm.

'I understand, Nana,' said Kendra. 'I've got to know Dad much more this past year or so and I've realised that he did what he thought was best for me. We have a very close relationship now, so if we can work it out, I'm sure he and Pops can resolve their differences, too.'

'I'm not sure, love. It's been such a long time; they've grown further and further apart, and your pops doesn't think your dad has made much of an effort. I hope he comes around, but I've been with him long enough to know what a stubborn old man he can be.' She laughed.

'Well, I thought it was time I paid a visit. We've had a hectic period recently and I wanted to get away for a few days. Is it okay if I stay here tonight, Nana?' Kendra asked.

'Of course, it is, child, you don't need to ask. I'll make up your old room for you.'

'Thanks, Nana. I wanted to visit Mum's grave, which I haven't done for a while. And I have a few questions for you and Pops, if that's alright?'

'Of course, darling. Go ahead,' said Martha.

'Dad mentioned a few things I didn't know about, and it got me thinking about her,' Kendra said.

Martha paused before responding, her voice lowered.

'Are you okay, my love? You haven't asked about your mother for such a long time. Why now?'

'Dad told me she didn't commit suicide and I believe him. I want some answers, Nana, and I think you can both help me find them.'

'None of us believed that she killed herself,' said Martha, 'but the police were adamant it was suicide so there wasn't much we could do. Luckily the coroner listened to us and gave an open verdict, but people ignored that and shunned us. What is it you're hoping to find?'

'I want to find the person who killed my mother and bring them to justice.'

CLIVE MAY NOT HAVE BEEN in the kitchen, but he was close enough to hear Kendra's announcement.

'What are you talking about, Kendra? What makes you

think you can find the truth after so long? It's been thirty years, girl, shouldn't you be moving on?' he said when he entered.

'No, Pops, I shouldn't,' she said calmly. 'The thought of someone being free and doing whatever the hell they want after killing my mum doesn't sit well with me. Nope. If I can find the person or persons responsible, I'll do everything I can to make sure they pay for their crimes.'

'I understand that you want justice, my love, but like I said, it's been so damned long you could be chasing shadows and ghosts for years,' Clive said. 'What makes you think you can do better than the police did?'

'For one,' said Kendra, 'we have much better technology now. Also, I have a great team of people who'll be helping me. They can work wonders and if anyone can help me find the truth, it's them.'

'Okay,' Martha added, 'what is it that you want to ask us, honey?'

'I just want to know what you remember about her death, whether the police gave you any snippets of information, whether Dad did, anything that can help me piece things together.'

'You know,' said Clive, 'we asked a lot of questions back then, and there was a lot of confusion and contradiction with what we were told. It left us none the wiser, and as the years passed, we just accepted it as being over and done, you know?'

'What sort of questions, Pops?' Kendra asked.

'Well,' he said, 'we were adamant that it couldn't have been suicide, but a couple of the cops kept telling us that it was, without telling us why.'

Martha stepped in. 'Then it got very confusing and mixed

up because of a chance meeting we'd had with your father a week or two before Amy died.'

'What do you mean?' Kendra asked.

'We were at Ridley Road market in Dalston one Saturday morning. It was the go-to place for Caribbean folk to gather, we used to dress up for the day and meet our friends. It was our favourite day of the week, wasn't it, Clive?'

'Yes, yes, get on with it, woman,' he said impatiently.

'That particular Saturday it was very busy, so we turned off the side road to take a short-cut to the bus stop, when we saw them.'

'Saw who?' asked Kendra.

'Your father, dear. He was deep in conversation with another man, a big fellow he was. Your dad was very surprised to see us, that's for sure.' She laughed at the memory.

'What has that got to do with Mum's death, Nana?'

'I'm coming to that, dear, be patient now,' Martha scolded.

'You can't blame her for asking, love, you're not the quickest at telling stories, you know,' Clive added.

'You can shush, too,' Martha replied quickly. 'As I was saying, before being so rudely interrupted, your father introduced this young man to us as Marvin, his *brother from another mother*, which I have to say I found rather rude. But anyway—'

'For heaven's sake, I'll finish the damned story,' Clive interrupted. 'The man was called Marvin Freeman; I'll never forget the name because of what happened after the inquest.'

'What's that, Pops?'

'The coroner listened to our pleas, and our insistence that Amy would not have killed herself. There wasn't enough police evidence to support suicide, just a strong suspicion.

There was no sign of a break-in or any signs of a struggle, all they had was a few drops of blood at the house.'

'So how did that involve this Marvin chap?'

'This is why I'll never forget the name. The blood the police found at the house was his. The police tried to explain it as a coincidence, but after the inquest, I approached one of the officers involved and gave him a piece of my mind.'

'Did you get into trouble?' asked Kendra.

'Not at all, he was quite charming. His name was Wellington, Detective Wellington, another name I won't forget. He was having a cigarette at the side of the court so not many people could see us. He pulled me to one side and told me his suspicions.'

'Carry on, Pops.'

'This Wellington chap told me they suspected this Marvin fella was simply visiting his close friend, your father, which could easily have explained the blood, you know, like from a paper-cut or something minor. When I pressed him, though, he told me that another theory being passed around was that Marvin had been having an affair with your mother. He told me not to believe it, and that other officers would give that explanation as a reasonable one for Amy committing suicide. The theory being that she was ashamed of the affair.'

Kendra was stunned by the revelation. It took a few seconds before she could summon up another question.

'Did Dad ever speak to you about that?' she finally asked.

'No, he did not,' Clive replied, his face a picture of fury.

'Stop it, Clive, getting angry isn't going to help anyone,' Martha chimed in.

'Your father took off and went back to work as if nothing had happened,' Clive continued. 'He seemed distracted after the funeral. Sure, he was upset, but once your mother was in the ground, we hardly ever saw him. And he hardly ever saw you. I was ashamed of him.' Clive's voice was still bitter from the memories.

'Pops, Dad did what he did to keep me safe. There's a lot you don't know about what happened and the only way for you to learn is to talk to your son and clear the air.' Kendra placed a hand on his arm.

'Not gonna happen,' he said, stepping back. 'I'm going to watch the match,' he said softly, and left the kitchen. Kendra could see it was a very sore subject for him and glanced at her grandmother.

'I told you, darling. He is a good man but as stubborn as a mule,' Martha said, shaking her head.

'There's a lot that you aren't aware of, Nana. Both of you. The easy thing would be for me to tell you, but I think it should come from Dad instead. There's a lot of healing that needs to be done here.'

Martha smiled at her granddaughter and nodded.

'You know, he sends us birthday cards and Christmas cards every year. Clive says that won't make up for abandoning his child, but I see him reading them when he thinks I'm not looking. When the time comes, he'll be ready, darling.'

'I hope so, Nana. Life is too short, you know? Especially when the whole story hasn't been told. I think it's time and I'll be speaking to Dad about it when I get back.'

'That would be the best present ever, my love. I'll pray for your success,' said Martha. 'Now, what do you fancy for dinner? I can make one of my famous beef stews that you like so much.'

'That would be lovely, Nana, thank you. I'll go and grab my bag from the car. Back in a minute, okay?'

When she returned a couple of minutes later, she passed the lounge where her grandfather was sitting, apparently watching a game of cricket. His eyes weren't really on the game, though, but on a photograph of himself and Martha with a young Trevor, all smiling at the camera. She stood and watched as he stared at it for several minutes, before she went back to the kitchen, leaving her holdall by the stairs. She was close to tears when she sat back down, her grandmother obliviously chopping vegetables.

'Nana,' said Kendra, 'I think I'm going to go to the cemetery now, if that's okay? I'll be back in time for dinner.'

Martha looked back at her and saw the sad expression on Kendra's face, the moist eyes, and she saw a vulnerable young granddaughter. She walked over and threw her arms around her in a much-needed hug, holding on for several seconds before letting go.

'You give your mum our love, you hear?' she whispered.

Kendra smiled and nodded.

'Of course, Nana. Of course.'

It had been many months since Kendra had visited her mother's grave. She walked slowly towards it, clutching a bunch of daffodils, which had been her mum's favourite flower. The grave was next to a fifteen-metre-tall rowan tree near the cemetery boundary, making it easy to remember where to go. Kendra loved that tree, its white flowers in spring turning into bright red berries in autumn. On many occasions when visiting she had sat under it, her back against the gnarly trunk, watching her family tidy the grave.

Standing in front of the aged granite headstone, with the

epitaph *'Beloved wife, mother and daughter. Forever with the Lord,'* Kendra teared up as she thought of all the things her grandparents and father had told her about the mother she couldn't remember. Amy March had been a strong-willed, intelligent woman who had done exactly what she'd wanted to do in her short life, a woman who Kendra could look up to and be proud of, a mother she had not been given the chance to bond with. She gently wiped some leaves from the top of the gravestone and tidied up the small patch in front of it, before placing the flowers into the vase that had been there since Trevor had brought it to the funeral.

'I doubt very much whether you can hear me, but it helps to talk to you when I visit, so I hope you don't mind,' she said, kneeling on the freshly cut grass next to the grave.

'I found out that you were probably murdered, so I wanted to tell you that I'll be doing my best to make sure that whoever is responsible pays for it. I hope it will make you rest in peace.'

She placed a hand on the cold granite as she made her vow.

'I promise that your death will not be in vain, Mum. I'll come and visit when it's done.'

She stood and brushed some cut grass from her jeans, and after one last look at her mother's resting place, turned around and left. She did not want her mother to see the steely, determined look on her face as she walked away.

2

THE CUBE

'You don't mess about when it comes to getting things done, do you, Trevor?' Andy said as he watched the lorries unload their cargo.

'Well, it just goes to show what you can do when you have the money, doesn't it? Thanks to the criminals we've had the privilege of crossing paths with, we can afford to do all of this and much more,' Trevor replied, rubbing his hands gleefully.

Andy's prowess as a hacker had allowed the team to amass a fortune, cleverly appropriated from the bank accounts of the criminals they had dealt with. Trevor, Andy and Kendra had collectively agreed to put that money to good use, which included buying a number of boxing clubs to help keep local youths off the streets; purchasing property for the growing team to live in, which they would own after time; establishing a legitimate security company in Sherwood Solutions, which had doubled up as a promising career path for many of the team; and now the new training centre and research development section next to the existing premises, affectionately nicknamed *the factory*.

'Yeah, I love that part, too. Every time I look at what we've done this past couple of years, I can't stop smiling at the irony,' Andy said.

'This new building is a great idea. Charmaine's proposal was inspired, and who would have thought that the equally inspired idea to add the training centre and showroom would have come from Amir?' Trevor added, smiling at the memory.

Andy laughed.

'They're growing into inspirational adults, Trevor. It shows we're doing the right thing here.'

'Yeah, I see that,' said Trevor. 'I guess it's all happened so fast, I remember Kendra bringing up the idea in the first place and me being horrified at the thought. It was almost as horrifying as finding out you were involved!' Trevor laughed and pushed Andy in jest.

'And just look at us now, eh? I can almost call you Dad, right?' Andy said, exaggerating a laugh and giving Trevor a sideways glance.

'You do that and I'll shoot you,' Trevor said, continuing to laugh but with steely eyes. 'You both decided to take a step back from your relationship, that decision was yours, so you are just colleagues for now. Don't mess with my daughter in any other way, you hear me?'

Andy nodded slowly, his sad expression evidence of his disappointment. He moved his eyepatch slightly and scratched behind it, giving him a momentary flashback of the time he had lost his eye. He could never understand how a missing eye would itch, but it did.

'Just because I agreed doesn't mean it doesn't upset me,' he said.

Trevor reached out and grabbed his arm, gently.

'I know I joke about it, but you did it for the right reasons, okay? Don't lose sight of that. Keeping your feelings in check will keep you both safe, and that's what matters while we are doing what we are doing.'

'I do appreciate you, Trevor, I hope you know that. Keeping feelings in check is bloody difficult, though.'

They both turned back to the two-acre site they had bought. As it was right next to the factory the plan was to fence it off entirely and share the one entrance at the front of the factory. This was an extra security precaution that would—at the very least—delay any attacks such as the one by the heavily armed Albanian gang many months earlier. As a result of that attack, the factory's security features had been significantly enhanced and now included bullet-proof glass and high-security doors that would require explosives to even make a dent. Andy had overseen the installation of extra CCTV cameras, including several that were hidden and on the approach to the factory as well as the perimeter. The team would have ample notice of any impending attack and would be able to get to safety much more quickly as a result.

'I spoke with the foreman, and he reckons they'll have the shell of the building up in three weeks,' Trevor said. 'It's all pre-constructed, like a kit that just needs bolting together.'

'We'll have to have a sit down with Charmaine, Amir, and Mo and discuss what they'd like to have in their respective departments,' Andy said.

'That should be fun. Luckily, we have Mo to oversee everything, and he'll keep them both in check.'

'In the meantime, there's not a lot for us to do. When is Kendra back?' Andy asked.

'She should be back tonight and at work tomorrow. I think we'll be meeting Rick tomorrow night for the first time as a team member,' Trevor said.

Rick Watts had found out about Kendra's involvement in apprehending two corrupt ex-police officers and a triad gang. He had challenged Kendra and subsequently volunteered to join the team, having seen the deeply rooted corruption within the police and government departments and feeling appalled with the number of criminals who avoided justice.

'He's gonna have a living fit when he sees me,' said Andy.

Rick had been Andy's boss before he was medically discharged by the police when he'd lost his eye and the use of his foot after tangling with the Albanians. He had purposely avoided contact with his old team to give the impression that he was a bitter and twisted man who wanted to be left alone. Rick had tried many times to visit and assist him but was always unsuccessful, which was part of the plan for keeping the team and its sometime-criminal activities a secret.

'Well, there's not a lot we can do now that he knows. I'd rather have him with us than against us, wouldn't you?' said Trevor.

'Of course, that's a no-brainer. Rick was a good boss; if anything, he'll enhance what we're doing, he's really well-connected.'

'Let's make him welcome but keep things to a minimum for now, until he's established. As with the rest of the team, let's not mention your secret ops room in the cellar, or anything to do with the finances in the Cayman Islands. That sort of thing needs to be kept between us two and Kendra.'

'You'll get no argument from me, Trev,' Andy replied, crossing his heart theatrically.

Andy had converted his cellar into a secret operations room when the trio had first started their quests of vengeance. It was fully kitted out and effective as an operations centre. They had upgraded to the factory after taking the Albanian gang's money and now only used the room as an emergency back-up. It was also their fallback position if the shit hit the fan in any way, which in their business was always possible.

Trevor was always good at planning for all eventualities, thanks to his undercover experience in the British Army, and he knew how important it was to have a back-up plan.

'Let's go and check on the factory. I want to make sure we only show Rick what we want him to see... for now,' he said, turning away and heading back towards the factory.

Andy walked alongside him, his limp now almost imperceptible despite his prosthesis. His decision to have the useless foot amputated and replaced with something that allowed him to be more involved in operations had been a success. He was now well used to it and barely gave it any thought or experienced any pain. Strangely, he frequently had the urge to scratch the missing foot, much like the situation with his eye.

'How come you didn't go to see your parents with Kendra?' he asked.

He'd been wanting to ask for a couple of days and had only now plucked up the courage to do so. He immediately noticed Trevor's expression intensify, a look he was now very familiar with.

'It's a family thing, Andy. Not something I want to revisit.'

'That's cool, I understand. I had problems with my parents too, especially when they found out I was a hacker.'

'How did they find out?' Trevor asked, his expression now back to neutral.

'I thought I'd do a good thing by paying off their mortgage, but when I told them, they freaked out.'

'I get that. They sound like decent people. Using stolen

money to pay off their mortgage was not great, despite your good intentions,' Trevor said.

'Oh, I never used stolen money. I made my money legitimately, but that wasn't the problem.'

'What was it, then?'

'It was the fact that I was only fifteen years old. I mastered the craft when I was very young, I told you I'm a geek. I made a small fortune from creating a software programme for security businesses. It was used in a lot of CCTV programmes for years,' Andy said casually.

Trevor stopped in his tracks.

'What? Fifteen? And you paid your parents' mortgage off?'

'Yes, sir. And that was what the problem was. My dad got pissed off that his baby had paid the house off. I didn't really need much money back then and wanted to help them. It's why I wanted to be a cop, to help people. I just learned how to be cool instead of nerdy and it worked out.'

'You're just full of surprises, Andy, you never cease to amaze me.'

'Why, thank you. Can I call you Dad, now?'

TREVOR AND ANDY were the only ones left at the factory when Kendra returned from her trip to her grandparents'. She met them in the canteen, where she gave her dad a hug and Andy a peck on the cheek, much to his continuing embarrassment.

'How are my two favourite men?' she said, taking a seat.

'We're good, love, how was your trip?' Trevor asked, deliberately avoiding any mention of his parents.

'It was great, thank you, Dad. I need to do it more often.'

'What time is Rick showing up?' asked Andy, his cheeks still crimson.

'He told me he'd be here for seven, so any time soon. Are you both sure you're okay with this? You know he's going to be especially surprised to see you, Andy,' she said.

'Yeah, I know. I just want to get it out of the way now. Hopefully he won't hold it against me,' Andy replied.

'Well, there's a lot riding on this, so let's just be cautious with what we say and how much we reveal to him. Just in case,' Trevor added.

The doorbell chimed. Andy checked the CCTV stream on his phone and nodded.

'Right on time, he's here.'

'I'll go and get him,' Kendra said. 'Get the kettle on, boys, this should be interesting!'

Rick smiled when she opened the double doors leading into the company reception area.

'Hey, Rick. Welcome to Sherwood Solutions,' she said, smiling back.

'It's impressive,' he said, 'I'm guessing it's just a shell company for what you've been doing?'

'No, actually, it is a fully functioning and viable security company that is doing very well at the moment,' said Kendra. 'If you play your cards right, you'll have a job here when you retire... if you want to continue working.'

'That's good to know,' he said with a laugh. 'With two kids just in university I can assure you I'll need to carry on working.'

'The guys are waiting upstairs. I thought it best you just meet with them first; we need to have a chat about what we'll be doing together and how it will work. Sometimes it's better to keep quiet about some aspects of the operation.'

'I get it, K, you don't need to worry about me on that score.'

'Good to know,' she said, as they approached the canteen.

Trevor and Andy stood as the pair entered.

'Rick, this is my dad, Trevor, and our mutual friend, Andy,' Kendra said, watching his face as Rick laid eyes on him.

'Holy shit, Andy Pike! How the hell are you involved in this?'

'It's a long story, but all you need to know is that it's all her fault,' Andy said, as he shook hands with Rick.

'How are you doing, Rick?' Trevor said, shaking the sergeant's hand.

'I'm very good, thanks. Have we met before?' Rick asked.

'I don't think so. Can I get you a coffee or a tea, or something cold to drink?'

'I'll have a tea please, thank you,' Rick replied. 'This is an impressive set-up you have here. Kendra tells me it's a functioning security company?'

'Yeah, we're growing quite nicely,' said Kendra. There's a lot going on here now, new buildings and expansion, that kind of thing.'

'Andy, you were a miserable old sod last time I saw you. I thought you were destined to be that way forever. The team was disappointed they never got to see you again,' Rick said, referring to the Specialist Crime Unit, where they had all worked together.

'I know, and I'm sorry about that. It was important to keep a low profile while we started this venture, and having a bunch of cops coming round regularly would have ruined that,' Andy replied.

'Well, I'm glad you're not the arsehole that people said you were,' Rick said, laughing.

'Rick, we appreciate you coming here tonight,' said Kendra. 'I've told Dad and Andy about our situation and how you found out about us, so the fact that you're willing to work with us here is a really good fit for us.'

'Look,' said Rick, 'I probably don't know a tenth of what is going on here, but I have figured out that what you're doing is helping a lot of people. That's all I want to do and I'm finding it increasingly difficult at work to do it legitimately. As long as innocent people aren't badly affected, and you're only taking on the bad guys, then you can count me in. Kendra told me how important police intelligence is to what you are doing, and I want that to continue being the case.'

'We're thankful for that, Rick, but as you can understand, we need to be somewhat cautious until we get to know each other better. I hope you're okay with that?' said Trevor, who had returned with drinks.

'Trevor, you can tell me as little or as much as you like. And you can involve me in as little or as much as you deem fit, too. I'm quite happy to assist from afar, passing on useful intel and helping out in any other ways that I can. Just tell me what you need me to do, and I'll do my best.'

'For now,' said Andy, 'the most important thing is that we keep the operation completely secret, Rick. We've been doing this for a couple of years now and have learned some harsh lessons, but we've been successful—we're making a difference. It might not always be that way, but we'll always try.'

'Like I said, count me in,' Rick said, taking a slurp of his tea.

'Okay, that's great. We've been focusing on the upgrades and expansion these past few weeks so we haven't got anything going at the moment, but now you're on board and Kendra is back at work tomorrow, maybe we can help with something soon,' Trevor said.

'Actually, there may be something we can start with while we're waiting for a bigger job to come along,' Kendra said.

'What's that, love?' Trevor asked.

'I want you to help me find the person who murdered my mother.'

3

RESEARCH BEGINS

'Well, good morning, Detective March, and how was your holiday?' asked DC Jill Petrou, Kendra's long-time desk-sharing partner in the Serious Crime Unit.

'I was only gone for three days, Jill, I wouldn't go so far as to call it a holiday!'

Working part-time had suited Kendra very well, allowing her to maintain relationships with her team, but crucially, it also gave her access to the national and international police databases which contained intelligence that was unavailable anywhere else. Just as important was the fact that she loved her job as a detective, and enjoyed working with her team, so this role allowed her to continue doing something she was passionate about.

'I know, I'm just messing with you. Mainly because I'm jealous about how much time off you have,' Jill replied.

'Then go part-time, like me,' Kendra said, laughing.

'I wish I could afford to do that, K, but as you know, times are hard and I have a huge mortgage and bills to pay.'

'Maybe it's time you took the plunge and moved in with Pablo, eh?' Kendra teased, referring to the ongoing relationship Jill was having with their fellow detective Pablo Rothwell.

'Shush, will you?' Jill whispered, looking around to see if anyone had heard. She was trying very hard to keep the relationship a secret.

'Oh please, do you honestly think nobody else knows? Come on, Jill, our team is flush full of smart cookies, you don't think any of them have worked it out by now? For one, look how Pablo's dress sense has changed this past few months, and how his confidence has improved. People have noticed that, and that's all because of you, Detective Petrou.'

Jill blushed, but smiled despite her embarrassment.

'Have you seen those skinny jeans he's started wearing? I'm not sure they were a good idea,' Jill said, laughing.

Kendra joined in the laughter, nodding in understanding.

'Well, that's exactly why you two should move in together, so you can stop him from making mistakes like that,' she said.

'I've been thinking about it, but I guess I need Pablo to come up with the suggestion, so I know he's serious about us, you know?'

'You of all people should know what he's like, Jill. Remember, it was you who instigated your first date, so you know he needs a nudge in the right direction. Don't wait for him, is what I say.'

'Maybe. We'll see. Anyway, welcome back to work,' Jill said, changing the subject.

'Have I missed much?'

'It depends on what you mean by that. If you mean missed much in the way of work, then no, it's been unusually quiet. There are rumours we'll be assisting other units in the

Met who are swamped, but for now we're topping and tailing existing cases and looking for cases we can take over from CID.'

'Okay, I guess I'll sort my emails out, and wait until we're tasked with something,' Kendra said, logging on.

'Have you spoken with Rick, yet? He was asking for you earlier,' Jill said.

'I haven't, I'll go and see him once I'm done here,' Kendra replied.

There were half a dozen follow-up emails that needed replying to, which took her less than ten minutes to sort out. Looking over her shoulder towards Rick's office, she could see that his light was on.

'I'll be back in a mo. Let's see what he wants,' she told Jill, getting up out of her chair and striding towards Rick's office.

She knocked on his door and entered before he could reply.

'Come on in, Kendra,' he said, looking up from his work.

'Jill said you were looking for me,' she said, closing the door and sitting.

'Yeah, I just wanted a quick catch-up. There wasn't much time to speak alone last night so I wanted to make sure you were okay with things,' he said.

'Everything's fine, why shouldn't it be?' she asked, raising her eyebrows.

'I ask because I don't think you saw the reaction on your dad's face when you dropped the bombshell about investigating your mum's murder,' Rick said. 'I say this as your friend and as a member of the team.'

'I don't expect him to be jumping up and down with excitement, Rick. It's something I'm determined to get to the bottom of, and I thought bringing it up like that was the best way to do it. You know, the good old shock and awe tactic.'

'I get that, and it was most effective. Do you honestly think you can solve a case that's thirty years old?' he asked.

'Honestly? Yes, I do. I spoke with my grandparents and already have some clues to start with. I'll speak with my dad later about it, hopefully he'll remember a few nuggets of information. It will all help, and with the tech we have nowadays, I think we'll find what we need.'

'Okay. It's pretty quiet at the moment so we can both work on it from here until things pick up. How were you doing it before without the potential danger of any trace of searches coming back to you?' Rick asked.

'You probably won't like this, but I used other colleagues' logins from the Intel Unit whenever I've worked with them. I was always careful to do so when they were on a break and from a computer that wasn't covered by a camera, just in case,' she replied.

'Sneaky but effective,' Rick said, smiling and nodding in appreciation. 'Well, I may be able to help in a similar way, Detective.'

'How's that?'

'As line manager, I have access to everyone's accounts and logins, so I can carry on doing the same thing from here,' he said smugly.

'Also very sneaky!' she said, laughing.

'I figure it's the best way for me to contribute to the team, with intel. I also have a few friends I can call upon for any specialist info and guidance. It will all come in very useful.'

'Thanks, Rick. It's gonna feel a little odd me asking you to do stuff, though, you sure you're okay with that?'

'You've always bossed me around, so why change the

habit of a lifetime?' He laughed again. 'Of course, it's fine. Just ask away.'

'Great, thank you. Can you start by searching the archives for any reports and files on my mum's murder? It'll be in the name of Amy March. The more we have, the more we can investigate. I'm especially keen to find out more about the investigators' recommendations and comments as I find it hard to believe they suspected suicide.'

'Leave it with me, K. The files should have been digitised by now, as with all cold cases, so hopefully everything will have been scanned.'

'Great, thanks, Rick. In the meantime, I'll do some searches into a chap called Marvin Freeman, whose blood was found at my parents' house. There's something strange about his involvement that I want to ask my dad about, too.'

'I'd probably want to do the same. Go down to the intel unit and see if you can find anything on Mister Freeman. Tell them I sent you to look for new cases, being that it's so quiet up here,' Rick said.

'Will do, and good luck on your end,' she replied.

'I'm on the case, Detective. You crack on with what you need to do, and we'll have a catch up later.'

'Thanks. See you later, Rick,' she said, standing.

'Again, I appreciate you letting me come on board, Kendra. There's nothing I want more than to put some of these bastards away for good,' he said, as she turned to leave.

'It's our pleasure, Rick, and welcome to our small family of justice... givers? I can't think of a better term,' she replied, waving as she left.

'THAT WAS QUICK, EVERYTHING OKAY?' Jill asked as Kendra returned to her desk.

'Everything is peachy, thanks. He just wanted to ask me if I could search for some new cases. I guess that's what being the part-timer gets you, eh? I'll pop down to the intel unit and do a couple of hours searching there. Hopefully I can find something interesting for us to do,' she said.

'Maybe catch up later for a coffee or lunch?' Jill asked.

'Sure, I'll give you a call.'

Kendra logged off and waved goodbye to her colleague. Taking the stairs down to the second floor Intel Unit, she soon entered the open-plan office, waving to the three people sitting at their desks.

'Well, if it isn't our favourite SCU officer! How's it going, Miss March?' Sam Razey asked.

'That's Detective March to you, Sam, and don't you forget it,' she said, smiling fondly at the former detective who had returned to the intel unit in a civilian capacity.

'It's always good to see you, Kendra, to what do we owe this pleasure?' Gerrardo Salla asked.

'I'm very well, thanks, Gerrardo. Rick asked me to come and search for some juicy cases for the team,' she said to the researcher who'd always had a soft spot for her. They had become firm friends despite his crush on her.

'You're always welcome. Pick any seat. As you can see, we're a bit light today, apart from the three of us,' he said, pointing to Sam, and Geraldine Marley, another civilian researcher.

'Where's Imran and Paul?' she asked, referring to the remaining two members of the intel unit.

'They're both on annual leave. Geraldine is most upset,' he said, looking towards the woman who was on the phone—

and who was now shaking her head and rolling her eyes at him.

'Ooh, more juicy gossip. You must tell me more later,' Kendra replied.

'My lips are sealed,' he said, miming zipping his mouth shut.

'I'll take this one here,' she said, taking the desk farthest away from the others.

She sat and logged into the system using her own login details. She started looking through recent crime reports, looking for patterns or anything serious that her team upstairs could get involved in. It was important to show that she was doing her regular job. The deception would only happen when the intel unit researchers went for lunch, when she would have time to log in as someone else.

As she knew they would, the three researchers got up to go to lunch at their usual time of twelve-thirty.

'You coming for a spot of lunch, Kendra?' asked Sam.

'Not yet, Sam. I may join you shortly, I'm just in the middle of something I want to finish.'

Kendra had picked her seat well; if there was ever any investigation, it would be difficult to pin it on her. She logged out and logged back into the national police database as Geraldine.

'Okay, where are you, Mister Marvin Freeman?' she muttered as she typed in his name.

Surprisingly, there were only a few dozen options for her to sort through. She amended the filter to remove anyone under the age of fifty, which narrowed it down to ten suspects. Two of them were now deceased, leaving just eight possible candidates.

'Okay, let's tweak these filters a little more,' she said,

changing the identity code to remove all males over the age of fifty, who weren't black.

That left just three men. She started to look through the first option and saw that the man had been released from prison twenty-five years earlier, having spent ten years in Pentonville Prison in London for manslaughter. At the time of her mother's murder, this man had been in prison.

The second man was a viable candidate, living in east London, and he was now sixty-nine and drawing a pension. This would have made him thirty-nine at the time of the murder, suggesting that he may have been too old to be the right man. She left his file to one side to review later, and opened the final one.

'Bingo!'

The third candidate was now fifty-seven and had lived in east London at the time, giving his address as a club in Dalston Lane, Hackney. Kendra knew immediately that this was her man. Everything seemed to fit into place, especially the cold, menacing eyes and the leering grin. His mugshot had been taken a year after the murder, when he had been arrested for grievous bodily harm on an off-duty police officer at a west-end party. He looked angry and vicious in the photograph, but his eyes were deeply disturbing, as if he was telling whoever was looking that he would find them and do them serious harm.

Kendra read the arrest report, which showed that he'd been in the company of a woman who had also been arrested, Robyn Hunt. They had gotten into a fight with a group of seven stockbrokers who were out celebrating a commission windfall. The office workers had been drinking heavily and had jostled the pair one time too many. According to witnesses, Freeman and Hunt were with two unidentified males who had had no part in the fracas, Freeman having shouted at them to back off. Freeman and Hunt had then waded into the group and beaten the hell out of them all, every single one of them. Three had ended up in hospital, two of them with severe injuries, including a fractured skull and broken arms. Their celebration had been quickly forgotten.

Unfortunately for Freeman and Hunt, there was another group there celebrating a recent promotion, a group of twelve detectives from West End Central police station. They were not yet drunk, having only just arrived, and they were all well-trained in self-defence, unlike the stockbrokers. Despite this, it still took seven of them to restrain Freeman and Hunt while the other five kept the crowd—and Freeman's two goons—away. They were both arrested and taken to the local police station whilst a number of the detectives stayed behind to take statements from two dozen people who had witnessed the fight.

The evidence was damning, but mainly for Hunt, who had caused most of the damage and whose striking appearance had meant eyes had been on her instead of Freeman. As such, she'd borne the brunt of the charges and was eventually imprisoned for six years, released after four-and-a-half. Freeman was given an eighteen months suspended sentence as there was no actual evidence of grievous bodily harm, just the lesser charge of actual bodily harm.

There was no further mention of Robyn Hunt after her release, suggesting that she was either dead or had kept clear of trouble. It was a very different case for Marvin Freeman, though, who featured in many subsequent investigations but with no further charges ever brought against him. There were half a dozen search warrants for his club in Dalston, with no significant findings. They had all been conducted after raids by specialist units acting on information from reliable informants. One lead investigator had commented that there was some suspicion they had been tipped off, as on each occasion there had been very few people in attendance and nothing illegal was found to charge him with. His comments to the raiding officers each time had been something akin to '*come in, officers, the tea is brewing*.'

'Yep, dodgy cops,' Kendra muttered as she continued to research the man.

She made notes and took photos with her phone to ensure she had everything she needed to be able to continue from home or the factory. She was uncomfortable staying too long in the system, so she logged off and logged back in to her own account, before locking the screen to return to later. She took out her phone and called Jill.

'Fancy lunch in the canteen? Great, I'll meet you there.'

As she left the office, she pondered on the intelligence she had gathered so far. There was more to do, and now she could have Andy delve further into other systems to see if they could find out what the elusive Mister Freeman was up to nowadays.

In the meantime, we need to find out what happened to Robyn Hunt, because I'm sure she has a tale to tell, she thought.

4

CONTACT

Trevor was waiting for her when she arrived home after her day's work.

'Hi, Dad. How's it going?' she said as she hung up her jacket.

Trevor's expression suggested he was not a happy man, something that Kendra had fully expected after her revelation the previous evening.

'I've been better, daughter. I'm hoping you can cheer me up by explaining what the hell it is that you're trying to do,' he replied, his voice sterner than she had heard it for some time.

Kendra sighed and sat down, knowing that she needed to get the conversation out of the way.

'Dad, you don't have to help me if you don't want to, but I've made my decision and I'll not stop looking until I've found the people responsible. It's that simple, and I'm sorry it makes you unhappy,' she said.

'I'm not unhappy, Kendra, I'm furious. Your mother's death has been hanging over my head for thirty years now, and you think you can just dive in and solve it after all this time and think I'd be okay with it?'

'Aren't you?' she asked.

'Darling, I don't have a problem with you investigating it. I have a problem with you not telling me or asking me about it before you announced it to the rest of the world,' he said, his voice softening.

'You mean Andy and Rick? *That* rest of the world?'

'Alright, alright, I exaggerated, but I should have been the first person you told.'

'Dad, I know what a sore subject it is for you, especially considering the relationship you have with Nana and Pops. I didn't want to add to that, and I'm not a little girl anymore who needs your protection or approval for everything I do,' she said, her voice now stern.

'Kendra, what happened to your mother is the worst thing that ever happened to me. The best thing was you. I can't bear the thought of losing you to the same people that took your mother away from us all, can't you understand that?'

Kendra moved and sat next to him, giving him a hug in the process.

'Dad, you've got to stop keeping things inside, it's a burden that always catches up to you. Look at what you've missed out on as a result. You barely saw me for most of my life, you've fallen out with your parents, you left the job you loved. All of that was because you thought you'd be able to deal with things your way, without telling your loved ones why you did what you did. I'm proud of you, because I now know the real you, and I want to make up for those lost years. You need to do the same with Nana and Pops and tell them the truth, so that they can understand why you did what you did.'

Trevor looked down, ashamed, knowing she was right.

'I'll go and speak to them,' he said, almost in a whisper, 'but there's one condition.'

'What's that?'

'You let me help you with the investigation. You let me help you find the man who killed your mother. And you let me deal with him when you find him.'

Kendra looked into his eyes and saw a steely determination that told her that anything but an agreement for this one condition would cause problems. She was fearful of what her dad would do, but she figured that she would be able to influence him when the time came.

'Deal,' she said.

HAVING AGREED to work together but before they started discussing the matter, they first enjoyed a chicken Caesar salad dinner that Trevor had prepared earlier, washed down with a glass of chilled Sauvignon Blanc. They ate in silence, anticipating the uncomfortable conversation ahead.

'Okay, Dad, let's not put it off any longer,' Kendra said, as she put the plates in the sink and sat opposite her father at the table.

'What do you want to know?' he asked.

'Everything, but most of all I want to know about Marvin Freeman,' she said, watching his expression change to one of mild shock at the mention of that name.

'Seeing as you've already made a start, I'll tell you what I remember. As you now know, I was an undercover operative in the British Army. At the time, we were working with Special Branch and the Secret Service, MI5, about a growing threat that nobody knew how to handle effectively,' he started.

'The Yardies?' asked Kendra.

'Yes, the Yardies. Vicious Jamaican gangsters who found ways to bring drugs and guns to the UK. They got involved in all sorts of things, corrupting everything and everyone they touched. They killed their own with a smile if they made the smallest mistake. They became a real threat to the nation.'

'How was it that the army got involved? I didn't think that was their thing,' Kendra said.

'It was one of those rare occasions when all government departments worked closely together. At that time, there weren't many black undercover officers in the police or MI5, and I'd been doing it successfully in Northern Ireland for a couple of years, which was ironic as there weren't many black people there. I was recommended by my commanding officer and asked to infiltrate the Hackney posse, as they were known. It took me three months to gain their favour because nobody knew me, but eventually I was accepted.'

'Wow, three months? How did you get in?'

'It was horrific, Kendra. I had to do things like rob businesses, beat competing drug dealers up, I even had to set fire to a shop. They made me do a bunch of things before they trusted me. I must've done a good job because Marvin Freeman finally took me under his wing.'

'How was he involved?' Kendra asked.

'He was the boss, love. He was nastier and colder than anyone I've ever met. Everyone feared him, *everyone*. He had his favourite lieutenants, an evil bastard called Banjo was one of them, and he always had his woman with him who was just as evil, a woman called Robyn. She was the odd one out, a white woman in a black gang. People thought that Freeman used her as a status symbol to show her off, but it wasn't like that at all. That woman could take on most men in a fight; she specialised in using her elbows.'

'I read something about her going to prison about a year after mum's murder,' Kendra said.

'I don't know about that, I was well gone by then,' said Trevor.

'Nana said that she and Pops saw you with Freeman just before mum was killed, they surprised you in a market somewhere?'

'Yeah, Ridley Road market. That was a bit of a shock, I can tell you. I was having a row with him. He wanted me to attack one of the stall owners there who was selling drugs on the quiet. He wanted me to do it in broad daylight in front of everyone, and the man had his child with him that day. I told him I couldn't do it and I think that was when he started having suspicions about me.'

'Dad, do you think he killed Mum?'

Trevor turned away and paused for several seconds before turning and facing his daughter.

'I'm sure of it, but it's more of a gut instinct, because there was never any evidence. I tried to find some, but I never did. I failed, Kendra.'

'Pops said they found some blood at the house, which was Freeman's. How was it the police didn't count that as evidence against him?'

'The police said that because of my *friendship* with Freeman, it would be assumed that he'd been to the house as a guest and somehow a tiny amount of blood from a graze or something ended up on the floor. Because there was no sign of a break-in or a struggle, it was assumed to be insufficient evidence. I was just happy that they hadn't gone upstairs and found you, because knowing that bastard as I did, he would have killed a baby just to teach a person a lesson,' Trevor said, burying his face in his hands as a result of the memory.

'Dad, how did the police know you were friends with Freeman?'

'I don't know, love, maybe they saw us together, maybe someone grassed me up, who knows?'

'And did you ever tell Freeman where you lived? I find it difficult to believe that you would have done.'

'No, of course I didn't. As far as he was concerned, I was a single man living in a Dalston bedsit,' he replied.

'Don't you see what that could mean, though?' she pressed.

'No, love, what?'

'If they knew so much about your relationship with Freeman, then could it not have come from an inside source?'

'You mean the police? You think someone told them where I lived?' he asked, now incredulous at the way the conversation was going.

'Yes, the police. If he was so influential, it wouldn't be a stretch that he had a bunch of cops in his pocket who would have tipped him off about raids; all of which were unsuccessful, I might add. Why not give intel on an undercover operation, too?'

'But only very senior officers were privy to that information, literally three or four people,' Trevor said, his voice almost a whisper as realisation dawned on him.

'I think one of them gave you up, Dad, which led to them finding Mum.'

'What can we do about it now, Kendra? They're all most

likely dead, I can't remember who was involved, how do we find proof?'

'We start looking for people who were there at the time, Dad, and start piecing it together. However long it takes, I think we can do it.'

'Where the hell do we start, love? I can't think of anyone who would be able to help after thirty years,' Trevor said.

'I can think of one person worth talking to, for sure. I'll have Rick and Andy start looking into them all, but I'm hoping that Robyn Hunt is as good a place to start as any.'

'Do you know where she is?' Trevor asked.

'Not yet, but I'm sure Andy will come through,' she said, 'he's pretty useful with things like that, as you know.'

'Yeah, yeah, I get it, he's a genius, blah blah, I like him, blah blah...'

'Dad! There's no need for that now, is there?'

'Never mind. Just let me know when you find her and I'll come with you,' he said.

'You will not. From what I've read of this woman she doesn't suffer fools gladly, so I doubt very much she'll respond well to someone who she thinks was a traitor. I'll go alone, I'll have a better chance,' she said.

'So, what do I do in the meantime? It sounds like everyone has a role except me, and it was my wife that was killed, remember?'

'Oh, you don't get off so lightly, Dad. You need to start thinking of who could have betrayed you, and you can go and mend your relationship with Pops and Nana. That's a decent place to start, isn't it? And if you have time, remember, there's a rather large building that's being built that you can check on. No excuses, Dad.'

'Fine, but make sure you keep me in the loop with everything, okay?'

'I will, I promise. Now, I need to get some sleep as I have a long day tomorrow, so I will bid you goodnight, Father.'

She kissed him on the forehead on her way out. Trevor sat for a few minutes, contemplating the tasks ahead.

Who the hell betrayed me? he asked himself.

KENDRA HAD JUST CLIMBED into bed when her phone pinged with a message from Andy.

'*Found him,*' was all it said.

'*Send me all you have,*' she replied, '*and good job, young man x.*'

'*Will do, young lady. Sleep well x.*'

A minute later, her phone pinged again, with a document attached. Kendra browsed through it quickly and nodded. She put her phone on silent and lay in bed thinking ahead to tomorrow. Now that she had some information, things would start moving, and with Rick's help, maybe they could get to the bottom of it soon.

Not much chance of that happening, she thought, experience telling her that nothing like this was ever easy.

THE FOLLOWING MORNING AT WORK, she went straight to Rick Watts' office, knocking on the way in.

'Morning, K, how's it going?' he said, looking up from behind his monitor.

'We're making a little progress on the investigation,' she

said, looking around to ensure there was nobody within earshot.

'You're okay in here, don't worry,' he said, smiling.

'Andy found Martin Freeman,' she said, handing over a piece of paper she'd printed off.

Rick looked at the document and raised his eyebrows in surprise.

'Wow, really? This is the same man?'

'Andy is pretty good, Rick, you know he wouldn't get this wrong.'

'So, you're telling me that the suspect in the murder of your mother is now a multi-millionaire, a respectable business owner?'

'It seems so,' she replied.

'Kendra, this man owns several hotels in London, a radio station, a football club, and a hundred-acre estate in Buckinghamshire. He's probably got a small army working for him and protecting him at all times. How the hell are we going to get anything from this man?'

'I guess we'll just have to think of something, won't we?' she said with a grin.

'Okay, so what do you need from me?' Rick asked.

'I checked the PNC and found a fair bit from the eighties, including a woman I'll be looking into, but there's not been much about him recently. Andy's gonna check all available records but I thought you could check other national records, maybe border force, Interpol, that kind of thing. See if there's anything hidden from public records,' she replied, referring to the Police National Computer database.

'Okay, I can do that. In the meantime, what will you do, K?'

'I'm here to work today, so tell me what you need, boss.'

'Okay, just sort your admin out and see if Jill needs any help. There's not a lot more to do at the moment, maybe use some of the time today to find something for the team to look at?'

'Will do. Just so you know, I'm waiting on Andy to send me some info on the woman, Robyn Hunt, so as soon as I get that, I'll pop in again and let you know,' she said.

'Okay, you can get back to work then, Detective,' Rick said.

'On it,' she replied.

5

THE SCAMMERS

'How's my favourite partner in crime?' Jill Petrou asked as Kendra sat at the desk opposite her.

'All is well in the world, Detective Petrou,' Kendra said, smiling at her friend.

'I saw you walk out of our esteemed leader's office; did you find out any juicy gossip?' Jill asked.

'No, why do you ask that?' Kendra asked, thinking it an unusual question to ask about Rick.

'He's been way too happy these past few days, so he's either cheating on Aileen or he's won the lottery,' Jill replied nonchalantly.

'Don't say that!' Kendra exclaimed. 'He'd never cheat on Aileen, and you know it,' she added, laughing at the suggestion.

'I'm just saying, he's happier than normal, so something has changed. You know I've a good nose for these sorts of things,' Jill said.

'You mean you're the nosiest person in the office, don't you?' Kendra giggled.

'Yes, well, you can laugh about it, but it has come in very useful, has it not?'

'I'm surprised Pablo hasn't said anything about it,' Kendra said, knowing she'd get a reaction.

It was Jill's turn to laugh.

'You'd think that, wouldn't you? He's actually worse than me, he just doesn't make a song and dance about it like I do.'

'Wow, you must have some very interesting chats over dinner,' Kendra said, still grinning.

'Not just at dinner time, my friend, not just at dinner time.' Jill winked.

'Yeah, thanks for planting that image, it's gonna take days to get rid of it. Let's do some work, shall we?' Kendra said, feigning disgust. 'What's going on in the manor?'

'To be honest, it's been quite boring these last few days. The usual robberies, burglaries, nothing too violent, nothing much taken, just opportunistic more than anything. There's been a couple of nasty assaults, one of them by a wife who beat the crap out of her drunken husband. We've had an unusual rise in victims of scams, which we've passed on to the fraud squad. Honestly, I don't remember it being so... *normal* here.'

'That's good news, Jill, it means we're doing a decent job, right?'

'I guess so. It's still boring, though,' Jill replied.

'I'm gonna sort my crap out and take a look for myself, fancy lunch later?' Kendra asked.

'Count me in, it's chicken curry day today and you know how much I love my curry!'

Kendra went through her emails and replied to those needing attention. She kept on top of her admin, so it didn't take long to finish. She logged into the system and started sifting through the crime reports over the past week. She came across the reports that Jill had mentioned, and her eyes were drawn to one of the reports of an elderly woman who had been scammed of her savings of three thousand pounds.

The poor woman, she thought as she read the reporting officer's comments. The victim had been taken to hospital when she had found out that her savings had been stolen, so intense was the shock.

Moving on, she found another, similar report, again an elderly victim, this time an eighty-five-year-old disabled man who had lost almost ten thousand pounds and who was now being looked after by his daughter due to a setback in his health—brought on by the theft of his life savings. Kendra went through and found that there were six reports just in the last week alone, and all had been submitted to Action Fraud, where the investigating officer had made a report online. Knowing that their success rates were low due to the majority of scammers being overseas, Kendra saw little hope in helping these victims—

She saw something on the report that piqued her attention. Going back to the others, she noticed an unlikely pattern.

Well, now, this is interesting, she thought as she discreetly wrote down the phone numbers from the reports along with other information that Andy would be able to use.

This'll keep him busy for a while, she thought.

TREVOR HAD SAT at the table with a piece of paper and a pen for the best part of two hours and had come up with just four names.

Four potential betrayers.

Four, one of whom had contributed to the death of Amy, the separation from Kendra, the estrangement from his parents, and the decision to leave the job that he loved. His life had undergone massive changes as a result.

Detective Superintendent Raymond Stanwick – Metropolitan Police, the man tasked as the lead of this mission, the man who had recruited the team tasked with infiltrating the Yardies.

Captain Bryce Harmon – British Army, a liaison officer who had attended the briefings with the other departments.

Detective Chief Inspector Keith Hamilton – Metropolitan Police Special Branch, in charge of the domestic desk that had dealt with domestic threats.

Steven Khan – Senior Manager at MI5, the man who'd handled many agents specialising in intelligence gathering.

Which one of you bastards did it? He thought back to the briefings held at a rented room above a barber's shop close to New Scotland Yard. He shook his head as he recalled the relationship he'd had with the men. He recalled the atmosphere in the meetings being cordial and professional, each of the four contributing to his mission ahead. He couldn't believe that any of them would betray him and the operation, such was the secrecy and national importance of the mission at that time.

Dropping the pen down, which he'd been twirling with his fingers, he leaned back and stretched his arms out, clearing his head of the four men, trying to look at things from a different angle.

Did I tell anyone? he asked himself, *did anyone see me coming here?*

Eventually he started pacing the room, his head starting to ache as he dug deeper into his past, looking for recollection of any incident that may have given him a clue. He couldn't think of one.

'I guess it's just one of you lot, then,' he said out loud, picking up the piece of paper and staring at it. 'Let's see how good you really are, Mister Pike,' he said, picking up his phone and typing a message.

TREVOR WAS surprised by how quickly Andy responded to his message.

'Really, old man? Is this the best challenge you could give me?' the message said.

Trevor rang Andy immediately.

'I told you what I'd do if you called me "old man" again, didn't I?' he told the young ex-detective.

'Ah, I figured that you're far enough away for me to avoid that smack on the head, plus it sounds funny when I say it,' Andy replied bravely.

'Lucky for you, I can't be bothered today, so just give me what you've found,' said Trevor.

'Okay, straight to the point, I like it. Starting with Detective Superintendent Raymond Stanwick, he died seven years ago in his sleep, lucky man, having retired twenty-seven years ago after thirty-six years' service. He was promoted to Detective Chief Superintendent the year after the operation, so basically took the credit for it,' Andy said.

'That's fair enough, it was his idea to pull everyone together,' Trevor said.

'I suppose so. Interestingly, his son Nelson is a member of parliament in north London and has done very well for himself.'

'They're not all bad, are they?' Trevor laughed.

'That's debatable. Next, we have Captain Bryce Harmon, your liaison officer. He is also dead, thirteen years ago, from cancer. After leaving the army twenty-one years ago, he became a pub landlord and moved around the west country from pub to pub until a year before his death.'

'He was a decent chap, from what I remember,' Trevor said.

'We then have Detective Chief Inspector Keith Hamilton, who retired from the police fifteen years ago and lives in Cornwall with his wife. He wrote a book about his memoirs which caused a bit of a stir, and he is still very much alive and kicking.'

'I remember him being quite young for a DCI, very clever man, also,' Trevor added.

'Finally, we have our friend from MI5, Steven Khan. He resigned from the service less than a year after the operation and set up a haulage firm in Ruislip. He started buying land and properties during the recession, especially from businesses and individuals who were in negative equity. That led to investments in developments at Canary Wharf, Bishopsgate, Bluewater; you name it, he has a slice of that pie. He is seriously rich now, Trevor.'

'I guess it was easier to borrow money back then, wasn't it?' Trevor said.

'Yeah, you'd think that. But guess what? He never

borrowed a penny. I found that he'd been investigated half a dozen times for potential fraud and money laundering, but nothing ever stuck. If I was a betting man I'd put my money on this chap,' Andy said.

'It sure seems that way, doesn't it?' Trevor replied.

'One other thing, he has strong connections to the government and has donated millions to their coffers, so expect some push-back if you go prodding; he'll likely throw everything at you, knowing how these mega-rich bastards are.'

'Thanks, Andy, I appreciate it, even though you've insulted me yet again. We shall speak about that soon,' he added, before hanging up.

Steven Khan, eh? I guess we need to speak, he thought, as he poured himself a drink.

'DETECTIVE MARCH, to what do I owe the pleasure of your lovely voice on this fine day?' Andy asked.

'Is that your posh voice?' Kendra asked, 'because you need to work on it a little more. You sound like a weird cockney James Bond.'

'Yeah, I've been working on it for days but can't get past the *weird cockney* vibe. Anyway, what do you need, K?'

'It's unrelated to what we're doing at the moment but something we should definitely be looking into. There have been a lot of scams in London recently and they are targeting elderly victims who have limited knowledge of the modern banking security systems, such as two-factor authentication and legitimate emails and links. On our patch alone there have been six in the past week, and that's just the ones that have been reported. I'm guessing it's in the hundreds in London alone these past few months,' she said.

'Sounds awful, what is my respectable ex-employer doing about it?' he asked.

'Sadly, the Met is advising victims to liaise with Action Fraud, and reports are being referred by investigating officers to them. We're not set up to deal with them directly at this time; I believe a specialist unit is being set up but in the meantime these bastards are scamming millions of pounds from vulnerable people.'

'The problem is that the scammers are based overseas, K. Unless you're looking at amassing air miles, I don't see how we can take these people on.'

'Here's the interesting thing,' she said. 'I looked into the crime reports and almost all the victims mentioned that they'd spoken to a woman with a London accent. That's not the usual MO of the overseas scammers, is it?'

'No, it's not. What are you thinking?' he asked.

'I'm thinking it's an operation that's being run here in the UK, which means that we *can* deal with them, right?'

'If that's the case, then absolutely we can. Do you have any intel I can use to start my searches?'

'Yes, I have some numbers that were recorded, and also the victims' details, maybe you can back-track through their phone records and see if they're connected in any way,' Kendra said. 'I also searched farther afield and have names and numbers of another thirty-five victims in the past three months, which may prove useful.'

'Okay, it's a start. Give me a few hours, though, as Rick has been in touch with some old files about your mum's murder investigation. I want to go through those first.'

'Not a problem, it can wait, but not too long. Have you heard from my dad? I think he was going to ask you to search for some people, too.'

'Yeah, I've already spoken to him and found the people he was looking for. I think he has one main suspect that may have been the betrayer,' Andy said.

'Okay, I'll call him and see if he needs any help with that. How's the rest of the team getting on?'

'The twins and Charmaine are busy with their project and the new build, and the rest are at the factory or out with clients on security assessments. It's pretty busy at the moment, lots going on,' he said.

'Okay, cool. We may need some of them to help with this scamming operation, so if you find anything, give them a shout, will you?'

'Will do. I'll catch you later, Detective March,' he replied, in his odd James Bond voice.

'Needs a lot of work, dude.' She laughed, and hung up.

'Everyone's a critic, eh, Miss Moneypenny?' he said to the small teddy bear at the side of his computer.

ANDY, busy as he was, always prioritised Kendra's requests, something that was unlikely to change any time soon. Instead of starting with Rick's requests he went straight to the information Kendra had sent him. Their sad but also humorous relationship had them both second-guessing their decisions to remain at arm's length for now, so as not to endanger each other, but it did not sit well with either of them.

He typed in the phone numbers and the other information Kendra had provided and started his complex unique algorithm search routine that had worked so well for them recently, something he had written himself. It involved searching the phone numbers, names, addresses and any other personal data to hand, whereby the algorithm created *invaded* computer systems that weren't currently using the most up-to-date security processes—which was most smaller companies and businesses. It was only a fleeting invasion, just enough to look for names and numbers before exiting and moving on to the next one. It was an expensive measure to keep up to speed with the ever-increasing security threats, especially in light of how sophisticated and genuine in appearance they had become. Andy's programme was fast and efficient and took just thirty minutes to find a solid connection between the victims.

'That's interesting,' he said, 'I guess that's where the scammers are getting their victims' information from.'

He spent the next hour and a half widening the search and confirming the connections, in addition to tracking the person or persons responsible for the scams. When he was ready, he called Kendra back.

'Before you say anything in your silly voice, please don't,' she said with a laugh.

'Hurtful, but okay. I know how the scammers targeted their victims,' he said, coming straight to the point.

'Oh, that was quick.'

'I started looking and things got away from me so I couldn't stop myself,' he continued, 'but I can categorically state that there are connections between the victims.'

'Tell me, oh wise one,' she said.

'That's kind, thank you. Before I do, I've found a possible address for Robyn Hunt, I'll text it so you can check it out.'

'Great, thanks.'

'Right, back to our scam victims, every single victim is a member of a social club, or a bingo hall, a bowling club or similar. Whoever targeted the victims did so by obtaining their personal data from the information they'd provided when they subscribed to the clubs,' he said.

'How did you connect them all if they're members of different clubs?' she asked.

'That's the thing. They may all be at different clubs but the subscriptions for those clubs were all managed by one company, MyClubSubs, a legitimate company that's been around for seven years now. All the subscribers' personal data is handled by this one company, hence the link.'

'You think they are part of the scam?' Kendra asked.

'I do, and I can even tell you why,' he said proudly.

'I can almost see the chest puffing out from here, Mister Pike.'

'Well, sometimes it's good to take pride in one's work, you know? Anyway, MyClubSubs is owned and managed by a Mister Andrew Crossbey, a former solicitor who was disbarred for some pretty shady dealings about ten years ago. Back then, he sent hundreds of letters to elderly people accusing them of copyright theft, telling them they had watched a movie or television show without permission of the owners. It was a big deal back then, involved millions of pounds. When he was found out, he was disbarred for two years and claimed poverty.'

'And now he's back doing the same sort of thing, preying on the elderly, who he knows won't be able to do much about it, let alone remember to call the police,' Kendra added.

'That's right. And from what I see on the public records, his company went from barely breaking even two years ago, to having assets of more than four million pounds in just the past twelve months. All seemingly legitimate, thanks to the MyClubSubs operation, which is effectively being used as a money-laundering operation as well as an intelligence gathering one.'

'That's pretty clever work. Don't you just hate it when those bastards get smart like that? What do you think we can do about it, Andy?'

'This guy knows what he's doing, so I'm guessing he's using top-grade security software and is likely to have measures in place to destroy evidence if raided. I've seen it before, where the removal of a computer triggers a weird self-destruct-type software that is completely unrecoverable,' he continued.

'So, with no evidence comes no conviction,' she added.

'Yep, that's the way.'

'How are we gonna get around that then, Andy?'

'It will involve someone getting close to the staff there. Basically, we target the weakest link and use them as a human Trojan Horse to gain access to the company records before they realise what is going on and erase everything,' he said.

'Okay, can I leave it to you to work that plan out? I'm guessing there aren't many staff, so whatever you can find out about them in the meantime will help move this forward.'

'Oh, don't worry, I already know who and how,' he said.

'I'm not going to ask, so just spit it out, genius.'

'Thanks to the marvel of social media, I've found the member of staff who we'll get close to. I can't find mention of anyone else so it may just be her and Crossbey, I'm not sure yet. She loves taking selfies and putting them online, complains about not finding a babysitter for her son, complains about not having much of a social life, she's basically perfect as the Trojan Horse. Her name is Kim Morgan.'

'I'm guessing you know who to use to get close to her, right?'

'Oh yes, it can only be Jimmy, our loveable gigolo from Walsall.'

6

ROBYN HUNT

Kendra stopped the car just short of the address that Andy had given her and walked over to the property, peering into the sizeable garden. The small house sat at the back of the garden, which had been well-kept. The high fence meant that you needed to get close to be able to look beyond, giving the place good privacy. The house itself was a freshly painted single-storey building with a pitched roof. The smoke from the chimney indicated that someone was there.

As she reached the gate, she saw a notice pinned to it that made her pause.

'Deliveries to side access. Thank you.'

She continued past the gate until she reached the end, where she saw the gravel track leading to another gate and then to a small wooden building behind the house. This gate also had a sign.

'Deliveries for Rushmore Studio.'

The wooden building was a decent size, approximately thirty feet in length and fifteen feet high, with a flat roof. It was also well-maintained. Kendra opened the gate and approached the green door, the top half glazed with tinted glass that gave no indication of what was inside. She pressed the doorbell, below which was a small brass plaque with *Rushmore Studio* written in a fancy italic style. She saw a shadow moving towards the door, which was then opened by a tall athletic woman in her early fifties, with wavy brown hair, striking blue eyes, and who was wearing a blue vest and brown shorts.

'Can I help you?' she asked, in an American accent.

'Hi, I'm sorry to intrude. I'm looking for Robyn Hunt,' Kendra said. Glancing down she saw that Robyn had been joined by two cats and a dog, a short-haired breed that Kendra didn't recognise.

'Don't worry about Mackie,' the woman said, 'she'll only get nasty if anyone attacks me,' she added calmly.

'Exactly what a good dog should do, right?' Kendra said, relieved.

'Can I ask who you are?' the woman said.

'Yes, of course. My name is Kendra March. I'm a detective in the Metropolitan Police and I'm here to ask you a few questions about something that happened many years ago,' she said, showing the woman her warrant card.

The woman looked at the card and then at Kendra, before glancing behind her as if to see whether or not she was accompanied.

'I'm alone; like I said, I just want to ask a few questions. Are you Robyn Hunt?'

'I am. What's this all about?'

'Forgive me, is there somewhere we can sit and talk? It's a sensitive subject and I'm hoping you can help clear something up for me,' Kendra said.

Robyn moved to one side and shooed the pets away, indicating for Kendra to come in. Kendra wiped her feet on the rug just inside the door and took off her coat. She removed her mobile phone from the coat pocket.

'Come to my office, the studio is a bit of a mess,' Robyn said, closing the door and leading her guest to the far corner.

Kendra saw three large easels with half-finished paintings: two landscapes and one of flowers. There was a large bench at one end, half of which was covered with shallow plastic boxes containing dozens of different coloured beads, glass and wood, along with longer boxes containing what appeared to be gold and silver wire. The other side of the bench housed several small display cabinets where the finished articles were proudly displayed.

Robyn indicated for Kendra to sit in a large armchair opposite hers. Kendra obliged, laying her coat over the arm rest and her phone on top.

'I make jewellery, and I paint, as you can see,' Robyn said as they entered the small office. There was barely room for the dark brown antique desk and chair, with another on the other side for visitors. Robyn's dog entered with them and sat facing Kendra, its eyes firmly fixed on hers.

'What breed of dog is she?' she asked.

'She's an Australian Cattle dog, also known as a Blue Heeler. She's getting on a bit now, but she is incredibly protective of me.'

'She's lovely,' Kendra said, smiling at the dog, which rested its snout on its paws but continued to watch the guest.

'Can I get you anything to drink before we talk?' Robyn asked.

'I'm fine, thank you.'

'So, tell me why you're here, Detective.'

Kendra paused for a few seconds, gathering her thoughts.

'Thirty years ago, my mother was murdered, and I believe you know who was responsible,' she said calmly, her eyes fixed on Robyn's, looking for any reaction that might help her.

Robyn Hunt barely reacted; one of her eyebrows twitched slightly, barely noticeable, but it was enough for Kendra to recognise that the woman knew something.

'I think you need to leave,' she said, standing slowly.

'Robyn, please. I'm not here to judge you or to accuse you of anything. To be honest, I'm not even here in my capacity as police officer. I'm here as a daughter who wants to find out what happened to her mum, that's all. Please understand that.'

'I'm not interested. That part of my life is over, and I've been trying to forget it for a long time now. I'm not that person anymore,' Robyn replied.

'Like I said, I'm not here to judge. I just want to know the truth,' Kendra said, 'please, try to understand.'

'I want you to leave, please leave. How can I forget the past if I have to talk about it again? Can't *you* understand *that?*' Robyn pleaded.

'I do understand, of course I do. But think of it as a way to cleanse those demons. If you can help me with the truth, surely that will give you some peace?'

Robyn sat down again, her gaze averted towards to the small window and the garden beyond. She nodded imperceptibly, her mind seemingly made up, and turned back towards Kendra.

'What makes you think I know who's responsible?' she asked.

'Thank you, I'm grateful,' Kendra said.

'I'll tell you what I can, but it was a long time ago, so my recollections may be a little hazy, and probably biased when it comes to some people,' Robyn said, grinning. She stroked the dog's head, comforted by her presence.

'I understand, and I believe I know who you may be biased against,' Kendra said.

'You do?'

'My money's on Marvin Freeman. I suspect it was he who killed my mother. Marvin Freeman, who at the time was your boss and your lover,' Kendra said, watching closely for more clues.

This time the reaction was one of anger, barely kept in check, as Robyn was reminded of something she'd tried for so long to forget.

'Marvin Freeman,' she spat, 'that was one evil bastard.'

'Was?'

'Was, is, who cares? I haven't seen him since he abandoned me. I went to prison for that bastard. Yes, he was my lover, but do you know how many times my lover came to see me in prison?'

'I'm guessing none,' Kendra replied confidently.

'You'd be right. He got away with it while I spent five years inside for something he started,' Robyn continued, angrily. Kendra saw this as a good sign.

'Why do you think he abandoned you?' she probed.

'Because he didn't give a shit about me, that's why. All along he was using me, like a trophy, showing my fighting skills off. It was great at the time, I got to beat the hell out of a lot of men, which he probably got off on. Once I was inside, he abandoned me in a heartbeat. I've never seen him since.'

'That must've been tough. How long were you inside?' Kendra asked.

'Five and a half years. It was brutal. The first month inside, I was fighting every single day just to impose myself, to show the evil bitches there that I wasn't gonna be bossed around. I just wanted to be left alone, didn't want to integrate or get involved in anything there. I just wanted to be left alone,' she repeated, her voice quieter, the anger gone, as the memories flooded back.

'It must've been lonely in there, all that time with nobody to talk to,' Kendra said.

'Yeah, it was for a while, but after a few months, everything changed. When I came to the understanding that Marvin didn't care, I realised that I had to make the best of it. I had to find a way to change my life, and I did that inside. I started to paint and then got into making jewellery. I know it sounds corny and soppy, but I found the peace that I needed and the future when I got released,' Robyn said, smiling. 'And here I am,' she added, her arm outstretched as she indicated to the workshop.

'You do some great work, those landscapes are breathtaking,' Kendra said.

'It wasn't easy. I had to find work and raise the money to buy this place. That took almost nine years. I did double shifts as a bouncer to pay the bills and have enough left over to save. But it was all worth it.'

'So, you've not heard from him at all?' Kendra asked.

'No. I didn't go looking, either. I wanted a fresh start, and he wasn't ever gonna be a part of it,' Robyn said.

'Did he kill my mother, Robyn?' Kendra asked, her voice soft, pleading.

Robyn looked her in the eye, still stroking Mackie's head with her left hand.

'Yes, he did. I'm sorry,' Robyn replied, turning away, embarrassed.

'What can you tell me about it?' Kendra asked, her voice almost a whisper.

'It's one memory I can never forget,' Robyn said; this time it was her turn to whisper. 'He threw her off that bridge as if she were a rag doll,' she continued, her eyes misting.

Kendra also welled up. She had seen the police report and knew about the manner in which her mother had died, but never wanted to believe it might have been suicide. Now she had someone who confirmed her mother had been murdered.

'I didn't know he would do that; I promise you. We were only taking her prisoner to bring her husband—your dad, out of hiding,' Robyn continued. 'I was a nasty bitch back then, but I would never have killed anyone, not even for that bastard. You may not believe me, but I promise you that much.'

'Why was he after my dad?' Kendra asked, remaining resolute.

'Marvin found out that he was an undercover cop who was trying to take his organisation down. He was angrier than I've ever seen him. Letting a cop into the posse was a sign of weakness and he wanted to do something about it quickly,' Robyn said.

'How did he find our house? Dad never told anyone about us or where he really lived, so how did Freeman find out?'

'Look, back in them days, the gangs had a lot of cops and politicians in their pockets, which is why they got away with so much and which is how they were looked after so well. I don't know any names but I'm pretty sure it was a senior detective who was on Marvin's payroll,' Robyn said. 'He had people in all walks of life calling him regularly at the club. I know because a few times, he asked me to man the phone when his regular guy wasn't there. I answered several calls each time I did it, from cops, local councillors, even from the government security services. I remember being impressed as hell by it,' Robyn said, 'it was how he was able to grow the posse so quickly.'

'How did he get away with it? They found his blood at the house, for God's sake,' Kendra said, her voice trembling with anger for the first time.

'Look, I don't know what else to tell you. His money covered everything up, don't you see? Back then, he could do anything he wanted just by waving a bunch of money in front of people. They were corrupt, dangerous times.'

Kendra nodded in understanding, calming herself down, hoping to squeeze every bit of information out of the only witness she was ever likely to find.

'I have to ask this. If the investigation was ever re-opened, would you be willing to give evidence at court?' Kendra asked.

'Absolutely not. I don't know where he is or what he's doing, but the Yardies are still around, just hidden from view. They'd find me and kill me within hours.'

'I understand. I had to ask, though, right?' Kendra said, her arm outstretched in an effort to placate Robyn.

'Look, I've told you everything I know. The demons won't go away, they'll always be there for me. I just want to spend whatever life I have left painting and making jewellery, with my pets for company. I don't want anything else,' Robyn said, shrugging.

'Before I go, can you tell me about any of the other people who worked for Freeman?' Kendra asked.

'There were only two that I remember, Banjo was his second-in-command, I don't know his real name. A brute of a man, took no prisoners, hated everyone and was hated by everyone. The only other one I remember was Calvin, who was with us when your mum was killed. I don't know his last name or anything else about either of them, sorry.'

Kendra stood and nodded in appreciation. She picked her phone up and then her coat, before turning to Robyn.

'I appreciate your help, Robyn, it can't have been easy, so I'm grateful,' she said, holding out her hand.

Robyn took it and they shook hands.

'Again, I'm sorry about your mum and I'm sorry about the part I played at your house. I hope you get that bastard,' Robyn said.

Kendra nodded again but didn't say anything, following Robyn out of the office and back into the studio. At the door, she put on her coat and then returned her phone to her pocket, before leaving with another nod towards the woman who had witnessed her mother's murder.

7

ELLIE MORGAN

Jimmy was one of the Walsall Six, as they were affectionately known, who had originally assisted the team successfully in the early days and who were now a permanent fixture on the team. Such were their contributions that they had all been given training and jobs with Sherwood Solutions, the legitimate security company that was based at the front end of the factory. Jimmy had proved himself over and over since the Walsall contingent's first introduction in London, and was frequently called out as the gigolo of the team, based on his experiences back in Walsall. Initially proud of the title, he was somewhat embarrassed by it now, as the last occasion he'd used his talents to enamour a young lady had eventually led to a relationship. It was a relationship that was still ongoing.

'Oh, come on, guys. Really? You know I'm still with Rhianna, right?' Jimmy said, when told of the next mission. His colleagues giggled in the background as Trevor attempted to explain.

'Jimmy, I get that, okay? I'm not asking you to sleep with

anyone, I just want you to get friendly with this woman who is cheating dozens if not hundreds of elderly people out of their savings. How would you like it if one of them was your nan?' Trevor pleaded.

'Dude, it won't be the same as it was with Rhianna, okay? Just get friendly, so that we can have her take your phone number, and then Andy will take over. That's all,' Darren, the senior member of the Walsall contingent, told him.

'You sure that's all I have to do? What if she wants a snog, or more?' Jimmy asked.

'If anyone can figure out what to do, it's you, okay? So, stop whining and say that you'll do it,' Darren laughed.

'Alright, alright, but I'm telling you now, if it doesn't work, I'm not taking it further, you hear me?'

'Good man,' Trevor said, patting him on the back. 'Now take this phone and memorise the number. When you get to the point where she asks you, or you offer her your number, this is the one you give her, okay? If she gives you hers, type it in on this phone there and then and call her on the pretext that you're making sure it works.'

'Sounds simple enough. Where do I find this woman? Can you tell me anything about her?' Jimmy asked.

'Her name is Kim Morgan, and she works for a nasty, bent solicitor called Andrew Crossbey. His firm is using names and numbers of elderly people supposedly held securely on their systems from clubs they have joined, and we believe Kim makes the calls to the victims to scam them of their savings. We grabbed some photos and info about her from social media,' Trevor said, handing Jimmy a folder that contained the photos.

'I thought these scammer operations used lots of people, how do you know she's making the calls?' Jimmy asked.

'A good question, that man. The operations you're talking about are more chance-based, where there are dozens of scammers calling random numbers, or numbers they've bought from illegal data miners. On this occasion, because they already have the target data, there is no need to call randomly, they are targeting effectively and efficiently. Using a woman with a posh London accent is unique and clever, very few will ever suspect her of being a scammer. It's a clever operation, whatever you want to say about it.'

'Fair enough. Do you know where this Kim Morgan lives?' Jimmy asked.

'No, but we know where she works, it's all in there. We can either follow her home from work or see if she goes anywhere local for lunch or drinks,' Trevor replied.

'Okay, that should be easy enough. I'm guessing these miscreants will be parked up out of sight and ready to follow?' Jimmy asked, pointing to his mates.

'Of course, and we'll have some CCTV footage to help with also, the office is at Canary Wharf, on the tenth floor, above the shopping centre. It's one of those serviced offices and we believe there's no other staff. We'll need someone on the ground floor to ID her when she leaves work, and a couple more on foot to follow her from there, which could easily be on the Docklands Light Railway, a cab, a bus, or on foot. There are lots of options, so we need to be switched on,' Trevor added.

'So, all I need to do is get her to call me on this phone? What happens after that?' Jimmy asked, still cagey and uncertain.

'Without making it too obvious that you're not interested in her, you can leave with whatever excuse you want. Just make sure she calls your number so that Andy's virus can transfer to her phone. Make an excuse and say you'll call her in a day or two, or something like that, leave her in a good mood.'

Jimmy shook his head again.

'Man, this stuff just doesn't sit well with me anymore, you know? But I'll do it, because like you said, she could be calling my nan or someone close to me, and that is much worse,' he said.

'Good man,' said Trevor. 'Darren, can you sort the team deployment on your end, and make sure the cars are plotted far enough away so as not to attract any attention?'

'Of course, leave it with me,' Darren replied.

'Amir, Zoe, and Charmaine, are you up for some foot surveillance?' Trevor continued.

'Count me in,' Amir replied.

'Us too,' said Charmaine.

'Great. Make sure you memorise her photos, and as soon as we make contact, make sure to get a good description of her: her clothing, et cetera,' Trevor said. 'The rest of you see Darren, he'll tell you where you'll be deployed.'

'What time do you want us on plot?' Mo asked.

'I think she works nine to five so if we can be in place by four-thirty, the footies can have a wander and familiarise themselves with the area; there's a lot going on at Canary Wharf, so recognising the hazards nice and early will be beneficial.'

'How are you getting on, Dad?' Kendra asked.

'It's been a bit of an eye-opener, to be honest, darling,

going back all those years and trying to figure out who screwed me over.'

'Have you made any progress?'

'I think so. One of the team that knew of the operation is now a billionaire landowner who never borrowed a penny to make his purchases. He was suspected of money-laundering and fraud but was never charged with anything.'

'I'm guessing you have Andy on the case digging into his life,' Kendra said.

'Yes, although it feels a little too easy, you know?'

'If it helps, I had a nice chat with Robyn Hunt, who you may remember as the Amazonian bodyguard that Freeman used to terrorise people.'

'You found her? Don't tell me, Andy?'

'Yep, he's doing us proud, isn't he?' she said.

'Yeah, yeah, we've been through this; carry on, please.'

'Robyn told me that Freeman had a bunch of police officers, politicians, and even someone from the security services on the payroll. She said that one senior detective in particular made regular calls into Freeman's club, but she didn't give a name.'

'That narrows things down very little. The security services guy could easily have been Steven Khan, and the senior detective could've been one of two who knew of the operation, one of whom is dead,' Trevor said.

'So, what's the next move?' Kendra asked.

'I'll keep digging away with Andy and see if we can find out more about the men on the list. What about you?'

'I'll wait for you to get something useful from Andy, and we can work on it together, if that's okay? In the meantime, I need to get back to the office where I'll speak with Rick and see if he can find anything about your suspects. Message the list over and I'll give it to him,' she said.

'Okay, love. I'll catch up with you later.'

'Cheerio, Dad. I'll call if I find out more,' she said.

It must be hellish going over this again after so long, she thought, concerned for her father.

THE TEAM at the factory had dispersed to retrieve the equipment they would need for the imminent operation. Darren and Mo prepared the two cars they'd be using whilst the three 'footies' made sure they had fully charged mobile phones, their only form of communication while they were following their target.

'Let's hope she doesn't stay underground for too long, otherwise we won't be able to let the team know where we are until we surface,' Zoe told Charmaine and Amir.

'I wouldn't worry about it,' Charmaine said, 'three of us should be enough to carry on following until the team catches up.'

'We'll have a problem if she gets an Uber, though. Two cars won't be enough to conduct a decent follow in London,' Amir added, 'but there's no urgency, so if she does that today, then we'll plan for it better tomorrow.'

'Right then, let's grab our lift down there and get to work, shall we?' said Charmaine.

The journey to Canary Wharf took just thirty minutes from the factory. The cars dropped Charmaine, Zoe and Amir as close as they could before moving away and parking in Milligate Street, a short distance away, and from which they could cover the main road leaving Canary Wharf. The three footies initially walked together as they approached One Canada Square, the fifty-floor tower block and the third tallest building in the UK.

'Where did you say their office was?' Amir asked.

'I believe it's the tenth floor,' Charmaine replied.

'It's not gonna be easy spotting her in a crowd of thousands, is it?'

'Nope. I think one of us should go up there and have a look around. You up for it, Zoe?'

'Yep, I can do that. What are you two going to do?'

'We'll cover the lifts and main exit. Give us a call if you see anything of note,' Charmaine said.

Zoe nodded and made her way towards the tower block. She entered the large lobby and walked towards the bank of lifts where a small crowd of people waited. She entered the first that arrived along with seven other people, pressing the button for the tenth floor. Only one person left before her, on the seventh, and then it was her turn. As she exited the lift, she saw signs directly ahead for a dozen or so companies, including MyClubSubs off to the right. Most of the offices were accessible via frosted glass doors and had similarly frosted glass partitions, allowing plenty of light in. As she reached her destination, she could see the outline of a person straight ahead at a desk. Zoe opened the door and strode confidently towards the woman at the modern steel-and-glass reception desk. The woman looked up as she approached and smiled.

'Good afternoon, how can I help you?'

'Hi. I was told there was a vacancy here for an admin assistant. I've come to see if there is an application form,' Zoe said.

The receptionist looked bemused.

'Vacancy? Who told you there was a vacancy?' she said, 'I deal with the admin here and there's only the boss and sales manager that require any admin. The tech guys don't.'

'Kelly told me,' Zoe said, frowning, 'she said you were short-staffed and were looking to recruit. I'm so sorry, I thought I'd jump the gun and see if I could get in first. I hope I haven't spoiled my chances.'

'Kelly? Do you mean Kim? When did she tell you?' the receptionist asked.

'Last night at the coffee shop downstairs,' Zoe replied.

'Please wait here, let me go and check with her,' the woman said, standing.

Zoe looked around the office and could see that the reception area was well-decorated and spacious. The offices were located to the right, where the receptionist duly walked along a short, wide hall where there were doors to four offices. The receptionist went to the third one along, knocked, and walked in. Thirty seconds later she came back out with another woman. Zoe recognised her from the photographs as Kim Morgan.

'Can I help you?' Kim asked, in a well-spoken London accent.

'Hi. Yes, I hope you can. Kelly told me there was a vacancy here as an admin assistant, so I thought I'd pop in and get an application form,' Zoe said, smiling confidently.

Kim was a tall, slim woman of approximately twenty-five. She wore tailored navy-blue trousers and a white blouse, along with black high-heels, nothing overly fancy but very elegant.

'Who is Kelly?' Kim asked, looking back and forth between Zoe and the receptionist.

'Kelly who works here, or I thought she did. Do you know,

I didn't even ask, I just assumed. I'm so sorry, I should've asked,' Zoe said, feigning embarrassment.

'Regardless, we don't have a vacancy here, so I'm afraid you've been misinformed,' Kim said, smiling.

'I'm sorry to have bothered you. I don't suppose you know whether there are any vacancies anywhere around here?' Zoe asked.

'No, sorry,' said Kim.

'Okay, thank you; and again, apologies for the intrusion.'

A couple of minutes later she was back in the lift heading for the ground floor. When she exited, she couldn't see either colleague, so she dialled Charmaine.

'Okay, she's about five-nine, with straight, shoulder-length blonde hair, wearing a white blouse, dark blue trousers and black high heels. I'll be able to point her out when she comes down.'

'Good work, Zoe. Won't she recognise you if she sees you again?'

'Don't worry, I have a beanie and will ditch my jacket, she won't recognise me.'

'Okay, we'll leave it to you to get the eyeball on her as she comes down, make sure you give us plenty of notice,' Charmaine said.

'Will do,' Zoe replied.

She took a beanie out of her pocket and put it on, along with a pair of thick-rimmed glasses, took a bright yellow woollen scarf from her coat pocket and draped it around her neck, and then tied her jacket around her waist, changing her appearance greatly. Grabbing a brochure from one of the displays, she found a seat opposite the lifts and sat, waiting for Kim Morgan to finish work. Nobody paid any attention to a young woman reading. Every time a lift reached the ground floor, she was able to get a good look at the people exiting. At a quarter-past five, Kim Morgan finally appeared. She was now wearing a navy-blue jacket, matching her trousers, and carrying a large brown shoulder bag. Zoe called Charmaine again.

'She's out and now wearing a dark-blue jacket and carrying a brown bag over her left shoulder, heading for the doors now. I'll stay on the line until you see her.'

'Thanks, Zoe. There's a small group walking out to the square now, she's probably in that lot. Confirmed, contact walking south. Amir and I have the eyeball, Zoe, join us when you can, I'll stay on the phone until we know how she's travelling,' Charmaine said.

Kim went towards South Colonnade, where she turned right. The road was relatively busy with commuters heading home, so Charmaine and Amir closed the distance between them to just a few yards.

'Zoe, foot traffic is very busy here so get in close. She's heading towards the station,' Charmaine said, referring to the Canary Wharf Docklands Light Railway station and one of its two entrances.

Zoe sped up and closed the distance, spotting Amir and Charmaine ahead of her in the crowd. Kim turned right under the triple-arched entrance to the station and headed for the gates to the platforms ahead. She took her purse out of her handbag and pressed it against the pad at the gate, which opened immediately for her. Amir, Charmaine and Zoe had no such means to enter. Charmaine looked at the board and saw they had four minutes until the next train. She nodded towards her colleagues and walked towards the ticket machines. She took out her debit card and selected a day pass at twelve pounds, repeating the process twice more.

Handing Zoe and Amir a ticket each, they went back to the gate and gained entry to the platforms, which were all busy.

'Split up and call if you see her,' Charmaine said. She messaged Darren to let him know they were travelling by train.

'Will message with a destination,' she added.

With a minute to go, Amir called Charmaine.

'Southbound platform, towards the far end,' he said, before ringing off and calling Zoe.

The unmanned train was coming into the platform when the trio were finally within sight of their target. When Kim Morgan got on and sat down, she had no idea that within twenty feet of her were three people watching her every move. She took out her phone and put earphones in to listen to music whilst checking for messages on Facebook. She paid no attention to the young Asian man who walked by her and sat three seats away, having surreptitiously glanced at her phone on the way to see if he could gather any further intelligence.

The train travelled south and stopped at a number of stops, picking up more passengers. Soon the carriage was full, with several people standing, giving the trio plenty of cover. As it continued, though, and passengers left the train, that cover soon disappeared and the footies elected to move slightly farther from their target to avoid detection. As they covered both sides of Kim, it was unlikely that they'd lose sight of her.

Thirty minutes and ten stops later, the train came into Lewisham Station, where it would terminate. Charmaine had messaged Darren when they had left the previous stop at Elverson Road Station, giving them a few minutes notice that they'd be getting off at Lewisham.

Kim exited the train and the station and then stood at the side of the road waiting for the cab she had ordered a few minutes earlier. She wasn't paying attention to the man approaching her from the left, who then suddenly grabbed her phone and started running.

'My phone! Somebody stop that thieving bastard!' she screamed.

Izzy had played his part and timed everything perfectly. She watched as he ran towards the road as if to cross, helpless. Just as he was about to cross, Jimmy stepped towards him and stuck a foot out, tripping him, and he fell heavily to the ground. Kim's mobile phone dropped from his hand to the floor and was quickly picked up by Jimmy, the hero that had stopped him. Izzy looked up and made it clear that this was a fight that he'd likely lose and so quickly got up and ran across the road, making good his escape, almost getting hit by a car as he did so.

Jimmy walked towards Kim and handed her the phone.

'I believe this is yours, Miss,' he said.

'Thank God for that,' she said, snatching the phone from his hand, checking for damage. She was suddenly struck by how handsome he was and was captivated by his smile.

'Are you okay?' he asked.

'I suppose. Sorry for snatching, this phone is very valuable to me,' she replied. 'They should hang scumbags like that,' she added, looking for the fleeing robber.

'Want me to call the police?' Jimmy asked.

'No, they're useless around here, they wouldn't do a bloody thing,' she snorted.

'Here, come and sit down,' he said, guiding her to a low wall.

She sat down, her hands trembling slightly from the adrenaline.

'That's never happened to me before,' she said, 'I've heard of a few around here, it's one of the reasons I want to get the hell away. Too many scummy people.'

Charming, Jimmy thought, as he tried hard to continue smiling at the cold, nasty woman.

Kim Morgan took a compact out of her bag and started to powder her nose. Jimmy ignored the strange act.

'It's okay, you got your phone back and you're not hurt. That's a good thing,' he said. 'What's your name?'

'Kim,' she replied.

'Kim, you may be in shock. Is there anyone you can call? Your husband, maybe?'

'No, I'm not married, the men around here are cretins... present company excepted, of course. I'll be okay, I just need a few minutes,' she said, smiling.

Jimmy looked away and then back to her, indicating towards a nearby coffee shop.

'How about we get a coffee, that'll help with the nerves. Seeing as you haven't got a husband, it won't be a problem, will it?' he said, laughing.

'I guess it would help a little, thank you.'

'Let me help you,' he said, helping her up and guiding her towards the coffee shop. They sat at a small table by the window.

'What will you have?' he asked. 'My treat.'

'Just a regular white Americano,' she replied.

'I'll be back shortly,' Jimmy replied. *A simple please or thank you would be nice*, he thought. *This is gonna be a tough one.*

A few minutes later he returned with two coffees and sat opposite Kim.

'Feeling better?'

'Yes, I am. You never told me your name,' she said, smiling at her handsome rescuer.

'It's Jimmy,' he replied. 'And before you say anything, I wish we'd have met under better circumstances.'

Kim laughed, clearly enjoying his company.

'I don't know,' she said, 'it's not every day you can have coffee with a hero, is it?'

I hope Izzy didn't hurt himself, Jimmy thought, thinking back to tripping his friend over.

8

JIMMY AND ELLIE

'How's it going, Charmaine?' Darren asked, 'we're on the plot and waiting for instructions. Is everything going to plan?'

'It certainly is,' said Charmaine. 'That Jimmy has some skills, I didn't even know he was on the train with us. He's with her now having a drink, so I'll call you when there's movement.'

Darren laughed knowingly.

'I know we take the mickey out of him but you're absolutely right, he has some skills, that boy. We'll catch up with you later,' he said.

'Shouldn't be long now, Darren.'

It was a little longer than they'd expected. Jimmy bought two more drinks as the pair continued to talk, the incident all but forgotten.

Eventually, Jimmy stood and held out his hand.

'I guess it's time to head off. It was really nice meeting you, Kim. Will you be okay getting home?' he asked.

She shook his hand, somewhat annoyed that he was leaving.

'Yes, I'll order another Uber, I need to make up for cancelling the last one,' she said. 'It's a shame you can't escort me home,' she added mischievously.

'I have to rush, sorry. Look after yourself, and stay away from phone thieves,' Jimmy said, ignoring her request. He turned and walked off.

Kim watched him leave, sighing more in lust than in disappointment. Her love life had been disastrous in recent times, and this had been the closest she had come to meeting somebody she thought would be good for her, with the added bonus of being very attractive. Her heart then skipped a beat as Jimmy suddenly turned back and walked towards her.

'Forgive me for being forward, but I really enjoyed your company, Kim. Do you fancy meeting again for a coffee or dinner, maybe?' he asked sheepishly.

'Yes, I believe I would,' she said, her heart pounding with excitement, 'took you long enough to ask.'

Jimmy chose to ignore the last comment.

'Great! When are you free again?'

'I'm free any time after work,' she said.

'Okay, can I give you a call tomorrow or the day after? I'm waiting to find out if I'm going up north for a few days, so I will call when I know. Is that alright with you?'

'Of course.'

Jimmy took out the phone Trevor had given him.

'Fab, what's your number? I'll call it now, so you have mine too,' he said.

She gave him the details.

Jimmy dialled the number, and her phone rang immediately.

'Got it,' she said, smiling.

'I'll call you soon. Looking forward to seeing you again,' he said. He then leaned over and kissed her gently on the cheek. 'See ya.'

The kiss took her by surprise, sending a shiver down her spine, a sensation she hadn't felt for a long time.

'See you soon, Jimmy,' she said, as he turned and walked away again.

She puffed her cheeks and raised her eyebrows at the impact the meeting had had on her, before calling for another Uber.

'I should buy that bastard robber a drink,' she said, and laughed out loud.

'OKAY, stand by, Darren. She's about to get into a silver Toyota Prius, index Alpha-Kilo-seven-three-Echo-Alpha-Juliet. The car is off and away, going south along Station Road,' Amir said from his vantage point near the pickup. 'I can give a direction at the junction, if you stand by. Okay, it's now right,right onto the A20, over to you.'

'Thanks, Amir. I have vision and it's now turning left, left into Elmira Street. I have one car for cover and we're continuing southbound at thirty miles per hour. Amir, call Mo to pick you and Charmaine up. I have Zoe.'

'Will do. I'll call back when we're on the move, shouldn't be long,' Amir replied.

Darren continued to follow the cab, which turned onto

Algenon Street.

Amir called back.

'We're with Mo, where are you?'

'We're in Algenon Street, southbound, indicating to turn left onto Vicar's Hill. And now indicating right onto the B236. Stand by, it looks like it's now turning left onto Chudleigh Road. Thank God for satellite navigation, eh? That's confirmed, it's left, left into Chudleigh Road. It's a lot quieter here, I'll have to fall back a little as I haven't any cover.'

'We're almost with you,' Amir said, 'maybe ten seconds behind you. Mo is a maniac driver,' he added.

'Okay, I have brake lights in the distance and the vehicle is pulling over to the offside. Stand by for a number as I drive past. The subject is getting out and walking towards a house. I believe it's number one-two-four, it has a green wheelie bin directly by the gate. I've now lost vision and the cab is away. I'll drop Martin off to do a walk-by,' Darren said. 'Will call back when we know more, if you can plot up nearby.'

'Will do, good job, big man,' Amir said, hanging up.

Darren turned onto Amyruth Road and stopped for Martin to get out on foot. Within seconds he'd disappeared onto Chudleigh Road and was walking past the house Kim was suspected to have entered. Martin took out his phone and called Darren.

'Definitely number one-two-four, the door is still open, and I can hear an argument of some kind, something about being very late,' Martin said. 'I believe she may be on the move again; you should call and prep the team.'

'Nice one, Martin. Stay out there as long as you can and see if you can keep an eye on the gate to see where she goes. It may be another cab.'

'Will do.' Martin crossed to the opposite side of the road

and sat on a low wall some fifty feet farther down, watching the house from an angle. There were a few cars parked so he would be difficult to see from number 124 when Kim did show herself. He rang Darren again.

'Okay, I have vision on the front gate and will see her when she comes out. If she turns left, I'll need to move, so you'll need to get someone else out to drop in behind her.'

'Thanks, Martin, shouldn't be a problem. Will you be able to see the car clearly if she's picked up by a cab?'

'Yeah, that won't be a problem. Stand by, she's out, out of the house and immediately crossing the road. She has a small child with her, maybe four or five years old, wearing a green puffer jacket, blue jeans and black baseball cap, a little boy. Okay, she's crossed over at a slight angle towards me and has turned immediately right, right into a road. I'll move and get a road name, but you may want to send another footie ahead,' Martin said as he walked briskly towards the junction.

He crossed the road so that he could square the junction, in case Kim and her child stopped for any reason.

'It's Foxborough Gardens, Darren. They're about to go out of my vision around a nearside bend. Is anyone down there?' Martin said.

'Yeah, I dropped Charmaine off further down and I'm parked up in a dead end, hopefully she won't come down here,' Mo replied. 'I'll hang up and call Charmaine now.'

'Okay, I'll continue and jump back in when Charmaine takes over,' Martin said. He hung up and called Zoe.

'Hey, Darren, I now have vision, she's walking towards a block of flats, the second one as you come into the road. It's five storeys and they're walking towards the entrance. Stand by, I need to get closer, will call you back,' Charmaine said.

It was a few minutes later when she called back.

'Sorry about that, I ended up talking to her. Anyway, she lives at number one-oh-five, it's on the ground floor. She's nice enough, although she speaks like a snob,' Charmaine said.

'Wait, what? You talked to her? Charmaine, that isn't what we taught you, is it? Surveillance doesn't involve talking to the subject, you know that, right?' Darren said. Charmaine laughed.

'I know, I know, I improvised, okay? They walked into the block and I lost sight of the straight away. If I hadn't run to catch them, I would have definitely missed them going into the ground floor flat.'

'If you saw them going into the flat, how the hell did you end up talking to her?' Darren asked, perplexed.

'She heard me fall and came to help me.'

'What? She heard you *what?*'

Charmaine laughed again.

'She heard me fall over before she'd closed her door and came to help me,' Charmaine said.

'Are you okay? Did you hurt yourself?'

'No, I'm fine. It sounded a lot worse than it was, just took me by surprise.'

'How the hell did it happen?' asked Darren.

'Like I said, I was running to make sure I got a door number. As I got to the block, I saw them heading for a ground floor flat and I was all happy that I'd seen them. I didn't notice the step and tripped over. Luckily, I stuck my arm out, otherwise it would have been painful.'

'And she heard you?'

'Yeah. Before I knew it, she was helping me up, asking if I was okay.'

'Did she say anything else?'

'She asked if I needed anything, so I asked for some water. She helped me into her flat and got me a glass.'

'You were in her flat?' Darren said, somewhat exasperated at the turn of events.

Charmaine laughed.

'Darren, none of this was planned, okay? It was accidental. Yes, I was inside her flat, which is very nice, by the way. I stood by the front door while she got me a drink of water. Her son's name is Adam, and she loves pink.'

'Pink?'

'Yeah, her walls are all painted pink. It sounds nuts but it kinda works, she has good taste in furniture, too. And her television is huge, must be eighty inches. Everything I saw was high-end, even the glass she brought me was crystal.'

'Yes, well, we know where she gets her money from, don't we? Okay, get yourself back to the junction with Chudleigh Road and one of us will pick you up. That's good work, Charmaine, despite breaking every surveillance rule in the book,' Darren said, laughing as he ended the call.

This job just gets weirder and weirder every day, he thought, as he moved the car to pick her up.

TREVOR LOOKED AT THE LIST, over and over, still unclear about the next steps. The same questions kept coming up, leading to the same conclusions.

I was betrayed by someone for money, I don't think there is any doubt about that, he thought. *The likeliest candidate is Steven Khan, who is now a billionaire property developer who didn't borrow any money to start his empire. Which means he was in bed with Freeman and the posse, which is where he got his start with money.*

But one question remained unanswered.

It was a detective who kept calling Freeman, which means it would be someone from the covert team, either Detective Superintendent Raymond Stanwick, now deceased, or Detective Chief Inspector Keith Hamilton, now retired. But which one?

It was a question that continued to badger and frustrate Trevor as he thought back to the operation. His dealings with all the men involved had been positive, with no hint of betrayal. He tried hard to think about the two detectives, to recall any occasions when he was alone with one of them. He did remember Steven Khan as having had a prominent role in discussions, but again could not think of anything that implicated anyone else.

'I guess there is nothing left to do except talk to him,' he said out loud, picking up the phone.

'Mister Giddings, to what do I owe the pleasure of this call?' said Andy.

'Why are you talking in that stupid accent?'

'What stupid accent? I'm trying to master my James Bond impersonation,' Andy said, offended by the remark.

'You are failing miserably,' said Trevor, 'so give up now. Anyway, I'm not calling to discuss your silly voice, I need a favour.'

'Sure,' Andy said, reverting to his normal voice, 'what do you need?'

'I need to speak with Steven Khan, so I need you to find out everything you can about his whereabouts, upcoming appointments, anything else which will help you find me a slot to meet him.'

'That's easier said than done, Trevor. I'll try my best, but unless we have a mobile number to call and implant a virus, that will be difficult.'

'You sound like Scotty from Star Trek, always bemoaning your lot when you actually know you can do it.' Trevor laughed.

'Yeah, well, he was a very underrated member of the team, that man. Like I said, give me a little time and I'll figure something out.'

'Okay, thanks. I also want you to find everything you can on the other two detectives, Detective Superintendent Raymond Stanwick, who's dead, and Detective Chief Inspector Keith Hamilton. One of them was on Freeman's payroll and probably worked with Khan. I want to know which one, so see if you can find any connection to the other.'

'Will do. How are things with Kendra and her involvement with this?' Andy suddenly asked.

Trevor paused before replying.

'I'd normally say that it's none of your business, but I guess it is now, isn't it?' Trevor said, before continuing. 'If you must know, it's opened some wounds I didn't want opening, but at the same time it's made me realise that some bastard, or bastards, got away with my wife's murder. Kendra has every right to chase them down, and I will do everything to help her. So, in answer to your question, things are difficult, but we'll get through it, I'm sure. We'll be just fine.'

'That's good to know, Trevor. And as ever, I'll do my best to help.'

'Just remember one thing in all this, Andy,' Trevor said.

'What's that?'

'We *will* get the bastards.'

9

OPTIONS

Kendra, as ever, knocked before entering Rick's office.

'Morning, boss man, how's it going today?'

Rick looked up from his computer and smiled at his favourite detective.

'Good morning, Detective Trouble, what can I do for you today?'

'Just thought I'd give you an update,' Kendra said, closing the door and sitting down.

'Why, thank you. I thought you'd forgotten about me already,' he said, arching his eyebrow.

'We've done no such thing, and you know it,' she said, 'so now who's the troublesome one?'

'I'm just kidding, what have you got?' he asked.

'Two things. Firstly, I spoke with Robyn Hunt, who confirmed that Freeman killed my mum. She won't come forward as a witness and wants to be left alone, so we need to come up with an alternative plan to get a conviction, which won't be easy after thirty years.'

'Sounds about right, I'll have a think on that one. What's the second thing?'

'We've housed the woman we believe is making the calls and scamming people for the bent solicitor. We're meeting up tonight to discuss our options on moving forward with that one, so if you're free, can you join us at the factory later?'

'Sure, I'll meet you there after work,' Rick said.

'Cool. Anything going on here?'

'Same shit, different day. You can help Jill out with an assault case, if you like. She needs to interview a couple of witnesses and could do with some back-up.'

'Consider it done, and I'll see you later,' Kendra said, waving as she left.

Jill was at her desk on the computer when Kendra sat opposite.

'How's it going, Missus Rothwell? How's Pablo treating you?' she cheekily asked.

'Will you keep your bloody voice down?' Jill blushed as she looked around to check if anyone had heard. Fortunately, Pablo and everybody else was working at the other end of the office, out of earshot.

'Oh, I haven't seen you blush like that for a while. That means something's happened between the two of you, so come on, out with it. Out with it, otherwise I'll be congratulating you on every social media platform within the hour,' Kendra said, rubbing her hands with glee.

Jill rolled her eyes and looked around again. Leaning over, she whispered her response.

'Pablo told me he loved me and wants to marry me. Actually, what he said was that when we're married, we can go on a round-the-world cruise together, which has always been a dream of his.'

'So, he didn't actually propose but talked about something in the future?' Kendra asked.

'Yes. So, making jokes like you do is really not funny, Miss Prissy Pants. I think he needs a bloody nudge with everything, that man. He can be infuriating!'

'But does he treat you right?' Kendra asked.

Jill blushed again.

'You know he bloody well does, and I know what you're bloody well doing, Kendra. Yes, he treats me great, and yes, we get on brilliantly, and yes, I know I have to nudge him more frequently. I get it, okay?'

'So, stop whinging and get nudging. You two are great together, so stop wasting time, woman.'

Jill rolled her eyes again and sat back down.

'You are a witch with evil powers,' she hissed.

'But you still love me, don't you? Now, Rick told me you needed some help, so tell me what you have, Missus Rothwell.'

Kendra narrowly avoided the pen as it whizzed by her left ear.

THE TEAM MET at the factory as planned that evening. As she parked her car, Kendra saw that a great deal of progress had been made on the new building behind the factory, which was to house the new training wing and showroom. The shell was up, and they had added a roof, so it was on schedule for completion in a month's time.

'It's looking great, isn't it?' Mo said as he pulled up alongside her car with his younger twin, Amir.

'Yes, it is,' she replied.

'We've been arguing in the car about Mo's role so far,' Amir said, putting his hand over his mouth to stifle his laughter.

'My brother can be a dick sometimes, sorry about that,' Mo said. 'Young Amir here doesn't see the value of project-managing something like this. He thinks everything goes to plan, always.'

'Bro, once the architect's plans are drawn up, how can it possibly go wrong?' Amir said, his arms outstretched.

'Because, little brother, you need to keep on top of the builders, you need to make sure the right materials have been delivered, that we aren't being screwed by anyone. If they know someone is overseeing it, then they don't try anything on, do they? You have so much to learn, honestly, I don't know how we're related,' Mo said, shaking his head in disappointment.

'He's right, of course, Kendra,' said Amir. 'I just don't let him off easily, it keeps him on his toes.'

'He also thinks that when it's finished, my role will be over, don't you, Amir?' Mo said, looking at his brother with a mischievous grin.

'What do you mean? It's mine and Charmaine's project, you won't be involved,' Amir replied.

'Won't I?' Mo said, heading towards the entrance.

Kendra laughed as she watched them walk away, arguing as usual. She looked back at the building works and nodded, pleased with the progress.

'Long may it continue,' she muttered to herself.

Everyone was gathered inside in the main room behind reception, waiting for the meeting to start. Kendra saw Rick speaking with Andy and headed over to them, where they were joined by Trevor.

'How's it all going, you pair of miscreants?' she asked, giving Andy a playful shove.

'We were just discussing your lack of manners, actually,' he said.

'Hello, K,' said Rick, 'we were actually just discussing our options about Freeman now we know there won't be a witness. We think a nice case of *creative* entrapment should do the trick.'

'Rick, you know as well as I do that entrapment is illegal, so what are you playing at?'

'We have a cunning plan, Detective,' he said, touching his forefinger to his nose and winking. 'We'll tell you after the meeting, if you have the patience.'

'Now who has bad manners?' she said. 'What about you, Dad? Everything okay?'

'Everything is not okay, as you know, daughter. Even this self-professed genius here hasn't come up with anything we can use or follow up on.' He pointed to Andy.

'I told you, I need some time. Have I ever let you down?' Andy said.

'Get your arse in gear and find something soon before we lose momentum,' said Trevor.

'I know it's frustrating, Dad, but if we're going to do this properly, then we have to have some patience. I'm sure we'll find something soon.'

'I know, love, but something is scratching the back of my brain, and I can't shake the feeling. Maybe it's nothing, but those instincts have always served me well, so I just need to learn to be more patient. Anyway, you ready to start the meeting?'

'Yes, want me to crack on?'

He nodded.

'Alright, everyone, settle down so we can start the meeting,' Trevor shouted. 'Kendra, over to you.'

The room became silent, and all eyes focused on her.

'Hello, everyone. Thanks for meeting at such short notice but we thought it would be good to brainstorm some ideas as to how we're going to move forward. As you know, we have identified the company and the individuals responsible for scamming millions from vulnerable, mainly elderly people here in the UK. We know where the two main individuals live but we haven't yet come up with a suitable way to deal with them.'

'Can we hang, draw, and quarter them?' Izzy asked, to much laughter.

'If only, eh, Izzy?' Kendra said, 'but you know how we operate, we don't do the killing thing, remember? We like to think that we're more creative in how we dispense justice, so has anyone got any genuine ideas? Don't be shy,' she added.

'Can we steal their money?' Charmaine asked, 'you now, how we've done before? Maybe give it back to the victims, like Robin Hood did?'

'Great idea, Charmaine, we will certainly be trying that. In fact, after this meeting, Jimmy here will be making a very important phone call, won't you, Jimmy?' Trevor said, winking at Jimmy, who made no effort to hide his displeasure.

'Really? You know I'm not enjoying this. I had to talk to her for ages last night, knowing she was evil. Please think of something soon so I don't have to do that again,' he replied.

'Don't worry, son, we're hoping to sort this little operation out sooner rather than later. Other than grabbing their money, what else can we do? Anyone else?'

'It's all about the money, Trevor, that's why they do this. If we hit their finances hard, then the job's done, isn't it? They'll be hurting pretty badly,' said Darren.

'The job's only half done, Darren,' said Rick, 'they need to pay a heavier price than just losing what they've stolen. That's what we need to decide on.'

'Fair enough. In which case, I would go with Izzy's suggestion,' Darren said, to more laughter.

'What do we know about the solicitor?' asked Charmaine.

'His name is Andrew Crossbey and he lives in a large seventeenth-century manor house in Brentwood, which is on the outskirts of London. He lives there with his husband Dilman Hussey, who owns a failing restaurant in Romford. We believe that Crossbey is funding the restaurant to keep it running for his husband,' Andy said, referring to his most recent findings.

'Anything else?' Kendra asked.

'Several, actually. I did a deep dive and found a couple of interesting things that may help us decide how to punish this piece of crap. Firstly, he has a planning application in with the local council to add a large extension and to convert a double garage into a granny annexe. I was able to access the plans and it's estimated to cost six hundred thousand pounds, mainly due to the building being listed and the specialist materials and labour required to build everything to the correct standard.'

There were several whistles from the audience.

'What's the other thing?' asked Trevor.

'He has a holiday booked to Australia; he'll be going away for almost a month with his husband. Believe it or not, I found out on social media; he put it on there and told everyone that he's hiring security guards to be on site while he is away. Can you believe that?' Andy replied.

'Wow, I'm already thinking of some ideas,' Amir said, rubbing his hands together.

'Yep, I think we all are,' Kendra said, laughing. 'What do you need to make things happen, Andy?'

'The first thing we need to do is send the virus to Jimmy's new friend. Hopefully that will reveal her contacts to us, the frequency of her calls to him, et cetera. More importantly, it will enable us to transfer the same virus to his phone. Once that is done, I should be able to access his network, both at home and the office. We can do a lot of damage while he is away,' he said.

'Okay, then, I guess it's over to you, Jimmy,' Kendra said, looking at the young gigolo, who continued to shake his head.

'Okay, okay, I'll go outside and call her right now. What do I need to do, Andy?'

'Call her and just chat normally for a minute or two, set up a date or something. When you're done, hang up and then send her the emoji of the thumbs-up jumping up and down. It's the only one in the photo album on the phone. The virus is embedded in that and will insert itself into her phone in the middle of the night when she's asleep. When she next calls Crossbey it will automatically send the same thumbs-up emoji to him, which he will hopefully open as it is from her. That's it,' Andy said.

'Okay, I'll be back in a few. Crack on without me,' Jimmy said, turning to leave. He received several slaps to the back from his friends on the way and was soon outside, calling Kim Morgan.

'Let's get this over with,' he muttered.

KIM SMILED when she saw it was Jimmy calling. She had hoped he would call and had bitten one of her fingernails almost raw with the anticipation. She picked up the phone and took a deep breath before answering.

'Hi, Jimmy, it's about time you called, it's not nice keeping a lady waiting,' she said.

'It's good to speak with you again, I enjoyed our talk the other day. My face is still sore.'

'Why, did the robber hurt you yesterday?'

'No, silly, it's from smiling constantly, from the time we met until now. That's why my face hurts, it has to get used to smiling so much!'

'That's a bit cringey but I'll take it as a compliment,' she said, rolling her eyes. 'Are you calling from up north?'

'No; luckily, that isn't happening until next week now, so I'm around for the next few days if you're up for meeting again,' he replied.

'I would, what do you fancy doing?' she asked, hoping for a plush dinner somewhere in Central London.

'How about a nice dinner and a movie, old-school,' he said.

'Erm… okay. I suppose that sounds like a plan. When did you have in mind?'

'How about tomorrow? I can pick you up around seven, if that's convenient?'

'Yes. I'll text you my address.'

'Fab. Anyway, I have to go, work stuff is calling. I'm looking forward to tomorrow, Kim. You have a great night,' he said.

'Okay, bye now,' she replied, hanging up. She sat, disappointed, hoping he'd have been whisking her away somewhere fancier than the cinema, until she remembered the text she needed to send. She typed her address and sent it to Jimmy, who replied almost immediately with a thumbs-up emoji that jumped up and down excitedly.

'Dinner and a movie. I haven't done that since I was a teenager. Maybe he needs a few dates to ramp things up a bit,' she said out loud, shrugging.

'So, what's this big plan of yours to take care of Freeman?' Kendra asked Andy and Rick after the meeting had finished. They sat in the canteen with Trevor, Amir, Mo, and Charmaine.

'I figured that since you two have become masters at lying your way through everything, I figured we should use those skills and get him to confess,' Rick said, keeping a straight face as he looked back and forth between Kendra and Andy.

'I've already argued my side, it's your turn,' Andy said to her.

'Rick, you're not going to forgive or forget for a while, are you?' Kendra laughed.

'Oh, I've already forgiven, don't you worry. As for forgetting, I'd rather not, but I do want to use the opportunity to make it difficult and uncomfortable for you two for some time, you know, milk it a little.'

This time he grinned, enjoying himself.

'Fine, you crack on and have fun. But two can play at that game, so if you want me to remind you of the times that we both had you over at work, then we can do that, too,' she said. She looked over to Andy and raised her eyebrows, smirking.

'Ooh, I didn't think of that; good one, K. Turn it back onto him, a neat skill,' Andy added.

'Honestly, you two can be a nightmare at times!' Rick laughed, shaking his head. 'Fine, I'll ease off on the reminders, seeing as you're so sensitive.'

'So, can you explain to me how you think you can legally get a man to confess to a murder that he committed thirty years ago?' asked Kendra.

'First off, this isn't a case of entrapment. As you should know, in English law there is no defence of entrapment, but it is considered an abuse of power for agents of the state to induce someone to commit an offence and then seek to prosecute them for it. The offence has already been committed, so a confession is the only thing that will work other than an eyewitness account, which we don't have and won't get,' Rick said.

'Okay, so entrapment isn't what we're looking for, then. How do you propose to get a confession out of Freeman that will be admissible in court?'

'That's simple, we lie through our back teeth and tape him confessing. I told you, use your strengths, Kendra.'

'I'm a little confused,' she said. 'Are we doing this as the team, or as police officers? Because if we do it as police officers, we will be scrutinised far more, don't you think?'

'Exactly, so we do it as a team. For clarity, police *are* allowed to lie when questioning a suspect. If the suspect wrongly believes the lies and confesses, that confession is admissible and can be used against them. Basically, that's what we should plan to do, think of a lie that will induce Freeman into admitting to the murder. We tape it and then send it to the Metropolitan Police, the National Crime Agency, Interpol, every law enforcement agency in the UK and Europe,' Rick continued.

'And the press,' Andy added. 'The press will put pressure on the police to act.'

'That's some good pressure there, but it will have to be a bloody good confession for it to work in court. And what if he gets off?' she asked.

'If he gets off, then we go to plan B,' Trevor said, 'which was my preferred option from the start.'

'What's that, Dad?'

'We beat the crap out of him and drop him off at the Triads. They hate each other and the Triads would skin him alive, which would still be too good for him,' Trevor said, his voice cold and emotionless.

'We have several options if he gets off at court, including our old favourite of dropping him off in Africa somewhere, where he can work in the mines for the rest of his life,' Andy said.

'Okay, let's hope we can do this with plan A, then,' Kendra said, shaking her head. 'I, for one, want that bastard locked away for life—and the world to know that he killed my mother.'

'Don't forget, he wasn't alone in this,' Trevor said, 'there's whoever is behind it all, one of the betrayers on my list.'

'I think we'll take each person as they come and deal with them as we see fit,' Andy said, 'otherwise we could be waiting a long time for justice to be served to people who have a ton of money and power behind them.'

'Agreed,' Kendra said, 'so we'll think of a way to get Freeman to confess, and you, Dad, need to come up with a plan to flush the betrayer out, for starters. How does that sound?'

'Sounds good to me. I'll be at the station and can help from there if you think of anything,' Rick said.

A short time later they dispersed and headed home. Trevor was quiet in the car with Kendra on the way home.

'You okay, Dad?' she asked.

'Not really, love. This has brought back a lot of painful memories, you know? But also, some really good ones that I'd almost forgotten. However painful this is, I'm glad we're doing it. Thank you, darling,' he said, reaching over and clasping her hand.

'Don't thank me yet, Dad. We still have to catch the bastards, remember?'

10

PROFILING

The virus planted in Kim Morgan's phone did what it was supposed to do and fully installed itself at three o'clock in the morning while she was fast asleep. It got to work immediately, transferring all data on the phone to one of Andy's secure caches. The second she phoned Andrew Crossbey, and he answered, the virus would transfer onto his phone and the process would repeat its instruction to install at three in the morning.

Andy's plan was to utilise the data on Crossbey and Morgan's phones to allow him access to their computers so that he could get up to some mischief, especially in the case of Crossbey while he was away on holiday. When he looked through the information from Kim's phone, he knew that he had most of what was required for him to access her computers, both personal and at work. He quickly cloned her phone so that he could intercept any messages such as two-factor authentication, likely required for access to secure accounts such as her banking as well as access to work servers, which were becoming more secure because of recent security advances.

By ten o'clock the following morning he had set everything up and had started putting measures in place specifically for Kim, preparing to do the same with Crossbey the following morning. He started sifting through the data that had been downloaded and was soon able to put together a comprehensive dossier of the woman whose voice the victims had trusted.

'Well, Miss Morgan, it seems you have many secrets,' he said out loud.

TREVOR HAD THOUGHT LONG and hard about how he was going to flush out the men Freeman had collaborated with. Despite having a strong hunch that Steven Khan was behind it all, he also knew that at least one police detective was involved, and it was this conundrum that had frustrated him so far. Having gone over his memories of the team thirty years earlier, he had not come up with anything that connected anyone to Khan thereafter. It was for this reason he had asked Andy to do a deep-dive into their lives, if only to find the most tenuous of connections so that he could plan the next step. While he waited for Andy to work his magic, he came up with a plan to confront Steven Khan, which wasn't easy given his high levels of security.

After much tinkering with his plan, he checked the internet and made copious notes about the man and his business empire. There was very little information about his private life on there, which didn't surprise him knowing the man's background in national security and intelligence. His property portfolio was significant, and Trevor found one article in the press that accused him of profiting from the poor by buying land and property on the cheap from those that were desperately in debt. There was no official response and nothing further as a follow-up article, mainly because, after more probing, Trevor found out that the journalist who had written the article had died in a mysterious fire at his London flat.

Trevor nodded, recognising that his task would not be an easy one. His phone rang and he saw that it was Andy.

'Find anything?' he asked.

'All I can tell you is that these people sure know how to cover their tracks. All of them,' Andy said.

'Working with MI5 and secret operations will do that to you, my friend. You haven't said no, so I'm guessing you found something?'

'It took some digging but the only connections I could find were large regular payments that one of Khan's shell companies makes to a member of parliament. The only reason I found it was because on one occasion it was logged by a person who works in his accounts department; I think they made a mistake using their name, probably thinking it would never be traced back to the main holding company.'

'Why did that one stand out? Isn't he known for making large contributions to the Government election fund?' asked Trevor.

'Yes, he is,' said Andy, 'but those are the ones he makes publicly, which anyone can see. This one is a contribution he makes several times a year, running it through various companies to distance it from his business, and he has done so for a long time. They clearly want it hidden from the public eye, hence using a shell company, and attempting to avoid any connection to Khan.'

'Who's the MP that's receiving the money?'

'That's the connection you asked for, Trevor. The MP is Nelson Stanwick, the son of the late Detective Superintendent Raymond Stanwick, the man who ran your undercover operation against the Yardies.'

ANDY HAD CONTACTED Kendra to update her with his findings from Kim Morgan's phone.

'So, you know where she lives and that she has a son, Adam, who is looked after by her mother, who lives in Chudleigh Road. That is now confirmed,' he told her.

'What else did you find?' she asked.

'Interestingly, the flat she lives in was only bought nine months ago and paid for in full, there is no mortgage or remaining debt.'

'That doesn't surprise me, the amount of money the bastard scammers are making. She is clearly doing well working for Crossbey, I can't imagine how much more he's making out of it,' she said.

'Hopefully we'll find out tomorrow when the virus works on his phone,' said Andy. 'She's already phoned him three times today, so it'll do its magic in the early hours. Once I have access to his accounts I'll know more. Much more.'

'So, she paid for her flat from her immoral earnings, what else?' said Kendra.

'You'll like this one. The father of her son is a teacher from the Birmingham area, who's going through the courts for joint custody of Adam, because she has denied access.

She's spent a small fortune on solicitors keeping him at bay, so it keeps getting postponed for legal reasons. By the time it gets heard, he'll be skint from all the legal fees, and she'll just keep denying access,' Andy said.

'She sounds lovelier by the minute, doesn't she?'

'There's more,' he said. 'She loves her social media posts, as you know from the bad luck with relationships, as she has made clear on so many occasions. She's not shy with what she says about people, that's for sure. Anyway, one of the things that keeps cropping up is her love of Dubai. She went there last year with a couple of friends and keeps mentioning how she's looking to move there one day, permanently. She's put a three hundred thousand pound deposit down on a flat there, in a complex at Palm Jumeirah, and she is in the process of getting approval for the mortgage for the remaining two hundred and fifty thousand. Crossbey is helping her fudge the paperwork so the mortgage will get approved. She's making the most of the scams while it's going well, isn't she?'

'We have enough to work with, for sure,' Kendra said, 'I think it's about time we put an end to their horrible scheme and dispense a little justice, don't you?'

'Bloody right we should. Leave it with me.'

'Do I really have to do this?' Jimmy asked Trevor on the call. 'You told me it would be a quick meet-up for coffee and then a phone call to upload the virus. Now you want me to take her out again?'

'I know, and I'm sorry, but if you don't do it, she'll know something is up and she'll put something on social media—

or worse,' Trevor replied. 'Just go for a movie and dinner like you said you would and then make some excuse that'll take you away for a few weeks.'

'What is it you need from her?' Jimmy asked.

'To be honest, we have more than enough to be getting on with,' Trevor said, 'but if you can find out more about her work or her boss it will all help later when we start putting our plans into action.'

'Alright, alright. I'll call her and take her out tonight. But, again, I hate this, it doesn't sit well with me at all. She's one nasty woman, that one. She needs arresting, I don't know why we don't point the cops in her direction,' Jimmy said.

'Come on, Jimmy, you know it'll take months before they do anything, and all that will happen is that the operation will quickly close and be moved somewhere else. They'll likely get away with it, knowing how much they spend on lawyers, so we need to be sure they pay for their crimes, literally.'

'Okay. I'll do what I can and will call you later.'

'Good man, Jimmy. Speak to you later.'

JIMMY PICKED Kim up from her flat in a metallic grey almost-new BMW 5-series, courtesy of Stav, whose garage supplied all the vehicles that the team ever required. He waited downstairs after sending a message that he was waiting for her. Kim appeared a few minutes later, wearing a pair of ripped jeans, black ankle boots and an olive-green jumper. She had a small handbag draped across her chest. Jimmy got out to meet her, opening the passenger door for her.

'You look great, Kim,' he said, giving her a peck on the cheek.

'I try, thank you for noticing. It's always nice to meet a real gentleman,' she replied, looking around the leather-clad interior of the car. 'Nice car, you never did tell me what you did for work.'

'This is one of the perks of the job, a company car. I work for a security firm as a consultant,' he said, putting the car in gear and moving off.

'Nice. What do you consult on?' she asked.

'Mainly on security systems for commercial premises, you know, like CCTV cameras and things like that. There's a big demand for it at the moment and the company is very busy. It's why I never know when I'm going to be around, they send me all over the bloody place,' he said. 'But enough about me, tell me more about what you do.'

'My job isn't as exciting. I work as an office manager for a company that handles online payments for businesses,' she replied. 'I basically order a bunch of people around and get paid a small fortune for it.'

'That sounds fairly interesting, why would you say that it wasn't exciting?' he said, probing for information.

'I suppose it is. I don't get bored, if that's what you mean, but it's just mainly dealing with clients, to be honest. I'm on the phone a lot and that part is never boring,' she said.

'Do you manage a lot of staff?'

'No, not really. In fact, it's mainly IT geeks that make sure the servers and software run smoothly. I help the boss a lot with his workload; he's always too busy to do admin so I help a lot with contracts, invoicing, that sort of thing.'

'That's cool. Sounds like you're much more than just an

office manager, you should ask for a promotion and a pay rise!'

'It's funny you should say that because I have asked for a raise and he's agreed, so I can't complain.'

'So, where do you fancy going for dinner?' Jimmy asked, changing the subject.

'Well, I was hoping for a fancy restaurant in London, but I'll settle for a nice little Italian restaurant I know in Bromley, if you don't mind a fifteen-minute drive,' she said.

'Sounds like a plan,' he said, 'I'm starving.'

During the drive to the restaurant, they continued with small talk, and Kim became more and more relaxed in Jimmy's presence.

At the restaurant, a small family-run business with a homely atmosphere and the delicious aroma of cooking, they both chose the spaghetti Bolognese sprinkled with plenty of grated parmesan, with a side of garlic bread.

'How boring of us,' Kim laughed, 'our first dinner together and we choose the most typical of Italian meals.'

'There's plenty of time to be adventurous with food later,' Jimmy said, raising his wine glass. 'Now, tell me more about yourself, I need to know what I'm letting myself in for.'

Kim laughed, now completely relaxed in Jimmy's company, and enjoying the evening very much.

'Didn't you want to see a movie?' she said.

'Not really, I'd much rather stay here or go somewhere quiet where we can talk more. I'm sure you want to know more about me too, right?'

'Correct. And I'm happy with that. I'd still like to be home by ten-thirty, though, I have a babysitter that needs relieving,' she said, taking a sip of wine.

'See? Right there, I have more questions already. Tell me

about your kids, where their dad is, I want to know everything,' he said, leaning forward exaggeratingly on both elbows. More laughter.

'You'll be happy to know it's just one special person, my four-year-old, Adam. His dad isn't around and won't ever be around, if you're worried—and no, he's not dead or in prison, either. I don't have a drug habit, I don't have any debt, and my weaknesses are my love of an Aperol spritz and holidays abroad, especially to Dubai. I work hard so I want to enjoy what spare time I have,' she said, biting the bullet and laying her cards on the table.

'Wow, okay. I guess I asked for that! I've never been to Dubai, it's hellishly expensive, isn't it?'

'It is,' she said, 'but it's worth it. I forget everything back home when I'm there, and I can afford it, so why not?'

'Fair enough. How often do you go?'

'I try and go every three months. Luckily my mum looks after Adam so I can go for ten days at a time.'

'Wow, you get a lot of annual leave, your boss must really like you,' he said.

'He should do, I earn him a bloody fortune. Honestly, I must spend six hours a day on the phone for him, talking bullshit to make him loads of money. I deserve every one of those days off,' she said, resentfully.

'Like I said, you should ask for a lot more money, sounds like you deserve it.'

'You know what, I think I will. He can't do what I do, and I don't think anyone else can. I work miracles for him and there isn't anyone else like me in this country. You have to go overseas to find someone like me, only my success rate is a hundred times more than they have there,' she said.

'You go, girl, I like someone who knows their worth. Good for you!' Jimmy laughed.

'Enough about me, young man. Now it's your turn, so spill,' she said. 'But before that, call that useless waitress over, will you? She's slacking and I want some more wine.'

Again, what a charming woman, Jimmy thought as he raised his arm to attract the waitress's attention.

'Come on, Jimmy, don't keep a lady waiting,' she insisted.

'Okay, here goes nothing. I don't have any kids and haven't been married. I work too hard, but it hasn't been a problem for me as a single man to be away from home so much. I'm starting to think it's gonna be a problem in the future, though,' he said mischievously. 'I love football, I support Walsall, my local club from back home, but I haven't been back for over a year. I love watching movies and sci-fi shows like Star Wars and Star Trek. Sounds like I'm a bit of a geek, doesn't it?'

'It does, and geeks are not great, Jimmy, but luckily you make up for it with your charm and good looks,' she said, laughing as he blushed. 'What's more worrying is that you support Walsall.'

He nodded knowingly.

'This is really nice, Kim, I'm very glad I was there the other night. Sounds nasty but I'm pleased you got robbed, otherwise this wouldn't be happening,' he said, taking her hand in his.

Kim raised her eyebrows and tilted her head to one side.

'Come on, Jimmy,' she said, 'it's a little early to be gushing like that, isn't it? Mind you, I wish I'd taken Adam to mum's for the night, now, instead of getting a babysitter. You're a bit of a charmer, aren't you?'

Jimmy smirked, knowing that his charms had worked—again.

'There's plenty of time for that, Kim. If anything, I love this part of getting to know someone almost as much as getting intimate,' he said.

'Really? That's a shame, I'm quite a fan of having a romp nice and early to see whether we're compatible,' she replied.

'Me too, I was lying through my back teeth,' he said, laughing again.

She grinned mischievously.

'But seriously,' he continued, 'I'm enjoying getting to know you. One thing, though, is that I won't rush into anything, so you can deal with this adventure however you wish.'

'Wow, I take it back, you're not just a charmer, you're a player too, aren't you?' she said, giving his hands an approving squeeze.

'Yes, I am. Now, how about you tell me more about your work, it sounds much more interesting than you made out earlier,' he said.

11

RECONNAISSANCE

'Any luck with Crossbey's phone?' Kendra asked when she called Andy the following morning.

'Oh yes, milady, lots of luck. That man is in for a world of complications in his life,' Andy replied, 'he won't know what hit him.'

'Excellent. When is he going away?'

'In a couple of days. I've already created folders on his house, his personal finances, his business and its finances, his husband's business, and all things miscellaneous. When he leaves for his trip, I will start putting things into place for Mister Crossbey, don't you worry.'

'Good stuff, young man,' Kendra said, 'are you coming to the factory today?'

'No, I'll stay home and work from here, I want to make sure I'm not distracted,' he replied.

'You mean by me?' she joked.

'Yes... I mean no, of course not,' he said, stumbling over his words. 'I meant by people in general, not just you. That's very mean of you, Detective March.'

He knew, of course, that although she was joking, it was entirely about being distracted by her.

'I know, I'm sorry,' she said. 'I miss the whole flirting thing so this way at least I get the odd laugh out of it.'

'Again, mean.'

'I agree. I'm meeting the rest of the team soon, so I'll call later to give you an update, if you're still talking to me,' she said.

'Fine by me, now leave me to my work and be off with you,' he said, 'before I'm tempted to flirt back.'

She ended the call, giggling.

Flirt away, young man, she thought, missing his presence.

TREVOR LOOKED at the address he'd written down on a piece of paper and looked up at the towering thirty-storey office block before him.

'Steven Khan, you have surely done well for yourself, haven't you?' he muttered, heading towards the entrance.

He had researched Khan's businesses and had elected to go to the head office of the parent company and try to make an appointment that way, as a start. It would also be a good way to explore the premises and assess Khan's security provisions.

The walls of the ground floor were entirely glass, so as he approached the looming building, he could see the large, lavish reception desk and the three receptionists standing behind it, all in matching navy-blue jackets. He approached the nearest of them, a tall Asian woman with impressively long straight hair, wearing blue spectacles.

'Good morning, sir. Welcome to Bluebell Holdings, how can I help you today?' she said with a smile and a nod.

'Good morning. I'm here to see if I can make an appointment with Steven Khan,' Trevor said, 'is it possible to see him today?'

'I'm afraid not, sir. Appointments with Mister Khan will have to be made via his personal secretary, who is not currently in the building. May I ask what this is about?' she asked, the smile now gone and suspicion clear on her face.

'Don't worry, love, I'm not here to cause any trouble. I used to work with Mister Khan, many years ago. I'm just an old friend dropping in to catch up,' he said, noticing the CCTV cameras behind the desk. He looked up at them deliberately, grinning and giving a wave.

'As I said, sir, Mister Khan's secretary is currently away. If you'd like to leave your details, I'll be sure to pass them on,' she added, passing Trevor a piece of paper and a pen.

'Sure, why not?' he muttered. 'As a matter of interest, which floor is his office on?'

'It's on the thirtieth floor, sir, but you'll always need to sign in here first, and they will only allow you access if you have an appointment.'

'Okay, thank you. Here's my name and number. Please have her call me,' he said.

'Not *her*, sir, it's *he*. Mister Khan's personal secretary is Mister Ralph Craig,' she said.

'Ah, my apologies, and thank you,' Trevor said, turning away from reception.

He headed towards the exit but veered away at the last moment and headed towards the lifts, instead, to see what sort of response he would get. As he reached the first lift, he pressed the button to go up.

'Sir, you cannot go up unless you have an appointment,' the receptionist said from behind him. He turned to see her standing there, flanked by two large security officers. They had moved with impressive speed.

'I just want to use the loo, if that's okay?' he said, continuing to press the button and turning away from them.

He counted to three before the security officers grabbed him firmly by the arms, one on each side.

'Please come with us, sir,' one of the guards said.

They dragged him backwards towards the exit. He saw the receptionist standing and watching him as he was unceremoniously pulled off his feet and then dumped outside the front of the building. He stumbled but quickly righted himself and looked back at the two guards, who watched his every move from behind the glass. He gave them and the receptionist a courtesy wave before heading off.

Before leaving the area, he made his way around the back of the building to check the security there. He noticed there were CCTV cameras on each wall, covering every side, with no apparent blind spots. He knew that his every move was being monitored, so he kept his actions to a minimum and walked around the block. The building had a car park, with the entrance and exit at the rear of the building. Both shutters were down, and he could see by the placement at each shutter that a key card was required to enter or leave. He also saw a security guard sitting in a small, raised room just inside the car park, covering the entrance and exit. The security was effective and modern, that was in no doubt, making it very difficult to plan anything involving this building.

Still, at least we know, now, he thought as he walked away.

KENDRA MET the rest of the team at the factory so they could catch up. The mood was positive as they had made good progress on the scammers, and they wanted to see them brought to justice at the earliest opportunity.

'Jimmy, do you want to kick things off and let us know how your date went? Did you get any interesting information?' she said.

'It wasn't a date, it was a fact-finding mission, part of the job, okay?' he said, to much laughter.

'My apologies, please do go ahead and tell us what you learned.' She grinned.

'Okay, first off, she is earning a lot of money there. She didn't tell me how much, but she goes to Dubai four times a year for ten days at a time, she has no debt, and she describes her job as unique, a job that nobody else in this country can do.'

'Did she tell you what she does?' Kendra asked.

'She started off by giving me some bullshit about being the office manager, but after a nice meal and a few drinks she let slip that she was on the phone for around six hours a day. No office manager would do that, but a phone scammer most certainly would,' he said.

'Good work, anything else?'

'Yeah, she has a four-year-old son called Adam and is estranged from the dad. He's not dead or in prison so he's out there somewhere but doesn't ever get to see Adam. Luckily for me she had a babysitter booked otherwise she was quite happy to take me back to her flat. I dodged a bullet there, so please don't ask me to do that again. Like I said before, she's a horrible person,' Jimmy pleaded, to more laughter.

'Don't worry about it, Jimmy, hopefully we'll sort these scumbags out very soon,' Kendra replied.

'Anything on Freeman, yet?' asked Charmaine.

'Kind of. We have a plan to try and prompt him to confess to the murder, which will mean coming up with a brilliant lie. That's what we're working on, the lie, so if any of you have any ideas, I'm open to them; the more we have to choose from, the better. If that doesn't work, then the only other option is to grab him and let the Triads deal with him.'

'What about the scammer boss, Kendra? Anything on him yet?' asked Darren.

'Yes. He and his husband fly out to Australia the day after tomorrow, so we'll have almost a month to carry out our plan. We'll need most of you to chip in with this one, we'll need at least four vans, maybe more, and somewhere to store a house full of contents,' Kendra replied. 'You may be asked to do a lot of lifting and carrying.'

The team nodded knowingly.

'What about the Albanian warehouse?' Mo asked, referring to the warehouse last used by the Qupi gang before the team had dismantled and then transported them to Africa.

'Sadly, the lease ran out, so we can't use that again. Do we have any room in any of the outbuildings here?'

'I think we probably do,' said Amir. 'We got rid of a lot of crap when the building work started, so we can use that space for now.'

'Good, okay, can I leave you to have a word with Stav about supplying the vans, Amir?' Kendra asked.

'Yeah, no problem, leave that with me,' he said.

'Great. That's about it, really, I don't think we're far off from sorting the scammers out, and I think we're a little closer to my mum's murderers now, so good progress, everyone, thank you,' Kendra said.

As the team dispersed, Charmaine and Zoe approached Kendra.

'How's it going, ladies?' she said.

'We're good, thanks,' Charmaine said. 'I thought I might run an idea past you that we had about getting a confession from Freeman.'

'Go for it,' Kendra said.

'It seems to me that pretty much all the people involved in the murder have moved on to bigger and better things, is that about right?' Charmaine asked.

'Yes. Freeman is a multi-millionaire now, and we believe the person he was working with has done even better. Why do you ask?'

'Do we know whether they are still in contact? Because from what you and Trevor have said, it doesn't sound like they are. Isn't that an opportunity to have them turn against each other?' Charmaine suggested.

'That's always an option, absolutely,' Kendra said. 'Did you have something specific in mind?'

'I figure that if you can lie and tell them that their ex-associates have already given statements or turned against them, wouldn't they all do it?'

'Maybe, it's worth a shot. We have to be very careful how we do it, though, otherwise it could very easily backfire,' said Kendra.

'I'm sure that between us we can come up with some creative lies to add to the mix, don't you?' Zoe added.

'Zoe, this team has shown me they are more than just brave people trying to do the right thing. You are all creative and all extremely brave, and that comes from being allowed to speak up and come up with ideas like this, even if they don't work. Don't ever stop. That's why what we are doing is working so well, isn't it?' Kendra said.

'We'll come up with something, don't worry, Kendra,' Charmaine said. 'We'll see you soon, take care.'

'Bye, ladies. See ya.'

Kendra watched them leave and nodded in appreciation of the team. She was right in her summation, the team was growing incredibly well, it was becoming more than just an efficient group of people looking to make things right; they were evolving into much more and she was very proud of that achievement.

We're getting close, Mum, she thought.

'YES, that's him. He hasn't aged well,' said Khan.

He was shown a number of still photographs taken from the CCTV footage in his building, photos of Trevor looking up at the camera, being challenged by security, and then walking around the building—obviously staking it out.

'So, you do know him, sir?' asked Ivan Abramovic, his head of security, an ex-special forces lieutenant in the Russian special forces.

'Yes, Ivan, I do. He was a very talented undercover officer in the British Army who worked on a very important case many years ago. Had he succeeded, we would not be in the position we are now. So, it begs the question, why has he turned up out of nowhere to my building?'

'I can find out, sir, just give the word. It won't take long to find him,' Ivan said.

'Don't waste your time and effort, Ivan. Mister Giddings

has kindly left a number for us to call, remember? Give me the phone.'

Khan dialled the number that Trevor had left with the receptionist. After two rings, Trevor picked up.

'Hello,' said Trevor.

'Well, if it isn't my old friend Trevor Giddings, alive and kicking. This is Steven Khan, responding to your visit. How are you doing, old boy?'

'I could be better, to be honest. I take my hat off to your security, they're very... efficient.'

'Yeah, sorry about that. If I'd have been here, that wouldn't have happened, so the least I can do is invite you back for a drink and a catch-up. When can you get back here?'

'How does ten minutes sound? I'm not far away having a coffee,' Trevor replied.

'Great, I'll see you in ten minutes. I'll warn them you're coming this time, so you won't get roughed up again,' he said, laughing.

'That would be good, thank you,' Trevor said, 'see you soon.'

Khan ended the call and turned to his trusted head of security.

'Prepare your men, just in case,' he said.

12

STEVEN KHAN

'Hello again, Mister Giddings,' the receptionist said as he approached the desk for the second time. Her smile was as wide as it had been the first time she had greeted him, as if nothing had happened. Professional to the very last.

'Hello again. Mister Khan is expecting me,' he said.

'Certainly, please follow me,' she said, as she headed towards the bank of lifts.

Having called for a lift, it was just seconds before the doors opened. She invited him inside and took a key card from her pocket.

'This will take you to the thirtieth floor, directly to Mister Khan's suite of offices. You'll be met there by a member of his team,' she said, tapping the top floor receiver with the card. She then exited the lift and stood facing Trevor, smiling.

'Thank you,' he said, smiling back at her as she watched the doors close. As soon as the doors were shut, he shook his head. 'Cold bitch, that one,' he muttered, as he looked around the lift for signs of CCTV. He spotted two cameras, in opposing corners, hidden behind the fake mesh grill ceiling, a faint blue light the giveaway that they were working. He grinned at one of them knowingly.

The lift took a minute to get to the thirtieth floor, giving time for Trevor to review in his mind what he was going to say to the man who may have played a significant part in the death of his beloved wife. He took deep breaths, calming himself in advance, so that his emotions would not be a part of the imminent conversation.

The doors opened onto a large reception area, thanks to the floor-to-ceiling glass that would cause panic to anyone remotely fearful of heights. A tall, well-built man stood waiting in front of the lift. He was dressed in a black suit, with a black tie and black shoes and had very close-cropped hair, so short it was difficult to determine the colour. Clearly a member of Khan's security team, the man beckoned Trevor forward.

'Good afternoon, sir. Mister Khan is waiting to see you, but before we go, I need to pat you down quickly. It's standard practice, sir, I hope you understand,' the man said.

'Sure, go for it,' Trevor said, raising his arms for the man to do his job.

The man was methodical with his search, putting each item he encountered in Trevor's pocket into a plastic tub that lay on a glass table next to the lift.

'May I ask what this is, sir?' he asked, showing Trevor the small voice recorder he had taken from the jacket pocket.

'That's a recorder, mate,' Trevor said, smirking.

'I'm afraid I'll have to hold onto that, sir, along with your phone, as we don't allow recordings in the building. I'm sure you understand. They will be returned when you leave,' the man said, placing the recorder in a different plastic tub on the same table.

Eventually the search was complete. The man then used a handheld scanner that he ran over Trevor's body to detect any foreign bodies such as hidden wire taps or recorders.

'Thank you, sir,' he said, 'you may put your belongings back in your pocket,' he added, holding on to the tub containing the recorder and phone.

Trevor nodded as he placed his wallet and notebook back in his jacket pockets. The bunch of keys he hung on a belt loop and his pen went back into his top pocket.

'Follow me, sir,' the man said as he led him through a glass door that led to a wide corridor with offices on either side, all glass partitions and no obstructions. Trevor saw people in offices at their desks but could not hear them; the sound-proofing was of a high quality. The farthest office and door were different, more private. The walls and door were solid so nobody could see what was going on. The man opened the door and ushered Trevor into a large, luxuriously appointed office. The far exterior wall was glass and offered a spectacular view overlooking London. A large mahogany desk with two computer monitors faced the door he had come through. To one side was a pair of dark-green Chesterfield settees, one of which Steven Khan was sitting in.

Khan wore a grey satin suit of exceptional quality, only to be expected from a billionaire. His shirt was bright white, and he wore no tie. Trevor recognised him immediately as he rose to greet him. Another man stood to one side, his hands in front of his body, his large build and posture suggesting he was another member of the security team. Khan held out his hand and smiled as he reached Trevor.

'Trevor, it's been a long time. You have aged well, old chap,' he said, shaking his hand firmly.

'You haven't changed at all,' Trevor said, looking at his adversary and hoping that his loathing didn't show.

'This is my head of security, Ivan, who insisted that he remain for this meeting. I hope you don't mind. These security people are very serious about their jobs, aren't they?' Khan laughed.

'I don't mind at all, I would have insisted on the same,' Trevor replied.

'Please, sit,' Khan said, indicating to the other settee opposite his own. 'Can I get you something to drink?'

'No, thank you,' Trevor said, looking around the office and nodding.

'Great view, isn't it?' said Khan.

'It sure is,' Trevor said, noticing a pair of abstract paintings by Salvador Dali.

'Yes, they are original,' Khan boasted, 'one of the luxuries I get to enjoy.'

'You have done very well for yourself, haven't you?' Trevor said, continuing to hold his temper in check.

'I got lucky with a couple of deals, the rest is history.'

'Lucky? My understanding is that you were in the right place at the right time and benefitted from some very... interesting alliances,' Trevor said.

'Really? Where did you hear that, Trevor? Actually, before you answer, please do tell me why you've shown up here after all this time,' Khan said, more business-like.

'Now that you come to mention it, I came to ask you some questions about the past, after some things have come to light that I wasn't aware of back then.'

'Like what?' Khan said, 'please, I'm intrigued.'

'A little birdy told me you're one of the people responsible for our spectacular failures, that you tipped off the Yardies about the operation and all the raids. I just wanted to know if that was true, that's all,' Trevor said, holding Khan's gaze.

'And what little birdy would that be, Trevor? I mean, it's been thirty-odd years, surely I have a right to know if someone is pointing a finger at me after all this time,' Khan replied, with a smirk.

'You know I can't tell you that, Steven,' Trevor said, 'but if it's true, well, you know that I can't just leave it at that, right?'

This time, Khan roared laughing.

'Seriously? I was expecting a lot more than this, I feel slightly offended,' he said.

Trevor smiled and lay back in the chair, relaxed and unconcerned.

'Okay, so let me get this straight. After thirty years, you think you can do *what* to me? Expose me? Have me arrested? You want to go to the press, is that it? Is this a shakedown, Trevor? Are you after money?' Because if you're a bit short, all you had to do was ask, I could spare a few hundred quid,' he said, laughing as he looked towards Ivan.

'Oh, I'm not after your blood money, Khan, I'm after vengeance. And don't worry, I'm not threatening to kill you, I'll just make sure that you go to prison for twenty-odd years. The view from their windows isn't so nice.'

Khan laughed again and looked to Ivan.

'Can you believe this guy? You know, Ivan, I didn't really like him back then, he was a cocky son of a bitch, and that operation was always destined to fail,' he told his man. He turned back to Trevor.

'Trevor, Trevor, you've come all this way to threaten me with prison? And what evidence, pray tell, have you unearthed after thirty years, that even implicates me in anything?'

'You'll just have to wait and see, won't you?' Trevor said. 'I thought I'd be polite and respectful first to see if there was any remorse or guilt, but clearly there isn't.'

With that, he stood and looked down at Khan.

'You are responsible for the death of my wife, you piece of shit. You can trust me that I will bring you down, if it's the last thing I ever do.'

Ivan moved and stood next to Khan, who rose from the lush settee.

'Don't come to my house and threaten me, you worm. Do you know how much power I have? Do you know how well-protected I am? I have the best lawyers in the world working for me, I have front-bench politicians working for me, I have the police working for me, and I have the best security you can find,' he spat.

'None of that will protect you, Khan. You're nothing more than a murderer who has profited from the misery of others. And before you threaten to kill me, please don't insult my intelligence and think I haven't left evidence for my lawyers to use, plus I did tell people where I am and to make sure to call the police if I'm not out of here in fifteen minutes. So, fuck you, both of you,' he said, looking back and forth between Khan and Ivan.

Ivan stepped forward towards him but Khan held him back.

'Don't worry about him, Ivan, we have time to sort this out... our way,' Khan said.

Ivan stepped back to his original position, watching Trevor like a hawk.

'This *is* just about your wife, isn't it?' Khan said, glaring.

Trevor's expression changed, flitting between anger and surprise.

'Yeah, I thought as much, the rest of it is insignificant to you. After all these years you finally realise that someone betrayed you, right?'

'It's the truth, isn't it?' Trevor said. 'You and Stanwick collaborated with Freeman, passed him all the intel he needed to keep us at bay and to allow them to grow strong. Just think what the police will do when they find out an ex-MI5 operative and a retired senior police detective passed on intelligence that led to the murder of my wife, that led to years of misery from the guns and drugs that Freeman brought over. They'll lap it up.'

Khan clapped his hands, nodding exaggeratingly in mock-admiration.

'I must admit, you did well to put all that together. Stanwick was a dick, by the way, it didn't take much to reel him in. All I needed was to get him onside and the rest was easy, he didn't have to do a thing, just keep his stupid, greedy mouth shut.'

'Good for you. Finding a senior Met police detective to act as your patsy must have given you a hard on. And I'm guessing the deal was that you kept giving money so he would keep his mouth shut, right?'

'It was worth every penny. I tell you what pissed me off, though, was that the arsehole passed on the information to his son, so we'd have to keep on sending money even after the shit died. I didn't give him the credit for that,' Khan said.

'I bet you're laughing now, though, aren't you? I bet that money you give Stanwick's son along with what you are contributing to other politicians has paid dividends, hasn't it?

I bet that gives you a boner too, doesn't it? Knowing you have police and politicians in your slimy back pocket.'

'Since time immemorial, Trevor, who am I to mess with tradition?' Khan laughed.

'Actually, the laws of the land might have a good go,' Trevor said, smiling at his adversary.

'Yeah, well, like I said, after thirty years you have no evidence, do you? Even if I admitted it, you can't do anything about it, can you?'

Trevor said nothing and his expression turned sour.

'There he is, the angry young—sorry, *old* man that I remember. You come to my house and threaten me and think you can get away with it, eh?' he spat, 'Well, here's how this is going to work. I'm going to let you walk out of here with your tail between your legs, empty-handed and angry as fuck, but with the knowledge that you were right about me.'

Trevor's eyes widened in surprise.

'Yes, Stanwick and I tipped the Yardies off. Yes, I told them where you *really* lived, about what you were doing under-cover, and about your lovely wife. Yes, I told them everything. Yes, I knew what that animal Freeman was going to do, I even encouraged it. And you can do nothing about it, you stupid man,' Khan continued.

'Fuck you,' Trevor said, moving towards him.

Ivan stepped in front of his boss, his arm outstretched in readiness. Trevor stopped.

'I haven't finished yet,' Khan said. 'You'll leave here untouched, but five minutes after you're gone, I'll be putting the word out that whoever can prove that they killed you will be given a reward of one hundred thousand pounds. You'll be looking over your shoulders for the rest of your short, miserable existence, while I live like an emperor in my kingdom. That'll make you feel good and proper, won't it, Trevor?'

'You're a piece of shit, Khan. You won't get away with this,' Trevor said, his voice not so confident.

'Trevor, Trevor, I already have, can't you see?' He indicated to his palatial office and view. 'See this loser out, please, Ivan.'

Ivan pointed towards the door and followed Trevor as he left the office.

'Your boss is a lovely man, a right piece of work,' he said, looking over his shoulder at Ivan. 'You know that?'

'Keep walking, Mister, through the door,' Ivan said, pointing towards the glass door ahead.

The first security man was waiting and opened the door for them. He led them to the lift where he used a pass key. He then reached over to the small table and retrieved the plastic tub that held Trevor's phone and recording device.

'Give those to me,' Ivan said, grabbing the tub before Trevor could. He looked at the contents and then at Trevor. He then tipped the tub and spilled the contents onto the floor. Before Trevor could reach down to retrieve them, Ivan smashed both devices with the heel of his shoe. He looked at Trevor for a reaction.

'Nice,' Trevor said, picking up the remnants of his phone, ensuring he had the SIM card.

'Don't come back,' Ivan said as the lift doors opened. Trevor stepped inside and was accompanied by Ivan's underling, who used the key card again.

Two more men waited on the ground floor to escort Trevor out of the building. There was no pushing or manhandling on this occasion, just silence as the doors were opened for him to leave and then closed behind him.

'Charming,' Trevor said, smiling as he looked back at the guards.

As he walked away, knowing he was still being watched carefully, Trevor smiled, pleased with the outcome.

One down, two to go, he thought.

'Hi, K, how's it all going back at the shop?' Andy asked, referring to the police station.

'It's pretty boring here, to be honest, just catching up with admin most of the time or getting witness statements. You know what Rick is like, he doesn't like us to be sitting around doing nothing, so he makes sure we're kept busy.'

'Fair enough, I'd be doing the same if I was him. Also, don't forget he has a big secret now, so he needs to keep up appearances, right?'

'So, what's going on? You didn't ring just to see how I was, did you? Or did you?' she asked, teasing him again.

'Stop it, you brazen hussy, I've called to update you on things, like you asked.'

'Go on then, update me,' she said.

'Our scammer chum is off tomorrow so I've taken the liberty of making a few changes to his plans for the building works,' Andy said, 'and there's a good chance he won't like them.'

'Uh-oh, something tells me you've reverted to schoolboy mode, and it sounds like you're enjoying it very much,' said Kendra.

'Yeah, well, there have to be some perks to this job, right? Anyway, I haven't finished. I've also researched his husband's swanky restaurant and found out that Crossbey has funded it to the tune of just over half a million pounds since it was opened. The building is leased, not owned by them, so it is an excessive amount of money for what it is, which suggests that it is one of the ways Crossbey is laundering the money he makes from his scams. By the way, the husband is fully aware of the way Crossbey makes his money and is party to it, so I have put some plans in place to address that situation also.'

'What about our smooth-talking mouthpiece, Kim Morgan?' asked Kendra.

'Ah, yes, the lady trying to get into poor Jimmy's pants. I've got something special in mind for her, and just like Crossbey, she won't be getting away with her crimes,' Andy replied.

'Okay, it sounds like you have everything under control regarding that lot, is there anything of note about Freeman?'

'Your father is being very cryptic about this one, I think he has something that he's planning, but it isn't quite finalised yet, if that makes sense. He told me he's going to send something over for me to work on, but first he was going to see a member of parliament. All very mysterious, don't you think?'

'You know Dad, he's always got something on the go. If the last couple of years have taught me anything it's the fact that he is a lot cleverer than anyone gives him credit for. I know for sure he'll have something very special lined up for Freeman,' Kendra said.

'Good. There's nothing like the sweet smell of justice, is there? I just wish it hadn't taken so long, for your sake.'

'Me too, Andy... me too.'

TREVOR HAD one more meeting that he was either hoping to arrange or *accidentally* have happen, which is why he waited patiently at a table outside a coffee shop near Leicester Square. He saw the press lined up across the street outside the cinema, waiting for the guests of honour to leave the preview showing of the political thriller that everyone had been talking about. Some of the foremost British and American performers were involved and the budget had been more than two hundred million pounds.

'Here they come!' shouted one of the paparazzi as they jostled for position from behind the temporary barriers erected by the police.

The first group of performers exited the cinema and walked along the red carpet that had been laid especially. Trevor could hear the camera shutters; ironic, as most of them were digital and the noise was purely for effect. There were questions shouted to the stars as they walked, waving to the crowds gathered behind a separate barrier. Some stopped to sign autographs or to take selfies with their adoring fans. Trevor finished his coffee, left a five-pound tip, and walked casually towards the throng. Knowing where they'd be heading, he bypassed the crowds and went straight for the waiting limousines, each one guarded by its waiting driver. He knew which limousine to aim for; his research and Andy's help had pinpointed it from many photographs available online.

'How's it going, mate?' he said to the driver, a tall, thin man in his fifties who was polishing the windscreen as Trevor approached.

'I'm good, thanks. What can I do for you?' the man asked, as he stopped his work and turned to face the stranger.

'I'm hoping you can do me a favour, mate, that's all,' Trevor said, his hands outstretched in a placating manner.

The driver stepped back, confused. Trevor saw this and stopped in his tracks, not wanting to scare the man.

'Mate, I'm not gonna do anything, okay? I just need you to pass on a note to your boss. I used to work with his old man many years ago and just want to connect with him. I'm gonna put my hand in my pocket to get the note, okay?'

Trevor carefully reached into his inside pocket and took out a piece of paper, folded in half. He held it towards the driver and then stepped towards the limousine. He then lifted one of the wipers and put the note under it before stepping back.

'That's all it is, mate, nothing to worry about. You can even read it, if you want, it's just a short note and a phone number for him to ring me, okay?' Trevor said. He then turned and walked away from the car, past some of the other vehicles that were now being approached by their clients. Trevor passed the couple that were heading for the limousine whose driver he had just placed the note with. The couple that had left the cinema after the stars were of no real interest to the paparazzi. The driver opened the door for the woman and then closed it behind her. Before opening the other door for her husband, the driver turned to his boss.

'Sir, someone left a note for you. He said he was an old friend of your father's, sir.'

Nelson Stanwick MP, son of Detective Superintendent Raymond Stanwick, got into the car and opened the folded note. There was a phone number and just seven words.

I know about Khan and your dad.

13

HYDE PARK

Kendra met with Rick the following morning for coffee and a catch-up, a regular thing for them, before the day's mundane police work that had been planned. Rick had been on the phone when she had walked in with their hot take-away coffees, one of which she placed on his desk as he spoke. It was a short call.

'Okay, that was one of my old diplomatic protection group mates, who now works as a port officer at Heathrow airport, and who just confirmed that Andrew Crossbey and his husband Dilman Hussey have just boarded flight BA7006. The bastards are flying first class, by the way,' Rick told Kendra.

'Damn, I hate those two, everything they do just seems to rub it in, doesn't it? I'm gonna ask Andy to see if he can change their return flights to something less luxurious,' she said.

'That I'd like to see,' Rick said, 'and remind me never to piss you off!' He laughed.

'Now that those two have left, we're going to start with

Crossbey and his house. Andy is also working on something for the restaurant and also for Kim Morgan, so things will start happening any day,' she told him.

'Great, the sooner we can sort them out, the better,' Rick replied.

'We've started a fund for the victims who have lost money to Crossbey's gang, it was easy to isolate them from the overseas victims. We're going to grab back as much as possible over the coming month while the bastard is sunning himself,' she added.

'Excellent, I like the way you think, Detective.'

'I don't suppose you've come up with anything, have you?' she asked.

'I hadn't, up until last night when I got an interesting call from a friend of yours,' Rick said.

'Oh yeah, who's that?'

'Detective Sergeant Jim Adair from the National Crime Agency, the chap who helped us with those corrupt wankers Eddie Duckmore and Dave Critchley. After everything was settled with the triads, he came back from Yorkshire and is back at work. He just wanted to thank us for our help and to offer his services moving forward, if anything juicy comes up,' Rick said, smiling knowingly.

'Oh, that is sneaky of you, Detective Sergeant Watts, I like it!'

'I'M GLAD YOU CALLED, Mister Stanwick,' Trevor said when he answered the phone.

'What's this all about and who the hell are you?' the MP said.

'Who I am is not your concern at this time. This is merely a courtesy call to arrange a meeting where I will supply you with evidence that you have been taking bribes for many years and that your father was a corrupt police officer. That's all.'

Stanwick was silent for several seconds as he contemplated a response. Trevor's revelation would likely end his political career, but much worse was the possibility that he could end up in prison. There was no upside to the situation.

'Where and when?' he replied simply.

'One hour, Hyde Park, by the Serpentine. Come alone, otherwise I go straight to the police and the press, who will both enjoy what I will give them,' Trevor replied, hanging up.

Nearly there, he thought as he prepared the next step.

TREVOR FIGURED that Stanwick was probably home by now in Camden Town, a twenty-minute drive from Hyde Park, so he went to the park early to watch for the MP's approach. As he expected, Stanwick was dropped off by a cab close to the Serpentine Lake, and not by his official driver. He got out of the cab and looked around casually before walking slowly towards a bench overlooking the lake. When he had sat down, Trevor set off from his vantage point and reached him a minute later, sitting at the other end of the bench.

'You're early,' Trevor said, looking straight ahead.

'Better than late, right?' Stanwick said calmly. 'Now, kindly tell me what this is all about.'

'What this is all about is very simple, Mister Stanwick. Your dear old father, who I worked with on a very important but secret operation, betrayed me and the people of London in exchange for money. That makes him a corrupt policeman, a snake of the worst kind. Payments were made regularly to him and then continued regularly to you after his death, suggesting that you are more than aware of the reasons for said payments. That makes you a corrupt politician, another really shitty type of snake. How am I doing so far?' Trevor said, finally looking over towards Stanwick.

Stanwick remained calm, not answering immediately.

'Those are some very serious allegations there, Mister...?'

'My name is Trevor Giddings, Mister Stanwick, and I used to work for your father as an undercover operative, I'm sure he mentioned me to you in passing. What you need to know is that I know everything about you. I know that Steven Khan is still lining your pockets through some bullshit shell company for some bullshit reasons. Oh, and he doesn't think very much of you or your dearly departed dad. He is, in fact, very resentful, so you should start watching your back.'

'That bastard would still be a pen-pushing civil servant if it wasn't for my dad. My dad made him what he is, so if anyone has a right to be resentful, it is me. Khan is nothing but a short, greasy, arse-licking wanker who was in the right place at the right time. The man is nothing but shit, so you can all go to hell,' Stanwick grunted, standing to leave.

'Okay, in that case, I'll send the evidence to the police and the newspapers later today, if you're not that bothered,' said Trevor.

Stanwick paused before sitting back down.

'What the hell do you want from me, just spit it out, will you?'

'I want you to write a statement confessing that you are aware of payments Steven Khan made to your father in exchange for intelligence that led to the murder of Amy

March, my wife. I don't give a shit about the rest, you can either leave it out or add it and hope they look at your confession favourably,' Trevor said.

'I want to see the evidence you have,' said Stanwick.

'I'm not stupid. I'll send it to you later,' Trevor said, 'and when you get it, you can leave your confession with your limo driver who can deliver it here to me tomorrow at midday.'

Stanwick shook his head, stunned.

'I'm sorry about your wife, okay? I had nothing to do with that, I was shocked when I found out about it, Freeman was a nasty, evil shit, by all accounts. He bragged to my dad about it to implicate him if anything went wrong, as insurance. Dad told me that he wasn't supposed to kill her, just threaten her to find you. As for the money, yes, my father told me all about it and put arrangements in place for it to continue after his death so it would help my career. I had no involvement in the murder, please believe me.'

'Doesn't matter. You knew about it and you knew who was responsible. You're corrupt and your dad was corrupt. You should not benefit from that, and my price is that you no longer benefit from that. Just be clear that you mention Steven Khan, otherwise our deal is off,' Trevor added.

'How will you send the information?' asked Stanwick.

'I'll have someone drop it off later, to your home address in Cobham Mews,' Trevor said, giving a mock salute and walking away.

Stanwick watched him go and then called for a cab to pick him up. He sat down and buried his head in his hands while he waited, knowing that his career was over.

Trevor now had the ammunition he needed to deal with Freeman.

'Two down, one to go,' he muttered.

'PHASE ONE IS COMPLETE, MILADY,' Andy told Kendra when she called for a catch-up.

'What's phase one, Andy?' she asked, 'or are you just making things up as you go along?'

'No, it's a real phase one, I decided to use them because there are so many elements it can get confusing. Anyway, I have changed the plans to the extension and outhouse at Crossbey's, so they are ready for use when the contractors turn up tomorrow.'

'Contractors?'

'Yes, he hired a company to do the work and I called them and made sure to tell them of the changes, and that if they needed to speak to Crossbey's representatives while he was away to speak to me, Ramon Gonzalez Junior.' Andy laughed.

'Seriously? Because Ramon Gonzalez wasn't enough?'

'If you're gonna do something, you might as well do it properly. They can't reach him directly because I intercept all calls to his phone and put a block on them, diverting them to me instead. I don't even think he's landed yet, it's a twenty-four-hour flight or something ridiculous like that, isn't it?'

'I don't care, just carry on, will you?' Kendra said.

'So, they're starting work tomorrow and I've offered them a huge bonus if they finish within three weeks, so they've agreed to do double shifts. Because the house is isolated from neighbours, nobody will complain or even know of the work after-hours, so they'll complete in time,' Andy continued.

'Nice work, anything else?'

Yes, ma'am, there is. I've started transferring funds from his accounts to a crypto account and then diverting it to a new account in the Cayman Islands. I'll then transfer the funds into the victims' fund that we set up, so by the time I'm done there should be a decent amount in there. I'm going to do the same with his business accounts and also the restaurant and all their personal savings accounts. It may even cover everything they have stolen, because ironically, his legitimate business is quite profitable. That's phase two.'

'My, my, you have been a busy bee. Anything else?' asked Kendra.

'I'm getting there; patience, milady. I've also started putting measures in place for Kim Morgan, but it's trickier, as she's still very much here and active. I'll be leaving that as a last-minute thing when we have more. That's phase three and my report is complete, boss,' Andy said.

'Just how many phases are there?' she asked.

'No idea. There's still plenty to do, your dad has got me working on stuff that he needs in a hurry, so I'll be getting on to that next. You okay?' he asked.

'Yes, all good this end, thanks. Just regular police work, you remember what it's like. I'll ring again later, if you're up for another chat,' Kendra said.

'I'll always make time for you, oh gracious majesty,' Andy said, laughing as he ended the call.

Kendra shook her head.

'I don't know why I put up with your antics, Andy Pike,' she said out loud, turning and walking back towards the station.

Who am I kidding, of course I know why, she thought, a big grin on her face.

'Hi, Dad, just checking in. Everything okay?'

Before returning to the office, she'd given Trevor a call to find out what he was working on with Andy.

'I'm good, love; better than good, actually. Where are you?'

'I'm still at work. I just spoke to Andy, and he mentioned that you've got him working on a bunch of things. Anything I should know about?'

'Yes, actually. I've sent him a couple of recordings that I want him to work on before I confront Freeman. I need one of them tonight so I can send it to one of the betrayers.'

'Oh, okay. What's the plan?' she asked.

'I've not thought it all through yet. I want to get these recordings sorted out and then hope to convince Freeman to turn on his associates. Not sure how I'm gonna do it yet but I'll figure it out,' he said.

'I think I can help you there, Dad,' Kendra said, her mind working quickly, 'we'll meet up later tonight and I'll tell you all about it. Are you meeting Andy at the factory or his house?'

'His house,' Trevor replied.

'Great, send me a message when you're there and I'll come and see you,' she said.

'You're getting more and more devious every day, daughter. I like it!'

'Dad, like I said, the apple doesn't fall far from the tree.'

'Don't you know it. See you later, love.'

And now we have a bloody good plan, she thought, walking into the station.

'So, what's this great idea of yours, daughter?' Trevor asked when they eventually met at Andy's house late that afternoon.

'Do you remember Jim Adair from the NCA who helped us out with Duckmore and Critchley?' she said.

'Oh, the Norwich City supporter?' Andy asked.

'Weird that's what you remember about him, but yeah.'

'What about him, love?' Trevor asked.

'He's been in touch with Rick to offer his assistance,' she said, 'and I reckon Mum's murder is the perfect case. His team work nationally, and they work with serious crimes, so we can justify using his services to address the historic arms and drug-smuggling that Freeman was involved with.'

'Okay, so what have you got in mind?'

'We brief Jim about the case and give him the evidence we have so far. He arrests Freeman and formally interviews him using what we've given him. It'll be official, on the record, so Freeman won't be able to slime his way out of it if we can make it stick,' Kendra said, her enthusiasm clear.

'I'm just gonna play devil's advocate here, K, so don't take it personally,' Andy said, 'but what physical evidence do we actually have? Other than what Trevor has sent me and what you have, which all amounts to hearsay, what will actually stick in court?'

'That's where we'll have to be clever. Remember, it isn't entrapment, because the offence has already been committed, and we're not using evidence to make him commit another. What we're going to do is cleverly introduce the evidence so that it looks like he's been screwed over. Also, police have rules to adhere to during interview, so passing what we have to Jim introduces it under legitimate circumstances. Jim will know how to handle it, too,' Kendra said.

'So, you're saying that the plan isn't to get a confession from him using regular interview techniques, but to get him angry and act irrationally based on hearsay and third-party confessions? Do you think he'll fall for it?' asked Andy.

'Actually,' she said, 'I don't. He's also going to have a top lawyer who may instruct him not to comment. The trick is for Jim to get him angry and for him to react thereafter, which may allow further opportunities to gather more evidence on everyone involved.'

'This is all giving me a headache, love. Is there no other way?' asked Trevor.

'Not that I can think of, Dad, not if we want to get a legitimate conviction for murder.'

'Damn, it sounds heavily weighted in his favour, doesn't it?'

'Think of it this way. Whatever happens, he'll know that *we* know. He'll know that others will have turned on him. What would you do if there was even the slimmest chance of getting convicted of murder?'

'I'd come out fighting, all guns,' he replied, nodding in understanding.

'Exactly, and that's what we should be planning for, because if there's anything I've learned about that bastard, he's as nasty as they come, and he doesn't think when he's angry... he acts.'

'Then I guess we should prepare for the worst,' Trevor said.

BEFORE HE LEFT, Andy handed Trevor an envelope.

'Thanks for sorting it out so quickly,' Trevor said, 'if this works, then we'll have taken care of some unfinished business and at least some justice will have been served.'

'No problem,' said Andy. 'I'll have everything else ready for Kendra tomorrow for when she meets with Jim Adair. Shouldn't take me too long.'

'Okay, I'll see you both tomorrow,' Trevor said, leaving.

'Will you need anything else for tomorrow, K?' Andy asked.

'No, I think we have everything we need for now. Will you be okay taking care of the Crossbey situation with the team?'

'Yeah, I've already spoken with Mo and Charmaine and they're ready to go tomorrow. Amir sorted the vans out and they'll be going direct tomorrow morning.'

'I guess that's everything covered, then. Goodnight, Mister Pike,' Kendra said, leaning over and kissing him on the cheek. She lingered for a second before stepping away and heading out of the door.

'G-goodnight, Miss March,' he said, his breath catching in his throat.

14

CONSTRUCTION

The four large vans on loan from Stav the garage man arrived at Crossbey's house at nine o'clock the following morning. Andy had checked and double-checked all the security arrangements that Crossbey had put in place and was able to pass on the alarm codes to the team. He had also paid in advance the security company who would send regular patrols during the month, from Crossbey's account, instructing them to start their patrols the following day. There were no concerns they would turn up while construction work was being carried out on the house, especially not on the day the team would be emptying the house of all valuables.

'Okay, everyone, remember what we discussed. In and out quickly, look for a hidden safe, and one of you check the garage for cars, we'll take them also,' Mo instructed.

There were three people in each van, twelve in total, so the expectation was that all four vans could be loaded and on the way in less than an hour. Amir worked his magic on the lock, which, like the house, was old and not very effective.

The alarm panel was behind the door and the code was typed in without incident.

Half the team went upstairs, and the rest remained on the ground floor, with one checking for vehicles. Within minutes, the vans were being loaded with everything portable, including computers, televisions, phones, smaller antiques and paintings, clothing; whatever could be carried by one or two people was stripped and taken from the house quickly. The safe was located in the main bedroom, behind an original Banksy, which was quickly taken to a van. The two-by-two-foot safe itself was forcibly removed from the wall using a sledgehammer, chisels and a crowbar, and two of the team members took it to the van.

Once the valuables were all loaded up, the team started on the furniture, mainly antiques, one piece at a time, which filled two of the vans and part of a third. They stripped the house completely in just under ninety minutes and the vans were soon underway in convoy, followed by the two cars found in the double garage, an almost new black Tesla and a fifty-year-old bright red MGB Roadster. The cars were driven to Stan, who would quickly dismantle them and sell the parts, more than covering any expenses he'd incurred.

The four vans made their way to the factory where they were unloaded, out of sight, into the recently emptied outbuildings, to be sold later and the funds added to the victims' account. The safe and the valuables were taken to one of the storerooms used in the past to hold some of the criminals they'd relocated. Mo estimated that the art alone was worth three-quarters of a million pounds. Once the safe had been forcibly opened, they found thirty thousand pounds in cash, a box containing twelve gold sovereigns, several Rolex watches, property deeds, provenance for the art, and other documents, adding a significant amount to the haul for the victims.

There was a good chance that Crossbey would be unhappy when he returned to an empty house!

Andy, in the meantime, had cleared the funds from several bank and savings accounts belonging to the couple, to the tune of eight hundred thousand pounds, all transferred to a crypto account and sent to the Cayman Islands, whereby it was then transferred back as funds to the victims' account, which was in a very healthy shape.

'Great job, folks,' Andy told them upon their return and once everything was safely stored away. 'That should put the cat amongst the pigeons, especially since I cancelled their insurance policies two days ago, while they were still in the country.'

The team roared their approval and dispersed, leaving Mo, Charmaine and Amir with Andy.

'What's next, Andy?' Mo asked.

'I'm still working on a plan for Kim Morgan, which shouldn't take too long. In the meantime, we need to switch our focus to helping Kendra and Trevor with their case. Things will soon be coming to a head with them,' he replied.

'Okay, call and let us know what you need, and we'll be there,' Charmaine said.

'Thanks, guys. I appreciate it. In the meantime, Amir, can you return the vans to Stav?'

'Sure thing, we'll do that now.'

They too dispersed, leaving Andy to his thoughts.

As much as I love it when things come together so smoothly, I also know that the hair on the back of my neck is an accurate forecast of things going wrong, he thought, going back to the operations room, where he'd scrutinise everything to make sure he hadn't missed anything obvious.

'Well, this brings back memories,' Jim Adair said as he sat opposite Kendra in the coffee shop where they'd met several times before.

'How's it going, Jim?' Kendra said, happy to see the Yorkshireman.

'It's going well, thanks primarily to you. The office was in a bit of turmoil after Duckmore and Critchley were killed and then JP handed himself in, but it's recovered well, and things are almost back to normal,' he replied, referencing JP Sisterson, who had helped the two corrupt officers and then turned himself in to thwart them.

'What happened to JP?' she asked.

'The investigation found him guilty of gross misconduct and he was dismissed from the force, but they decided not to charge him, mainly because he turned himself in and admitted to making silly choices,' Jim said.

'That's fair enough, I suppose. So, what are you up to nowadays?'

'I'm cracking on with the usual cases, but volunteered to be the point man from my team with Met Police serious crime units such as yours. That's why I called Rick, so I can offer our services if anything decent comes along,' Jim replied.

'It's funny you should mention that, Detective Sergeant Adair, but something serious and very interesting has come up, if you're interested,' she said.

'Please, tell me everything, Detective March,' he replied.

'Okay, enough of that formal shit, it just doesn't sound right. We have a cold case from thirty years ago which we have worked on unofficially. The plan was to collect all the evidence and then send it to the NCA and the press so that the case can be officially opened again. So what I'm about to disclose is, at the moment, confidential and for your eyes and ears only, because it is somewhat sensitive,' Kendra said.

'Sounds interesting. What is it?'

'It's the murder of my mother, which was never investigated as such, but judged to have been suicide. We know who did it, and we have some evidence that will likely be deemed as hearsay, as nobody will come forward to give evidence in court. You still interested?' she asked, watching for his response.

'Wow, I didn't see that coming, the murder of your mother? Wow. I'm so sorry. But please, go on,' Jim said, leaning forward.

'There's no physical evidence, so all we have is hearsay from people who were there or who were involved in some way. The man who killed her is a nasty bastard and we think that having him arrested and interviewed where some of that hearsay is presented to him may make him angry enough to retaliate and do something stupid. Are you up for it?'

'Absolutely, I'm up for it. I love these older cases where there was no DNA or bullshit that nobody understands, and this sounds wonderfully deceitful,' Jim said, nodding appreciatively.

'That it is,' Kendra said.

'I'm guessing that... officially, you're not involved in any way?' asked Jim.

'That's correct. The information will be passed on to you anonymously and you'll have to start from scratch. Hope that's okay? I don't want to make things awkward for you, but it is genuine, and you'd be helping me out a lot,' she replied.

'Kendra, I'm more than okay with it. I know how this shit works and you helped *us* out a lot, remember?'

'I don't like to take advantage, though, Jim, but from working with you before, I know that you're a good cop who wants to put nasty people away, and bending the law a little is acceptable. I hope I was right in judging you that way,' she said, nervously biting her bottom lip.

'No problem. Just give me the nod and I'm all over it,' he replied, not changing his expression in any way.

'Great, thank you. I'll give you a call when I have everything you'll need, which will be within the next few days.'

'I look forward to it. Now, are you going to bother offering me a coffee, since we're here? It's the least you can do, right?'

TREVOR SAT on the bench by the Serpentine Lake as he had done so the previous day. He looked around casually, prepared for the worst, including police turning up along with any heavies sent to intimidate or hurt him. He had no identification on him, no money, no weapons, nothing to incriminate him in any way. He was simply there to pick up the letter that he hoped Stanwick had had the sense to write.

He saw the car approaching from the southern entrance, heading towards the car park located close to the Princess Diana memorial. The vehicle stopped and the driver got out, who Trevor recognised from the previous day. Dressed casually in jeans and a black jacket, the driver looked anonymous, as was the silver Ford Focus he had driven here, probably his own vehicle. The man looked around and saw Trevor at the bench. Trevor raised his arm briefly in acknowledgement and waited as he walked over.

'How's it going, mate?' Trevor said as the man sat down.

'It's been better. I don't know what you're doing or what you said to my boss, but I've never seen him so down before. He's a changed man. What the hell did you do to him?'

Trevor looked at the man, waiting for him to finish.

'Mate, I don't know you from Adam, so I'm not gonna bullshit you. Your boss is a gigantic dick who screwed up badly and who needs to pay. So instead of ranting at me I suggest you do what you came to do and then piss off home. Oh, and I'd recommend you start looking for a new job soon, too,' Trevor said, holding the man's gaze.

The driver averted his gaze and put his hand into his inside jacket pocket to retrieve an envelope. He handed it to Trevor, looking away as he did so, as if ashamed by his actions.

'There you go. Thank you,' Trevor said, 'now you can go and tell your boss that you did your job.'

The driver walked back to the car park without another backwards glance, his deed complete.

Trevor opened the envelope and scanned the letter. He nodded and then put it back in the envelope. He waited for the Ford Focus to leave before he stood and walked towards the car park and his car.

Okay, the dominoes are starting to fall, he thought as he drove away.

TREVOR REALISED as he approached his home that someone was waiting for him. He counted three cars, two men in each, at strategic locations surrounding his road. It was where he would have placed a surveillance team to cover his address, so he always had the habit of checking every time. He called Kendra.

'Darling, I have three cars plotting up my address, so I thought I'd let you know before I give them the run around,' he said calmly.

'Are you going to be okay, Dad? What can I do?' she asked.

'See if you can round any of the team up. If you can, I'll lead this lot to a location where it will be a fair fight. Can you do that for me?'

'Of course, I'll call you back,' she said.

Trevor figured correctly that they'd be lying in wait to try and ambush him when he got out of the car, so he slowed down and drove around the block purposely, so that they could see him. He also made a point of making eye contact with the driver of one of the cars, nodding at him as if to let him know he was aware of their presence. The driver looked angry as he started the car and began to move out of his spot to follow. That was Trevor's cue to make progress away from the area.

Kendra called back.

'Dad, I have Darren and his team making their way to you, shouldn't be more than ten minutes, in three cars.'

'No, tell them to make their way to the Tesco car park in Cranbrook Road, to the far end by the clothing bins, it'll be quicker and easier. I'm going to get them to follow me there.'

'Will do. I'll get Darren to call you when he's ready. Be careful, Dad, do you know who they are?'

'I have a feeling it's Khan's mob, he put the word out that whoever took me out would get a hundred grand, so they'll be professionals. I'll be fine, though, don't you worry,' he said.

'Okay; I'll ring off, but make sure to call me when it's all over, promise me,' Kendra demanded.

'Of course, I will, I promise.'

As Trevor drove away, he could see that all three cars were now in convoy behind him.

'Okay, people, let's see what you have,' he muttered, and sped up.

His phone rang; it was Darren.

'How's it going, Trev? How far away are you?' he asked.

'I'm not more than five minutes away. Did you bring your kit with you? This lot are professionals, Darren, so warn the others to be careful. I'm gonna lead them to you so that you can take out their tyres, okay?'

'Yeah, we're all kitted up and each car has a stinger, so we'll be ready to use them as they come past the bins,' Darren said.

The stinger system employed hollow steel spikes that would penetrate the tyres on any vehicle and deflate them quickly but safely. The trick was the way they were deployed, which wasn't easy. Fortunately, Darren and the rest of the team had practised many times, so Trevor was confident they'd get the job done.

'Listen, Darren, I don't want you engaging with this lot, they're probably armed. Just take out the tyres and do what you can to stop them in their tracks, okay?'

'Not a problem, Trev, I have a cunning plan,' Darren said.

The drive took six minutes and Trevor allowed the following cars to close in, ensuring that they stuck with him. As he approached the superstore in Cranbook Road, he drove around the perimeter road on the right-hand side towards the rear where Darren and the team were waiting. His eyes were constantly on the mirror as he wanted to ensure that the distance between him and his pursuers was enough for the team to do their thing. As he approached the end, he saw the team hiding behind parked cars, spaced out and ready to deal with all three cars.

As he slowed, he saw in the mirror that the coordinated efforts of the team had worked. Darren had deployed the stinger, disabling the leading car, with all four tyres pierced. Behind that, Izzy and Martin had done the same with the other cars, with the same result. All three cars came to a stop, the drivers confused. In the moments it took for them to realise what was going on, Jimmy, Clive, and Rory had approached the passenger side of each car and smashed the windows with the hammers they had purchased a few minutes earlier in the superstore. The passengers had no time to react before Darren, Izzy and Martin each threw in the contents of a two-and-a-half-litre tin of white emulsion paint, also purchased from the store, covering the passengers and drivers, along with some on the windscreens.

The team members walked casually away and were out of sight of the superstore inside thirty seconds, leaving their targets immobilised and unable to do a thing. Before they were able to leave, the police, whose place of work was less than a hundred yards away, were at the scene, having been called by several members of the public. It would be several days before the cars were removed and the paint cleaned. The six men, who were found to be in possession of firearms, would be locked up for months before their day in court.

Not a single one of them had a clue what had happened and who was responsible, other than their original target, Trevor Giddings.

15

PLANS AFOOT

The team met at the factory shortly after the incident, where Kendra wanted to address them all.

'As much fun as that was, we now know that Khan is deadly serious about putting a bounty on Dad's head, and as you saw, the team he sent were professionals. We must all be more careful, so make sure you keep your eyes peeled, use different routes, and just watch for anything or anyone that looks out of place. Is that clear?' she told them all.

'You're right, it was fun,' Darren said, 'but knowing they were all armed and looking to kill Trevor puts a different spin on things. How are we going to do this, other than keep a look out?'

'There's only one way to deal with this,' Trevor said, looking around at them all, 'we take the fight to Khan. If he wants to play that game, then we can, too, only in our unique way. We still need to be wary, of course, but he is not expecting us to retaliate, he thinks he's too powerful. While we're working on getting him arrested, we can kill two birds with one stone and cause him some damage, both financially and to his reputation.'

'Ooh, I like that plan,' Amir said, rubbing his hands. 'What did you have in mind?'

'You know we've done a lot of research while putting the case together, so we have a bunch of business addresses and several premises that he calls home. I say we start visiting them and leaving him something to think about, something that will cost him a fortune and attract the wrong sort of attention. And while we are doing all that, we can also collect more evidence that the press can use to discredit him. What do you think?'

'Crikey, he is gonna be royally pissed, isn't he?' Andy said.

'He is, but remember, he has some serious security muscle behind him, including some Russian dude who's built like a brick shit-house. He's ex Russian military so he knows how to hurt people, we need to be very careful.'

'Where do we start?' asked Charmaine.

'I think we start with his fancy palatial residence outside London,' he replied.

'Why there, Dad?' asked Kendra.

'It's only one of the homes he owns, but it's the largest and most valuable. Ironically, he hardly ever stays there, he usually stays in his London penthouse. I thought the palace would be the best choice as it will take the longest for anyone to respond to, and will make a big statement that he isn't untouchable.'

'Fair enough. I think there's no guessing who you want to take this one on, is there?' Kendra winked. They all turned to the door that Amir had just entered through. He looked up from his phone to see the entire team grinning at him.

'What?' he said.

Kim Morgan checked her phone again, willing for it to ring or even announce a message from Jimmy. It had been several days since they had last seen each other, and despite knowing he was likely to be away working, she was desperate to meet with him again, and this time there would be no babysitter or child at the flat to intrude on the intimacy she had been planning. She had contemplated calling or sending a message to see if that would trigger something, but quickly promised herself not to fall into the trap that she'd fallen foul of several times by coming across as too keen or too needy.

'Ring, dammit,' she said, before tossing the phone onto her desk and sighing in resignation.

She sat at the desk and scrolled through the latest list she'd been handed, a list of the fifty-seven members of the Howland Green bowls club.

'I guess I may as well do some work, that apartment isn't going to pay for itself,' she muttered, thinking of her future in Dubai.

Picking up the mobile phone allocated to her this week, she started to ring the first number, readying her crib sheet. On one side of the paper was the script that she used, and on the other, space to record information, bank account details, and anything else she could use to con the victim out of their hard-earned money. The call was answered.

'Hello, is that Mister Albert Regis?' she asked.

'Who's asking?' came the reply.

'Hello, sir, my name is Samantha Palmer and I'm calling from the Pension Service in Wolverhampton. If you can confirm that you are Mister Albert Regis, I can tell you why I'm calling, sir,' Kim replied.

'That's me, what can I do for you?'

'Oh, good. Hello, Mister Regis. Before I start, I just need to go through some security questions with you,' Kim continued.

'This again, every time I speak to someone, I have to go through this. Go on then, fire away,' he said.

'Please tell me the first line of your address and your postcode.'

'15 Trelawney Gardens, IG7 4NE.'

'Thank you, and your date of birth?'

'February twenty-seventh, nineteen-fifty,' came the answer.

'And your national insurance number?'

'Alpha-Bravo-nine-four-one-two-four-three-delta,' he answered.

'And can you tell me how often you receive your pension payments?' she asked.

'Every two weeks.'

'Finally, tell me the last four digits of the bank account your pension is paid into.'

'Nine-nine-eight-eight,' he replied.

'Thank you, Mister Regis. That completes the security check. May I call you by your first name?'

'Yes, you can.'

'That's great, thank you, Albert. I actually have some good news for you today. I've been notified by your case worker that we have underpaid your pension to the tune of thirteen pounds a week for the past three-and-a-half years, which works out at two thousand, three hundred and sixty-six pounds,' she claimed.

'That's bloody marvellous, isn't it? Makes a change to me owing money, that does,' a happy Albert replied.

'It is good news for you, yes. Now, we have two options for you and it's entirely up to you how you wish to proceed,' she continued. 'We can either send you the entire sum owed, or we can repay it back at thirteen pounds a week on top of the revised rate, making it an extra twenty-six pounds a week, that's fifty-two every fortnight, until the sum is paid off. Which option would you like to choose?'

'Well, that extra twenty-six pounds a week is a good difference already, but by the time you pay it back I may not be here, so I'll take the full amount and splash out on a nice holiday, I think,' Albert replied happily.

'Thank you for letting me know your preferred option. Just to confirm, you'd like the deficit paid to your bank directly rather than the fortnightly reimbursement?' she asked.

'That is correct, thank you.'

'You're welcome, Albert. Now, I'll need you to confirm the name on the account, the sort code and the full account number,' she asked him, 'along with the security code on the back of your card.

'Okay, give me a sec while I get that for you,' he said.

There was a pause for a few seconds before Albert returned.

'Okay, here we go,' he said, reading out the information she had requested.

'Thank you, Albert. Now, this will probably make your account within the next seven to ten working days. You might well receive it sooner, but we have to advise you of that potential waiting period just in case. I've also updated your records to include the fortnightly increase, to start from your next regular payment. So, by then, everything will be in order, with your deficit paid in full and your revised fortnightly amount now correct,' she said.

'Thank you so much, Samantha, you've made my day,' said Albert.

'WHAT IS IT, ANDY?' Kendra asked.

'I just checked and saw that Kim Morgan has been preying on the elderly again.'

'How do you know that?' she asked.

'When I uploaded the virus, I was able to access the computers, as you know, so I added a similar program to the cloned phone one. Basically, I can see what keystrokes she uses, and she has just added a bunch of bank information to a spreadsheet on her desktop.'

'Shit,' Kendra said, 'we need to stop that bitch from doing any more harm.'

'I can disable her computer, if you like. Well, I say disable, I can change the password to one that she'll never guess, which will keep her from doing anything with this particular computer.'

'Yes, please do that. Can she use her laptop or any other company computer, though?'

'She can, and also her phone, but I think we need to keep that going. I can disable her laptop using the same thing, but it needs to be switched on, which it isn't at the moment,' he said.

'Okay, do what you can for now, I have to think of a way to stop her from calling anyone else,' she said.

'Don't tell him I told you, but you should get Jimmy to call her and keep her busy for a bit, until we can send the evidence to the police,' Andy said.

'Damn, he's gonna go batshit,' she said.

'NO WAY, Kendra, you promised me that was the last time!' said Jimmy.

'I know, and I'm sorry, Jimmy, but that woman is causing carnage and needs to be stopped. She likes you a lot, so if you can keep her busy for a day or two it would give us the time to get the police on her.'

'Two days? Two days? Are you serious? It was bad enough being with her for two hours, what the hell am I supposed to do for two days?' he shrieked.

Kendra smiled, trying hard not to laugh, and took a few seconds to reply.

'Jimmy, if anyone can keep her occupied for two days, it's you. You don't have to spend the night or anything, just make something up about taking it slowly and respecting her, that usually works.'

'Does it? Does it really? Is it something you've experienced, is it? No, I didn't think so, because that's a load of crap. She'll never fall for that, not in a million years.'

'Jimmy, we need you for this, please.'

'Dammit, Kendra, do you know how hard it is to keep smiling and being nice to a horrible person? It's exhausting, and it is bloody difficult!'

'Can you help or not?'

Jimmy paused before responding.

'Yes, I'll help, but I want you to know that I'm doing this under protest, and I don't wish to be considered for similar roles in the future. You can send Izzy next time, he's just as good with the ladies,' he replied.

'Deal. Thanks, Jimmy, you're helping a lot of people by doing this,' she said.

'Like I said, it's the last time.'

TREVOR, Charmaine, and the twins arrived at Khan's country house, just outside the village of Cuffley in Hertfordshire, some fifteen minutes outside London. The twenty-four-acre estate was enclosed within ten-foot tall, sturdy iron fences that Khan had installed when he'd bought the house fifteen years earlier at great expense. The entrance to the estate was via an ornate wrought-iron gate with a coat of arms that Khan had purchased around the same time, making him Lord of the Manor of his Cuffley estate. There was a rear entrance for deliveries, and for staff to use, which led to a small car park next to the sprawling house. Online research had revealed that it had eight bedrooms and ten bathrooms, along with a ballroom, a library, three drawing rooms, and a huge kitchen and pantry, not forgetting the wine cellar that Khan had installed. The entire house had been renovated to the tune of two and a half million pounds, completely modernised, with only the exterior indicating its two-hundred-year heritage.

'Okay, you know the drill,' said Trevor. 'There are cameras covering the main entrance and at sporadic intervals along the boundary of the estate, covering what they perceive as weak points. Amir, you know where they are, so where do you want dropping off?'

'There's an area of dense bush near the rear entrance that isn't covered by the cameras as it is overgrown, so I'll work my way through that and walk the long way around to the house,' Amir replied.

'We haven't seen any sign of dogs or security guards roaming around so I guess there will be a minimal presence,' Mo added.

'We can hope, brother, otherwise your favourite twin will be running for his life, right towards you.' Amir grinned.

'What about infra-red cameras, won't they spot you?' Charmaine asked.

'They probably would, but I don't see any modern cameras like that, they all look to have been installed at least ten years ago when he modernised everything, so I think we'll be alright,' he said.

'Okay, we'll park down the road until it's dark, and drop you off. While you're in there we'll check the perimeter and for any activity that may be a problem, so make sure you have your phone switched on so we can warn you,' Trevor said.

'But on silent, bro!' Mo laughed.

Amir shook his head and rolled his eyes before taking his phone out and making sure it was on silent.

'I'm good, bro.'

An hour later they were back, the area in near-darkness, only a few lights visible from the ground floor of the house. Trevor drove them to the rear, where Amir had asked to be dropped off. He stopped the car momentarily, and within seconds, Amir was out of sight, as Trevor continued driving.

'I always get nervous with things like this,' Mo said, as he watched for signs of his younger sibling.

'It's because you care about your brother, Mo,' Charmaine said, patting him on the shoulder, 'brotherly love and all that.'

'Don't you dare tell him that, Charmaine, I'll never hear the last of it,' Mo said, as he turned away quickly.

Trevor drove away from the estate. He returned to their original parking spot and turned the engine off, putting them in complete darkness as they waited on Amir to call for pick-up.

'DAMN IT,' Amir said as he put his hand in a badger's droppings. Fortunately, the droppings were days old and dried out, so it didn't leave too much of a smell on his hand once he had wiped it on some grass.

He eventually managed to struggle through a small gap in the bushes before coming to the railings, which he climbed carefully before landing softly in the gardens. As always, Amir took stock of his surroundings, looking for opportunities that would help him get into the house, such as trees that were planted close to the house, or older-style doors on the ground floor that he could easily open. In this instance he could see no weakness, nothing that would make his mission easy.

'The hard way it is, then,' he muttered, as he walked slowly around the perimeter back towards the house.

There were two lights on that he had seen: one at the front near the large wooden door to the house, the other next to the rear entrance. He assumed that the lights indicated a security presence at either end of the house, which would suggest a minimum of two guards. As he approached the rear, through the window with the light on he could see the head of one guard watching a television that he had placed next to a monitor that showed the CCTV footage, his feet up on the table as he munched through a family bag of crisps.

Naughty boy, Amir thought, shaking his head at the guard's shoddy work.

Despite the lack of opportunities, Amir knew that a good old-fashioned drainpipe was always an option. It was a tricky option, but his prowess as a successful and highly skilled parkour athlete made climbing drainpipes easier for him than most. Looking up towards the second-storey window that he wanted to try and enter through, Amir plotted his route, recognising that it would take a jump of around six feet from the pipe to the windowsill. For that to work, he'd need a good footing, and that would mean jumping from a section of the drainpipe that had a junction, on which he could firmly plant his feet. That junction was three feet higher than the windowsill, so he'd be dropping fast, as well as trying to get a solid purchase on the sill six feet away.

Looking around one last time, he took a deep breath and leapt across, dropping swiftly. He had originally wanted to land on the narrow sill, but his feet missed, so he had one chance only to grab hold with his hands. He grabbed and held onto the sill, hanging on until he was ready to lift himself up. Being relatively slight, Amir managed to perch his backside on the sill before lifting himself and then standing. He listened intently for any noise coming from within, and was confident nobody was there, before he slowly and quietly pulled down the sash window. The window was a good size, five feet in height and three feet across, so Amir had plenty of room to manoeuvre himself and climb into the room.

Before dropping to the floor, he stopped again to listen, and only when he was happy did he drop down quietly. He noticed the floor was tiled and as his eyes adjusted, he was able to see enough to know that he was in one of the bathrooms. He walked to the door, putting his ear to it before silently pulling it open to see what was beyond. It was a long dark hallway, with several doors on each side and a wide staircase halfway along, leading both downstairs, and upstairs to a third floor. Amir had no idea which room was Khan's, and which room likely had any valuables worth taking. Taking valuables which would be sold, and the proceeds used to contribute towards the victims' fund was but one objective. He went to the sink and inserted the sink plug before turning on the tap. He did the same with the bath plug. He then left the bathroom and walked along the hall, repeating the process twice more in the opulent bathrooms, each one linked to a bedroom via an internal door.

Amir checked the entire first floor, where there were four bedrooms—apparently all guest rooms, the beds neatly made with a pair of towels laid out ready for the next guests—and four bathrooms. He moved quietly to the top floor and repeated the process, checking every room, blocking all the sinks and turning on the taps. One of the bedrooms was larger than the others and appeared to be Khan's, so Amir checked the wardrobes and found them full of clothes, confirming his guess. It had a large en-suite bathroom with gold taps and fittings, navy blue tiles, and lots of mirrors. Before blocking the sinks, he placed all Khan's clothes into the bath and the shower and then ran the water.

Satisfied with his work, Amir went back downstairs to see if he'd be able to take anything of value before leaving. He didn't want to take any chances knowing that there were at least two security guards on site, so he was cautious, wary of the water that was likely to start dripping through the ceiling.

Before he'd reached the ground floor he heard voices, which he presumed to be the guards.

'Dave, I've just lost power to the monitors and the telly, is yours still on?' shouted one of the guards.

'Nah, mine's gone too, Bill. Can you check the fuse box? It's in the pantry, mate,' Dave said.

'Will do,' came the reply.

Amir decided to exit stage left and went back to the first bathroom. When he opened the door, he saw that the water had started overflowing and was now making its way out of the door towards the staircase. It was only a matter of time before the guards realised what had happened. He quickly went to the window and left the way he'd come, only this time, instead of aiming for the junction three feet higher, he leapt for the drainpipe, grabbing it with both hands and balancing his feet against the wall. From there, it was easy for him to drop down and make his way towards the perimeter and his exit point. He called Trevor on the way.

'I'm out, pick me up at the same place,' he whispered.

'Blimey, that was quick, we'll be there in a couple of minutes,' Trevor replied.

Amir climbed the fence and then worked his way through the dense bush, remembering to avoid the badger droppings. When he eventually freed himself from the bush, he walked along the single-track road towards where he knew Trevor would be coming from. Thirty seconds later he was in the back of the car, and they were on the way out of the area.

'How did it go, bro?' asked Mo.

'There were a couple of guards who were both awake, so I couldn't do much, really.'

'What did you do, then?' Charmaine asked.

'I left them a little present.' He smirked and explained

what he had done, knowing that he would be causing Khan a great deal of trouble and expense.

The guards both attempted to fix the fuse box in the pantry, wrongly thinking that was the problem, and were unable to turn the power back on, so it was some time before they realised that water was gushing down the stairs. When they ran to the first floor to investigate, hundreds of gallons had already flooded each floor, damaging the electrical circuitry, the flooring, the ceilings below, and more. It would be months before the house dried out properly and repairs carried out, at the cost of several hundred thousand pounds.

'Great idea, Amir. That should get his attention. We'll have to be a bit clever with the next one, he'll probably increase security now,' Trevor said.

'Which one will be next?' Charmaine asked.

'The one he'd least expect us to target, his headquarters in London,' Trevor said.

'Um, didn't you say that the security there was great? That he's got some super-soldier Russian dude running it? How are we gonna pull that off?' Charmaine was concerned for the team.

'Oh, we won't be doing it ourselves, I forgot to mention that,' Trevor said.

'Come on, Trev, put us out of our misery, will you? Who's gonna be doing it?' Mo asked.

'The Yardies, that's who.'

When Khan was informed of the incident, he sent Ivan Abramovich to investigate, recognising that the attack was a clear message to him.

'I'm telling you, Ivan, that bastard Trevor Giddings is behind this. Find out what you can and then try and track him down, I want him out of the way before he does any more damage.'

'Yes, sir, Mister Khan,' Abramovich replied.

When the call was over, the Russian smiled, looking forward to his favourite pastime: hunting humans.

16

MARVIN FREEMAN

Marvin Freeman was enjoying his usual breakfast: tropical fruit granola and yoghurt with a mug of sugary tea when there was a knock on the door of his Buckinghamshire residence. His housemaid, Sylvia, answered the door to a police detective who held his warrant card up for her to see. He was accompanied by three uniformed police officers.

'Good morning, madam. My name is Detective Sergeant James Adair from the National Crime Agency, and I'm here this morning to speak with Mister Marvin Freeman. Can you please tell him that we're here?'

'Yes, sir, one moment,' Sylvia said, closing the door. She dashed to the morning room where Freeman was eating.

'Mister Freeman, the police are here, sir, and they want to speak with you.'

For a few seconds, Freeman said nothing.

'What the hell do they want?' he said, standing.

'They didn't say, sir, they asked to see you,' Sylvia replied.

Freeman made his way down the hall and opened the front door.

'How can I help you, officers?' he said to the waiting police.

Jim Adair showed his warrant card again.

'My name is Detective Sergeant James Adair, I'm from the National Crime Agency, Mister Freeman. I'm here to arrest you for the murder of Amy March. You're not obliged to say anything unless you wish to do so, but it may harm your defence if you don't mention when questioned something which you later rely on in court. Anything else you say may be given in evidence. Do you understand?'

'What? What the hell is this all about?' One of the uniformed officers made a note in his notebook of Freeman's response.

'Sir, please come with us. We'll be conducting a formal interview at the police station,' Adair said.

'Answer my question, dammit, what the hell is this all about?' Freeman repeated.

'Mister Freeman, like I said, I am arresting you for the murder of Amy March thirty years ago, and we are taking you to Thames Valley Police headquarters in Kidlington, where you will be interviewed after you have been booked in. I suggest you make arrangements for your solicitor to have him meet you there.'

Freeman turned to Sylvia.

'Call Brian Hampton and tell him what's happened, and to hurry to the police station for the interview,' he told her.

'Yes, sir,' she said, going back inside.

'Let me grab my jacket,' he told Adair, reaching for his green Barbour jacket from the coat stand.

As he stepped out onto the porch, one of the uniformed

officers placed Freeman in handcuffs behind his back, before grabbing his arm and escorting him to one of the two waiting cars. He was placed in the back seat, with Adair sitting next to him.

'Seriously? You're arresting me for something I allegedly did thirty years ago? My solicitor is going to rip you to shreds, you know that, right?'

'He can give it his best shot, sir,' Adair replied, enjoying Freeman's discomfort.

'What the hell has happened that you've come after me now? I know about that woman, she committed suicide, as your colleagues from the past reported,' Freeman added.

'New evidence has come to light, sir, as you'll be informed during the interview. You could, of course, confess now, which would be looked upon favourably by the court,' Adair said.

Freeman laughed.

'You lot are crazy. You honestly think I'm going to confess to a murder? Man, Hampton is gonna tear you a new one, you'll be lucky to keep your job after this. I'm a respectable businessman and I have hundreds of people below me, you do know that, right?'

'That doesn't entitle you to evade justice, sir,' Adair said, 'if you're found not guilty then you'll be a free man, but there is a formal legal process, and you will be going through it.'

Freeman shook his head and sat back in the seat, uncomfortable and agitated, thinking back to the murder, and trying to figure out what had changed after all this time.

What the hell have they got on me? He thought.

THE POLICE HEADQUARTERS at Kidlington was forty minutes' drive from Freeman's home and the rest of the journey had been made in silence. When they arrived, Freeman was taken immediately to the custody suite where he was booked in by the custody sergeant, which included removing his belt and taking his phone, watch, rings and wallet, which were all sealed in a tamper-proof bag and placed in a safe.

'What is he here for?' the custody sergeant asked Adair.

'He was arrested at nine-fifteen this morning for murder, to which he replied to caution...' Adair looked to the officer who had recorded the response.

'..."What? What the hell is this all about?"' the officer quoted.

'His solicitor should be on the way, Sergeant, and we intend to interview him as soon as he arrives,' Adair added.

'Very well. Take him to cell five, please,' the custody sergeant told the officer, who proceeded to walk Freeman into the cell block.

'I'll be in the canteen until the solicitor arrives, if you can give us a shout,' Adair said.

'Will do,' the custody sergeant replied.

Jim Adair grabbed a sandwich and a coffee in the canteen while he waited for another forty minutes, whereby he was summoned back to the custody suite. Freeman was sitting on a bench, flanked by a uniformed officer and a stocky, grey-suited man. The custody officer summoned them over, where they joined Adair.

'DS Adair will be conducting the interview, please use interview room three,' he told them. The uniformed officer, the same one that had recorded the response to caution earlier that morning, led Freeman and the solicitor to the interview suite adjoining the custody suite, entering room three as instructed. Freeman and his solicitor sat opposite Adair, the uniformed officer closing the door behind him as he left the room.

Adair reached over to the recording device that was secured to the wall and desk and started preparing for the interview. It took a minute or two to enter the information required and turn on the recording device, before he turned to the two men facing him.

'My name is Detective Sergeant James Adair from the National Crime Agency and I'll be conducting the interview this morning, which is being recorded. The time is now ten fifty-three in the morning. Can you please state your names for the record,' he said.

'Marvin Freeman,' came the first reply.

'Brian Hampton of Hampton Cruikshank Barnes Solicitors, representing Mister Freeman,' came the second.

'Thank you, gentlemen. Before I start, I want to remind you of the caution, Mister Freeman. You do not have to say anything, but it may harm your defence if you don't mention now, something which you later rely on in court. And anything you do say may be given in evidence. Do you understand?' Adair asked.

Freeman looked to Hampton, who nodded.

'I do,' he replied.

'Thank you. Mister Freeman, you were arrested at your home address this morning by me at nine-fifteen for the murder of one Amy March. Can you please tell me what you recollect of your dealings with the victim thirty years ago?'

Freeman looked to Hampton, who shook his head.

'No comment,' he replied.

'Did you know Amy March?'

'No comment.'

'Did you ever meet Amy March?'

'No comment.'

'Okay, let's try something different. You had a few run-ins with local police in Hackney for drug possession and assault amongst other things, did that all happen when you were leader of the local Yardie gang?' Adair asked, changing tack.

Freeman again looked to Hampton, who again shook his head.

'No comment.'

'Do you not even want to acknowledge your police record, Mister Freeman? It's not a trick question, sir.'

'No comment.'

'Okay, so my guess is that you'll be making 'no comment' replies to all my questions, is that correct?'

'No comment.'

Adair smirked.

'I should have seen that one coming. Okay, let me try something else,' he said, reaching into his jacket.

He removed two small voice recorders from one pocket and a third from another, placing them in front of the two men on the desk.

'What I have here are three separate recordings that I'd like to play to you,' Adair said. He turned on the first one.

The unmistakable American voice of Robyn Hunt played.

'Marvin Freeman... that was one evil bastard... I haven't seen him since he abandoned me. I went to prison for that bastard. Yes, he was my lover, but do you know how many times my lover came to see me in prison? ... He got away with it while I spent five years inside for something he started... he didn't give a shit about me, that's why. All along he was using me, like a trophy, showing my fighting skills off. It was great at the time, I got to beat the hell out of a lot of men, which he probably got off on.

Once I was inside, he abandoned me in a heartbeat. I've never seen him since.'

Jim leaned over and switched off the recorder. Freeman was looking at Hampton, his expression having changed from that of a confident man to one who was angry and frustrated.

'This is bollocks,' he said, before Hampton put a hand on his arm to placate him.

'I will add that she also confirms that you killed Amy March, I just want you to hear that we have the recording. Let me play you another,' Adair said, turning on the second device.

Steven Khan's voice was loud and clear.

'Yes, Stanwick and I tipped the Yardies off. Yes, I told them where you really lived, about what you were doing undercover, and about your lovely wife. Yes, I told them everything. Yes, I knew what that animal Freeman was going to do, I even encouraged it. And you can do nothing about it, you stupid man.'

'What the f...' was all Freeman said before Hampton stopped him and Adair switched off the recording.

'Detective, may I ask how you came by these recordings?' Hampton asked.

'You may ask, and I shall decline to tell you. If you want to know, then ask for full disclosure and you'll get a formal response,' Adair said. 'I have one more I'd like you to hear.'

He turned on the final recorder.

Nelson Stanwick MP's voice was also clear.

'I'm sorry about your wife, okay? I had nothing to do with that, I was shocked when I found out about it, Freeman was a nasty, evil shit, by all accounts. He bragged to my dad about it to implicate him if anything went wrong, as insurance.'

'This is bullshit!' Freeman said angrily, standing. Adair stood and faced him, prepared for any violent response.

'Sit down, Mister Freeman,' Hampton said, trying to pull him down.

'You can go to hell, how is this allowed? Those arseholes have all turned on me, after all I did for them. They'd be nowhere without me, and now they're blaming me for everything that I did for them?' he shrieked.

'Stop talking, Mister Freeman!' Hampton shouted.

'Shut the hell up, this is a set-up. The police have made deals with those bastards to put me away. What the hell did you promise them, eh? Immunity? Witness protection? What?' he asked Adair, before turning to Hampton. 'Can they do that?' he asked.

'Please, will you sit down, you're making things worse,' Hampton pleaded.

Freeman glared at Adair as he sat down. Jim followed.

'If I may continue, Mister Freeman, it seems that you may be correct in your assumption. You have choices, though, which I suggest you consider very carefully,' he said.

'What choices?' Freeman asked, before Hampton could stop him.

'You can help us with our investigations against Steven Khan by giving us a full statement of his involvement in all the activities and the murder of Amy March, confess to a lesser charge of manslaughter, or you can take your chances in court where your solicitor here will have to try and convince a jury that all three recordings you have just listened to are not genuine. Your choice,' Adair said.

Freeman looked to his solicitor, no longer confident, still angry, and now very frustrated.

'I pay you a lot of money, Hampton, you'd better give me

some good advice here. You know the consequences...' was as far as he got before Hampton again stopped him and nodded. The solicitor turned to Adair.

'I need to confer with my client before he makes his decision. He has nothing further to say until I can discuss his options.'

'Very well. This interview is concluded at eleven thirty-one,' Adair said, reaching over and turning off the recording device. He stood and knocked on the door, which was opened by the uniformed officer that had accompanied them earlier.

Adair left the interview room and went to report to the custody officer, asking the uniformed officer to remain outside the interview room until the occupants had finished their discussion.

That went as well as could be expected, Adair thought as he went to grab a cold drink from the canteen. *Things are about to get very interesting indeed.*

17

ATTACK PLANNED

Trevor knew the instant he'd checked the office block that the team would suffer excessive casualties were they to attempt to strike at Khan's office block. The physical security was of high quality and the personnel were highly trained, with the brute of a man leading them, Ivan Abramovic. There was no telling what that man might do.

Trevor had managed to fool them by taking a decoy voice recorder and phone to the meeting with Khan, knowing those would be confiscated, and instead using covert equipment, a pen camera and miniature recorder on his keyring. Getting into the block and causing damage was a whole different prospect and he thought long and hard about a solution. He wanted to hurt Khan, and he knew that an attack on his flagship premises would do that, even if the damage was minimal. In the end, his plan was a long shot, but one that he realised would be worth the risk if he could pull it off.

Early on, when he'd asked Andy to research the potential enemies responsible for betraying him thirty years ago, he'd also asked him to check on some of the members of the Yardie posse that Freeman ran, namely Banjo and Calvin, whom he knew had been around when Freeman had killed Amy. The resulting intelligence had been very interesting and had surprised Trevor.

Banjo, whose name was Roland Ash, had moved on with Freeman and had become an integral part of his successful business ventures. He was now Head of Security for the hotels and the football club that Freeman owned.

Calvin Thompson was now head of the posse in Hackney, where their presence was now low-key and included several legitimate businesses, including two taxi firms, a dozen rental properties, and three car showrooms. They did not want to do anything to attract attention to themselves anymore. Andy had found that some members of the posse were still showing up on stop-and-search records but in the main they were keeping out of trouble.

Interesting, Trevor thought, reminiscing about his days with them. He remembered both men well and thought long and hard about how he could deal with them and Khan in a single stroke. His plan was ambitious and daring, but if it worked, it would cause damage to both parties, with no actual risk to the team.

Trevor's plan centred around the fact that Freeman had been arrested and was likely to be kept in custody for at least several days while interviews and further investigations were concluded, before being bailed to attend court for a first hearing sometime in the future. With Freeman in custody and incommunicado, Trevor decided to contact Calvin Thompson, knowing that he still had strong connections with him, and point the finger at Khan as being responsible for the situation now affecting Freeman. It wasn't difficult for

Andy to get a contact number for Thompson, which he called.

'Who is this?' Thompson answered.

'A blast from the past, Calvin. Maybe you remember me, maybe not. This is Trevor.'

There was a long pause while Calvin digested the information.

'I thought you were long dead, Trevor. It's a shame you're not, you traitorous bastard.'

'Oh, don't be like that, Calvin, I liked you back then. We were buddies, remember?'

'Why the fuck are you calling me?' Calvin asked.

'I just wanted you to know that your boss Freeman has been nicked for murder. You know, the one you witnessed. I know you were there that night, Calvin.'

'What the hell are you talking about? That was thirty years ago, nothing's gonna happen to Marvin after all this time.'

'Well, you'd be wrong about that. You see, Steven Khan and that detective's son, the MP, and even your old pal Robyn have all turned against him and gone full-blown witnesses. He's going away forever, Calvin, and you'll be going with him,' Trevor said, hoping his lies would be convincing. 'All that hard work you've put in all these years will go up in smoke while you're sitting in your prison cell.'

'Go screw yourself, traitor, you're talking crap.'

'Really? Why don't you call Freeman's house and ask his staff where he is? Better still, why don't you call Khan's place of business, you know, that big glass tower block in London, and ask them why they're looking after the witnesses there, all nicely secure in the plush suite that Khan uses for his whores. He plans on looking after them very well so that he can screw your boss over and grow his empire even more. He'll probably take on your businesses, too, that'd be ironic, wouldn't it?'

'What?' Calvin growled.

'That's right. Steven Khan, the filthy-rich bastard that you lot helped make so powerful is now feeding your ex-buddies the best cuisine and giving them the best protection until Freeman is sent away for the rest of his life. He pulled some strings with his government connections, paid a few of them, and on top of growing his business empire he's also receiving immunity for turning witness. You have to admire his business acumen, he's a slimy one, that fucker, isn't he?'

'If what you're saying is true then why are you telling me all this shit?' Calvin asked, probing.

'Because I want justice for my wife, Calvin. Once Freeman is put away, I'll make sure you're next. You may not have killed her, but you were there, you helped that bastard, and you kept quiet for decades. You'll be next. I'll make sure you get an honorary mention from the witnesses. You're an accomplice to murder, my friend.'

'Nothing's gonna happen to me, you fifth-columnist shit. Marvin will be released, and it won't even go to court, you'll see. He has some powerful friends, too,' Calvin said confidently.

'I have three witnesses who say otherwise. So, I'll be seeing you in court, we can watch Marvin being escorted out of the court in chains, never to be seen again. Catch you later,' Trevor concluded, ending the call.

Fingers crossed, he thought, hoping that the carrot was juicy enough for the Yardies to spring into action.

CALVIN CALLED Freeman's house immediately.

'Hello, Sylvia. This is Calvin Thompson, can you put the boss on, please?'

'I'm sorry, Mister Calvin, but Mister Freeman isn't here,' Sylvia replied.

'Where is he, Sylvia?'

Sylvia paused before replying.

'It's not my place to say, sir.'

'Sylvia, I'm going to ask you one time and I need you to be honest with me, okay? Is the boss with the police?'

Sylvia paused again, unsure of whether to disclose anything.

'Sylvia, answer me! I've been told that he's been arrested, is it true?' Calvin insisted.

'Y... yes, sir, It's true. They came and took him away this morning.'

'Shit! What for, Sylvia? What did they arrest him for?'

'I heard them say it was for killing someone thirty years ago, Mister Calvin. Is that possible, they can do that after such a long time?'

'Thank you, and yes, they can,' Calvin replied, hanging up.

He leaned against the wall, stretching his back and looking up at the ceiling, thinking of the potential problems ahead. He dialled another number.

'Banjo, the boss has been pinched for killing the traitor's wife thirty years ago,' Calvin told his friend.

'What? Are you messing with me?'

'No, sir, I am not. I just spoke to his housemaid, and she told me that the police took him this morning. But that's not all, we have bigger problems.'

'What's that?' Banjo asked.

'That traitor bastard Trevor called me and told me. He said that Robyn, Khan, and the detective's prick son have all turned witness against him. Khan is looking after them in his London offices.'

'Shit, you know what that means? If they get the boss, we'll be next, you know that, right?'

'I do, which is why I'm calling to ask for your help,' Calvin said.

'What have you got planned?'

'I'm gonna send those snitch bastards a message they can't ignore, so they'll know what will happen to them if I ever get hold of them. They won't say shit to anyone once they get the message, you can count on that, old friend.'

'Tell me what you need, brother.'

'DETECTIVE MARCH, I didn't expect to see you back again,' a surprised Robyn Hunt said when she answered the door.

'I'm sorry, but there's been a development that you need to be aware of, and I came to warn you,' Kendra said.

'Oh? What development?'

'Freeman was arrested this morning for the murder of my mother. I told the arresting officer what you told me and that you wouldn't be willing to give evidence, but he told Freeman that you and a couple of others have turned against him. I think he's hoping that Freeman confesses or something,' Kendra said.

'Shit! I knew you were bad news the second I saw you,' Robyn said, turning away in disgust.

'You need to go into hiding, Robyn, or give evidence and go into protective custody,' Kendra added.

'Damn you!'

'I'm sorry, but actually I have no sympathy for you, Robyn. You watched that man kill my mother and did nothing to stop him. In my mind, you're just as guilty as he is. I've told you what your choices are: run and hide, or come with me and give evidence against him,' Kendra pressed.

'He won't stop until he finds me and kills me; you know, that don't you?' Robyn pleaded.

Kendra shrugged.

'Like I said, I don't care, and you'd be the same if you were in my shoes. You should think yourself lucky that I came to warn you, because unlike you or Freeman, my conscience is clear. By the way, did you know that I was upstairs sleeping in my crib when you came and took her away?'

Robyn's head dropped in resignation.

'I'm so tired of it all, this bullshit has had me looking over my shoulder for years, isn't that enough? Surely you can't expect me to give evidence and think I'll walk away unharmed. Is that what you really want me to do?' she finally said.

'What I want is for you to go to hell,' Kendra said. 'I don't care how.'

She turned and walked away, not looking back, not caring if Robyn decided to give evidence, satisfied that her conscience would remain as it was: clear and prepared for the worst.

Jim Adair walked back into the custody suite to see Freeman and his solicitor sitting on the same bench. They looked up and caught his eye as he walked in, and immediately Jim sensed that Freeman's defiance would be an obstacle.

'How's it going, Sarge?' he asked the custody sergeant. 'Which room can I use for our esteemed guests?'

'You can use room three again,' the sergeant replied, indicating for a uniformed officer to escort Freeman. As it wasn't an interview, there was no need to turn the recording device on, so it was a discussion, mainly to see whether Freeman would cooperate.

'So, Mister Freeman, have you given any thought to my offer?' Jim asked.

Before replying, Freeman looked to his solicitor, who gave a short encouraging nod.

'I have, and I respectfully decline. I think I'll take my chances in court,' he said, defiantly.

'Very well. In that case, there is nothing further to discuss,' Jim said, standing.

He knocked on the door for the officer to let them out, whereby they returned and stood in front of the custody officer.

'Sarge, Mister Freeman has decided to take his chances in court, so we'll be waiting on the Crown Prosecution Service to send a charging decision soon,' Jim said.

The custody officer addressed Freeman.

'Mister Freeman, do you understand what that means? As you have been arrested for murder, we have to wait for a decision on charging you from the CPS, meaning you have to stay in custody until that happens. Do you understand?'

'I understand,' Freeman said. 'I understand very well that I'll be out of here soon.'

'Well, you'll have to wait for that decision in the meantime, sir,' the custody officer replied, nodding to the uniformed officer.

Freeman was taken back to his cell to await the CPS decision. Once he was out of hearing, Hampton turned to Jim.

'So, you'll not tell me how you got those recordings, eh?' he asked.

'That would be giving up our methods now, wouldn't it, Mister Hampton? I'd rather wait until you went through the correct channels with disclosure, then we may give you an inkling… if indeed it is appropriate. We must, after all, protect our sources and our methods, right?'

Hampton made no reply, instead turning towards the custody officer and nodding curtly, before turning to the uniformed officer.

'Please escort me out of here, officer.'

Once Hampton was out of the custody suite, the custody officer turned to Jim, one eyebrow raised.

'Think you've got enough to get a charge?' he asked.

'If our witness comes forward then we will have a slim chance. If not, then no chance at all,' Jim replied. 'I appreciate your assistance, Sarge, I'll let you know what the CPS decision is as soon as I know.'

He waved as he left the suite, making his way back to the canteen for another coffee. He was on his third slurp when Kendra phoned.

'How did it go?' he asked.

'No good, I'm afraid. She's frightened witless and thinks her life is over now. I told her that Freeman knew she'd told us.'

'Ooh, that was naughty,' Jim said.

'Yeah, I know, but sometimes you need to shock people into making a decision, it just didn't work this time. My guess is that she'll be packed up and on the run by tonight,' Kendra added.

'Well, there goes our case for murder,' Jim said, 'we'll have no choice but to bail him now.'

'I know. I appreciate you for doing this, Jim. Is there any chance you can stall for a bit, keep him in the cell until tomorrow morning?'

'Honestly, I'm not sure. His brief has left, which would have helped him, and it's pretty late in the day. I'll give it a go.'

'Thanks, do whatever you can. Sorry, Jim, I was hoping for a better result for us both.'

'You know the old saying, Kendra. You've got to be in it to win it,' Jim replied.

'Thanks, anyway, I'll catch up with you soon,' she said, ending the call.

'Damn it,' he muttered, staring at the phone.

He was not looking forward to breaking that news to Freeman.

I guess I can wait until the CPS sends word. Freeman can sit in his cell for a little longer, he thought.

'THANKS FOR THE HEADS-UP, LOVE,' Trevor told Kendra once she had updated him. He was disappointed but knew that there was a back-up plan.

'What do we do next, Dad? He'll be walking out of the station soon with a smug look on his face; I hate that he's getting away with it again.'

'Don't worry about that, love, he won't be getting away with it. I planted a seed with his chums in Hackney that should be working wonders any time soon.'

'Oh? And what, pray tell, will that seed be growing into, Father?' she asked, knowing that he had planned something unconventional and spectacular.

'Like I said, you won't have to wait long to find out,' he replied.

'Is this likely to cause some blowback on us, Dad? Because if it is, then we need to know so that we can be ready.'

'Oh, I'm expecting retaliation, don't you worry. I've spoken to Andy and Charmaine and they're plotting something suitably devious, just in case.'

'Okay, well, you can tell me too, I'm on my way home, so meet me there,' she told him.

'Alright, love, you can buy the pizza today.'

18

THE YARDIES

Trevor's estimate wasn't far off.

The Yardies chose the early evening to make their attack, knowing that the horde of commuters heading home from work would help them make their getaway. The three-and-a-half-ton box van they had chosen was stolen from the overnight car park at the South Mimms service station in North London, where the owner had parked it overnight while he slept at the nearby Premier Inn. It was a simple task to change the number plate to a similar vehicle to avoid the automatic number plate recognition systems prevalent around London.

Banjo had been true to his word and had provided the small amount of deadly Semtex along with the remote detonator required to initiate an explosion. Calvin had given his instructions to the four-man team that he'd sent on what he called *a mission of great importance that would ensure the future of the posse*. As the van approached the giant glass tower block, now fully lit in the dimming early evening light, the driver banged three times on the panel behind him.

The three men in the back of the van pulled down their balaclavas and readied themselves, knowing what was to come. The driver turned onto the road leading to the rear car park of Khan's office block and stopped just short of the ramp. The shutters of the van were pulled up and the three men jumped out and ran towards the car park barriers, brandishing firearms and shouting at the stunned guard beyond. He ran for his life, not waiting for the armed men to get close.

The first man on scene pressed the button that raised the barrier, while the second sprayed the CCTV camera overlooking the entry. The third man walked in and watched for any witnesses to their arrival. There were none, and he signalled to the waiting driver. As the van entered the car park, its high roof just making it past the entry, the third gunman pointed towards the door and the stairwell close to the middle of the car park. The driver followed the instruction and drove slowly and parked close to the door. He exited the van and opened the door to the stairwell, jamming it open with a wedge of paper.

He then turned and walked back to his waiting colleagues who were all scanning the car park for potential threats.

Before they exited the car park and walked up the ramp they removed their balaclavas, pulled up scarves around their necks to cover their faces, and put their handguns back in their pockets. As they reached the top of the ramp, they heard the alarms go off from within the tower block; the guard had found help. The driver removed the phone from his pocket and dialled the number he had been instructed to call when the van was in place.

The explosion was deafening, and even though they were now walking along the street with other pedestrians and were a good hundred yards away, they were stunned by the noise and the shockwave that almost knocked them over, showering them with tiny shards of glass shrapnel. The Semtex had done its job effectively, destroying everything within its initial blast range. The firebomb and shock wave made their way through the wedged-open door and up the stairs, blowing the doors to the reception area off their hinges. Everyone in reception was blown off their feet, and one unlucky guard who had ventured close to try and listen for the invaders was killed instantly by the fireball as it crashed through the doors.

Every single glass window and panel in reception was shattered, spraying glass for hundreds of feet, injuring many people in the street. Those on the ground floor were screaming in pain and those out in the streets were wailing, trying to get away as quickly as they could. The four gunmen split up into pairs and headed off in opposite directions where they would eventually be picked up by colleagues that waited in streets where there were no cameras or nosy neighbours. It would take months of investigating and trawling through hours of CCTV footage to pick out the four men responsible for the atrocity, but none of them were recognisable due to the scarves they wore. They tracked them as far as they could using CCTV footage but were never able to identify them or any vehicles that picked them up.

KHAN WAS in his penthouse suite overlooking the Thames when he received a call from the security manager on duty at his offices.

'What do you mean, an explosion?' he said, sitting

upright, 'what the hell was it, a ruptured gas line or something?'

'No, sir, it was a bomb. We were attacked by four armed men who drove a van into the car park. We don't know exactly what happened because they sprayed paint on the CCTV camera, but we think there was a bomb in the van. One of our men was killed by the blast and seventeen of our staff taken to hospital, some with serious injuries from the blast,' the manager replied.

'A bomb? A bloody bomb? Who the hell would do that? What the hell for? And how the hell did they get in so easily, I pay you lot a bloody fortune to keep the building safe,' Khan screamed.

'They were armed, sir,' the man said, 'we have sticks. There's nothing we could have done to stop them. You can't expect our men to engage with armed men, sir.'

'The money I pay you suggests that I bloody well can. I'm on my way over with Ivan, we'll speak about this more when I get there,' Khan said, ending the call and storming off to get changed. He called Abramovich.

'Get to the office as soon as you can, someone's bombed the place, Ivan, and I'm guessing that Giddings has something to do with it. I'll meet you there, just leaving the flat now,' he said.

'Yes, Mister Khan, I'll be there in fifteen minutes.'

'Be there in ten. We're going to war on that bastard.'

'HELLO, SARGE,' Jim Adair answered, 'what can I do for you?'

'We've had a call from the CPS, who have confirmed that we can charge Freeman with the murder. I guess having a witness tipped them in our favour, eh?' the custody sergeant remarked.

'Ah, well, I was just about to pop down and see you about that, Sarge. I'll be there shortly,' Jim replied.

Jim swore a dozen times before he reached the custody suite, angry that Freeman was likely to walk free. It had always been a long shot, but knowing now that the CPS were happy for a charge based on the witness just made it more frustrating all around.

'What's going on then, Detective Sergeant? I thought you'd be pleased with the decision, but it seems not to be the case, so tell me,' the custody sergeant said.

'I've just received word that the witness is refusing to cooperate and come in to give a statement. We've tried to change her mind but she's running scared, she thinks Freeman will hunt her down,' Jim replied.

'Well, that's put the cat amongst the pigeons, hasn't it? How do you want to deal with it? Do you need more time? As it's now outside office hours I can hold him for a little longer, maybe even overnight, but tomorrow morning, first thing, he is out of here.'

'If you can hold off till the morning, I'll write it up and we can bail him. We can't charge without the witness so we'll just bail him to come back while we look for more evidence, which could take months,' Jim said.

'Okay, we can do that. Forget we spoke, I couldn't reach you so I have no idea about the witness, you can break the bad news tomorrow morning to whoever is custody sergeant. That work for you?'

'That's perfect, I appreciate it, Sarge,' Jim said, leaving the suite. He was straight on the phone to Kendra.

'THAT WAS Jim Adair from the NCA. He's just told me that Freeman is going to be released tomorrow morning and bailed to come back some time in the future. So, what the hell is going on, Dad?' Kendra asked.

'Sweetheart, you always knew it was a long shot, so don't be too pissed off about this, okay?' Trevor replied.

'I'm just frustrated, Dad, the CPS were happy to charge him with a witness but now there's no way he can be charged,' she said.

'So, we just revert to plan B, like we always knew would happen. I've spoken to the Yardies, their posse leader is one of the men who was there that night and he remembered me. I basically told him that there were three witnesses who have come forward to snitch on Freeman and that I'd be going after him next.'

'What does that all mean, Dad? So what?'

'I haven't finished, love. I told Calvin, that's the leader, that the witnesses were being held in some sort of protective custody at Khan's plush offices, and that Khan was one of them and had made a deal for immunity in exchange for Freeman.'

'Still not with you,' she said.

'I've basically goaded him into attacking Khan to protect Freeman and his own skin. He won't be able to resist it, they've all got too much to lose now, with legitimate businesses worth millions.'

'You think he'll go for it?' she asked.

'I do. When you get into work tomorrow you can check and see if anything's happened overnight.'

'Fair enough. What if he doesn't go for it?'

'Then we try plan C, love, and we'll keep trying until one of them works. That bastard won't get away with it, none of them will, I promise.'

'That's good to know, Dad, thanks,' Kendra said.

'Now, hand over a slice of that pizza, that pineapple looks very tempting.'

KENDRA DIDN'T NEED to go to work the following morning to find out if anything had happened. As soon as Trevor had left, which surprised her as she thought he'd be staying the night, she got a call from Andy.

'Turn the TV on,' he said.

'Okay, want to tell me why?' she asked, using the remote to do as he asked.

'Go to the news channel and you'll see.'

Kendra did as she was told and immediately sat up straight in shock at what she was seeing.

'*...and nobody has come forward to claim responsibility*,' the reporter said, as several firemen walked up the ramp in the background, from the still-smoking car park with their hoses, their job seemingly done. '*The attack took place while the area was busy, shortly after office workers in the vicinity started to make their way home. There have been many casualties, currently believed to be forty hospitalised and one confirmed dead, but that number is likely to increase as police go through the building looking for missing staff.*'

'That's Khan's building, isn't it?' she blurted.

'It sure is. Any ideas who did this?' Andy asked.

'Yep. Dad clearly hasn't told you yet, but he lit a match

under the arses of the Yardies and this is them responding,' she replied.

'I spoke with him earlier, but he didn't tell me anything about this. Has he told you about the bounty on his head?' Andy asked.

'Bounty? No, what has he told you?'

'He really pissed Khan off, who told him that he's putting a bounty of a hundred grand on his head. We spoke about it and his expectation of retaliation by Khan, so we made some plans about how to deal with it,' Andy replied.

'He's started doing it again, not telling me everything so that I don't worry, hasn't he? Leave it with me, I'll have a word. In the meantime, you tell me everything that you know so that I can help,' she demanded.

'Fine by me,' Andy said.

'Maybe we can make our own plans and not tell him, eh? See how he likes it.'

'Whatever we do, let's do it soon because this attack on the office block is only going to make things worse with Khan. And knowing your dad, it's exactly what he wants to happen, for them to come after him,' Andy said.

'Agreed. So, what do you think we should do?' she asked.

'First off, I need to tell you what we discussed, which gives us an idea of how he's thinking about dealing with the problem. He told me that he's cleared one of the boxing clubs and spread the word that he's working and sleeping there for the time being. He's asked the twins to help him with a few traps there, and I sent him some miniature CCTV cameras so that we have live footage of the outside and inside of the club. I think he's looking to do this quietly and quickly by himself, which doesn't sit well with me.'

'Okay, that explains why he left tonight, I thought he'd be

staying as usual, but he's obviously planned this tonight and is expecting something to happen. He thinks that he's drawing them away from us and that he can deal with them without our help,' Kendra said.

'I have no doubt he's skilled enough to take on a handful of men, but Khan's security chief is one nasty piece of work, ex Russian special forces and as skilled in killing as they come,' Andy said.

'What traps has he set for them; do you know?'

'He took gas masks, some CS gas, three tasers, and some oil, so my guess is that the twins will be staying with him to help take out whoever turns up at the club.'

'Ordinarily, that might work, but from what you've told me about the Russian dude, anything could happen. I don't like it one bit,' Kendra said.

'What do you have in mind? Like I said, these guys are as skilled as anyone we've ever dealt with, so we need to think very carefully about this, Kendra.'

'Then I guess that's where we start, we expect the worst and plan for it,' she said. 'What kit have we got that we can use?'

19

AMBUSH

'I guess we're ready then, gents,' Trevor said to Mo and Amir.

'Yep, everything is in place, so now we wait,' Mo replied.

'You both have full kit on, right? There's a good chance whoever turns up will be armed.'

'We know that, Trev, we aren't stupid. I don't even want to see these people when they turn up, are you sure what we are doing is enough?' Amir said.

'Let's go over it again then, shall we?' Trevor said, 'we've laid the oil down near the front door, which will cause them a few problems, right?'

'Check,' Mo replied.

'The same for the back door, some oil just inside, right?' Trevor continued.

'Check,' Mo said.

'Yeah, yeah, they'll slip and fall over, blah, blah, then what? You think tasers are gonna be enough?' Amir asked.

'If you let me finish, you'll get your answer, Amir,' Trevor said, 'don't forget, we will also be using CS gas, which is why I asked you to bring the masks. That and the tasers should disable them enough for us to zip-tie them.'

'What if they're also wearing tactical gear, like us? The tasers won't work, will they?' Amir continued relentlessly. He loved to play devil's advocate, and in this scenario, he wanted to push his points as far as possible.

'That will present a problem, yes, which is why I also asked you to bring the stun guns. We'll have to get in close but if they have any exposed skin, they'll do a good job,' Trevor said, showing the powerful Tiger Xtreme stun guns that Andy had bought on the dark web along with other equipment and weapons that were illegal in the UK.

'Trevor, you said they'd likely be armed, so if we can't taser them, won't it be dangerous for us to get in close to try and stun them?' Mo asked, seeing where Amir was heading with his questions.

'It will be dangerous, Mo, of course. That's why you're wearing the full kit, your vest will stop almost any calibre bullet, and your mask will protect you from the CS gas. I'm hoping it doesn't come to that, which is why I also stocked up on this stuff,' he said, patting one of the three handheld cordless spray guns that were on the table. The Graco Ultra Airless sprayer was expensive but having seen how effective the team had been in the past using larger sprayers to disable attackers using toxic wood preserver, Trevor had figured that something smaller and more portable would be just as useful.

'Can you tell me again what they are?' Mo asked.

'This is a handheld spray gun that is used for smaller projects, as it only holds one litre of high-strength bonding glue. I've mixed some red acrylic paint in with it as the glue is clear and we want something a little more effective. You need to remember that it only holds one litre, so use it only if you have to and aim for the head to blind them. You won't have to get as close as with the stun gun, but it will buy you some time to disable them,' Trevor added.

'You keep finding these toys to use, let's just hope it's enough,' Amir said.

'Amir, you know where we stand as a team, we don't kill, we disable and either leave the police to deal with them or in some cases deal ourselves, but nothing fatal, remember?' Trevor reminded him.

'I know, and I remember. What will we be doing with this lot? I mean, if we take them out, won't the police just ask you questions again, as in how come the boxing clubs keep getting attacked?' Amir asked.

Trevor paused, reminded of the last occasion when his close friend, handler and mentor, Charlie, had been killed when Albanian gangsters had attacked his other club.

'I'm aware of that, Amir, and it's a very good point. We'll have to cross that bridge when we come to it, okay? I'm sure I can deal with the police.'

'Okay, it's your funeral,' Amir said, his arms raised in supplication.

'Good, then we wait,' Trevor said, 'and again, I appreciate you both for helping out with this.'

'Don't be surprised if your daughter doesn't rip you a new one when she finds out,' Mo said, giggling.

'Yep, she certainly will, which is why I've kept it from her. We can handle this quickly and quietly; she doesn't need to know.'

Amir shook his head again, knowing full well that if anyone were to find out, it would be Kendra.

ANDY PARKED MARGE, the specially equipped camper van, fifty yards away from the boxing club, where they had good vision on the entrance. When he saw that it was clear of passers-by, he quickly moved into the rear, joining Kendra, Darren, Jimmy and Izzy. It was a little more crowded than usual, but they were able to sit and monitor the screens that Andy had so cleverly set up. Two monitors covered the front door and part of the interior of the club, and which he had set up for Trevor. Another monitor showed the rear entrance.

'The boys are in place at the rear,' Darren said, referring to Clive, Martin, and Rory, who were parked behind the club covering the back door, out of view but ready to deploy quickly.

'Great, so now we wait,' Kendra said, 'everyone is kitted up, right?'

'Yes, including masks at the ready as per your instructions,' Darren replied.

'My guess is that Dad will deploy the gas as soon as they get attacked, so the last thing we want is for us to get caught up in it,' she added.

'We have tasers at the ready and zip ties to disable them, but tell me again what these are?' Darren asked, referring to the two cylindrical objects each of them had been issued with.

'They're smoke grenades,' Andy said, picking up one of the EG:18 Wire Pull smoke grenades he'd recently acquired.

'They give out a really dense smoke for around ninety seconds, with a simple ring-pull ignition,' he added.

'Ah, I see, that's why you asked us to bring the Nightfox goggles, so we can see when we deploy them.' Darren nodded.

'Yeah but remember that Dad and the twins haven't got a clue we're here so don't get them mixed up with the baddies. We want to get in and out quickly without any casualties,' Kendra said.

'I'm more worried about what those three will do to us, to be honest,' Jimmy said, 'should we warn them when we go in?'

'Yes, but only once you've dealt with the attackers,' she replied.

'Okay, sounds like a plan,' Jimmy said, 'of sorts.'

'There's not much more we can think of doing ourselves, gents, this is as good as we can do with what we have, which to be honest is more than most,' Andy said.

'Okay, let's keep our eyes open. If anything's gonna happen it will be from now,' Kendra said. 'Andy, can you add the live feed from the van to the monitor, please?'

'No problem, I'll do front and back,' he said.

A fourth monitor flicked to life, showing the view ahead of the van towards the club, which was flanked by a carpentry business and a van hire company, both businesses closed along with all the others in the street. The last, fifth monitor now showed the view from the rear, as far back as the junction with the main road. The quality cameras Andy utilised gave crisp, uninterrupted feeds that would give them the heads-up if there was an attack.

'And now we wait,' Andy said.

ANDY SCRUTINISED the monitor with the rear view. 'Stand by,' he said, 'we have two incoming SUVs.'

'Rory, we have a potential threat in the street, stand by,' Darren said on the phone to his colleague.

The SUVs pulled up at the front of the boxing club and double parked. Three men got out of each vehicle, wearing dark tactical clothing and balaclavas.

'Are they carrying guns?' Kendra asked.

Andy zoomed in.

'Yes, handguns,' he said. He quickly picked up his phone and typed Trevor a message.

As he did so, one of the men, a gigantic brute of a man, pointed to the alley next to the van-hire business and two of his men ran towards it.

'Incoming, six men, handguns, beware. 4 front 2 rear,' Andy's message warned.

'Rory, you have two armed men running towards you and the rear, beware,' Darren said.

The remaining four walked purposely towards the door to the club. The leader looked around to confirm there were no witnesses before he kicked the door violently, splintering it in its frame. He moved to one side and the other three men ran inside, with him following, their guns raised in preparation.

'Go, go, go,' Kendra said.

Darren, Izzy and Jimmy left Marge urgently, their tactical masks on, and the night vision goggles in place, ready to be used when needed. They ran towards the club a few seconds behind the attackers.

'Let's hope we aren't too late,' Kendra said.

Andy reached over and squeezed her hand.

'They'll be okay, the team are well-trained now, K.'

'I hope so, Andy, I hope so.'

'THEY'RE HERE,' Trevor said calmly, as he saw Andy's warning and then heard the door being smashed open. 'Six men, four from the front and two to the rear. Amir, can you handle the rear?'

'I can try,' the younger twin answered, slipping on his mask and sliding away silently.

They were both hiding behind the boxing ring in the centre of the large gym, which they had reinforced with wooden boxes filled with weights and other dense, heavy equipment, giving good protection from any gunfire.

'You ready, Mo?' Trevor asked.

'Always,' Mo replied, as they both pulled their masks on.

Trevor readied a CS gas canister as he watched for the attackers. He heard a commotion as the armed men came into view, two of them sliding on the oil and tumbling over as the others held back cautiously. Trevor pulled the pin and threw the can, aiming for the gap between the four men.

Before it had even started to release its noxious contents, the two men that had slipped on the oil pointed their guns towards the direction that the canister had come from and opened fire from the kneeling position they had assumed within seconds of falling. Their training was clear to see; they were dangerous professionals.

Trevor and Mo ducked, bullets ricocheting around them but missing, thanks to the protection of the boxes. Trevor peered over for a look and saw the gas was now having an effect, the two men that had been firing now retreating quickly, slipping and falling again in the oil, blinded and choking. They avoided rubbing their eyes and retreated out of sight blindly, listening to their colleagues' voices and heading for them.

'Shit!' Mo suddenly said, grimacing in pain.

'Are you okay?' Trevor asked, as he looked over and realised something was wrong. Mo was holding his left forearm.

'I've been shot, Trev, so I'm gonna say no,' Mo replied. He lifted his right hand for Trevor to see that there was a hole in the tunic he was wearing, and blood flowing freely from it. Mo needed medical attention urgently.

'Keep the pressure on it, Mo, we need to get you to the doc so he can sew you up. Turn your arm around, let me see.'

Mo did as he was told and Trevor breathed a sigh of relief when he saw that the bullet had gone straight through.

'You'll be okay, but you have to keep a tight hold so you don't lose too much blood, okay?'

'I'll be fine,' Mo said, reaching for a roll of duct tape. 'Here, wrap me up, I can still move it, so it missed the bone, this will help with the bleeding.'

Trevor glanced towards the attackers before taking his gloves off and wrapping a good length of duct tape over the wound.

'Is that tight?' he asked.

'Yep, that'll do it. Now, pay attention to those bastards, Trev, I don't wanna get shot again!'

Trevor nodded and put his gloves on, ready for whatever was going to come next.

Ivan Abramovich had quickly assessed and appraised the situation with the CS gas and pulled up the cloth mask from around his neck to protect his mouth and nose. With his eyes closed, he put on the tactical glasses used in firearms training, which gave some protection. It wasn't perfect but it was better than nothing.

'Masks and glasses on, now!' he shouted.

His men, all ex-special forces soldiers from various armies around the world, followed his orders. The two that had already been affected poured water in their eyes in an attempt to clear them and so stayed back while Abramovich and his other man edged forward. Having noted the oil on the floor, he slid his feet carefully forward, peering around the wall to gauge the situation. The room was in darkness, and he couldn't see Trevor, who he correctly assumed was responsible for the gas. He waited for his two men to gain entry at the rear and so bided his time.

'I'm coming for you, Mister Giddings.'

AMIR HID behind another barricade they had put up to cover the rear door, with boxes stacked up and filled with equally dense materials as those in the front, which would hopefully stop bullets getting through. He had slightly different plans for the two men that were about to smash through the back door, and the oil on the floor was going to help. As the door was shattered by a hefty kick, the two men ran through... straight onto the oil. Amir, Mo and Trevor had bound their shoes with cloth, so as soon as the attackers slipped and fell to the ground, Amir moved in with his own unique response, his feet steady despite the oil, a dumbbell in each hand, which he quickly used to crack the heads of the gunmen. Both men collapsed to the ground in agony. Amir threw the dumbbells away and reached for the portable sprayer, which he then proceeded to spray onto the heads of the groggy gunmen, who tried and failed to get up. They spluttered and tried shuffling away from the danger.

Blinded by the glue-and-red-paint mix, they were badly disoriented as well as in agony, and tried in vain to remove the unusual concoction, clawing at their faces with their gloved hands. Amir, having quickly emptied the one-litre spray gun, took out the small stun guns; having seen that both men wore protective vests he knew that the tasers would be ineffective. He quickly stunned the first man by applying the device to his neck, giving him a nasty, powerful shock, before doing the same to his colleague. It was over in seconds, with the only sound being the door smashing open. Amir quickly zip-tied both men at the wrists and ankles, doubling up on the wrists to make it almost impossible for them to escape.

'Better go and help the oldies,' he said to himself, moving towards the main gym.

DARREN, Jimmy and Izzy reached the door to the club as the firing started. Darren quickly put his arm up to hold his men back while he assessed the situation. He could see along the corridor that two men were now scrambling backwards, affected by CS gas, and two others, one being the leader, were moving cautiously forward. As he watched, he heard a crashing sound from the rear of the building and realised that the back door had been caved in. This seemed to be the signal the leader had been waiting for, as he beckoned his remaining man forward and they ran into the main gym, firing towards the ring as they attacked.

Darren, seeing this happen, ran inside towards the two remaining attackers who were pouring water from their canteens into their eyes to clear the CS gas. The two men were completely unaware of the three men heading their way and before they could respond they were being stunned into unconsciousness and zip-tied like hogs. Darren took out some duct tape and sealed their mouths shut so they wouldn't shout any warnings when they came to.

Having secured the first two, he moved forward, Jimmy and Izzy close behind. The gunfire had been brief, and they couldn't see much ahead in the darkness. The trio put on their night-vision goggles and immediately saw what was transpiring ahead of them.

'I don't believe it,' said Darren.

TREVOR AND MO, having had the advantage of wearing the night-vision goggles, had been able to see Abramovich and his man attempt to storm them and force them out of their hiding place by firing wildly towards them. He could see they were well-protected with vests and tactical gear, confirming that tasers would not work on this occasion. This created a problem for Trevor as he realised quickly that the only way to deal with these men now would be to get close, meaning there would be a very high risk of further danger to himself and the twins.

'How are you doing, Mo?' he asked.

'I'm fine,' he replied. 'I can't use my left arm much, but the right is still good. How's it looking there?'

'I can see two men, one of them is that bastard Ivan, I'm sure. They're wearing protective vests and other tactical gear similar to ours, so the tasers won't work. We have to figure out another way of disabling them before the other two recover from the gas.'

'Got any ideas how?' asked Mo.

'Not really, but I'm sure...'

Before he could finish his sentence, Trevor saw two large medicine balls fly over from the rear of the gym and strike both attackers, flooring one of them and bringing Abramovich to his knees. The Russian aimed his gun towards the direction they had come from, but before he had a chance to fire, a five-kilogram dumbbell hit him square in the head, knocking him down.

'Don't just stand there watching, get down there and secure the bastard,' Amir shouted.

Trevor rushed forward, a baton in one hand and the stun gun in the other. Abramovich's colleague was starting to get up, so Trevor quickly smacked him over the head with the polypropylene police baton and then stunned him to unconsciousness with the stun gun. He was suddenly aware of someone rushing towards him from the front entrance and stepped back, ready for Abramovich's remaining men to attack, thinking that he was in big trouble.

Darren was first on scene and quickly stunned Abramovich, who was groggy and starting to come to. The effects were immediate, and he fell back to the ground, unconscious.

'You know what to do, boys,' Darren told Izzy and Jimmy, who proceeded to zip-tie and secure the two men.

'I'm very happy to see you guys, but where the hell did you come from?' Trevor said, taking his mask off.

'We thought you might need some help, and it turns out that you did. You may need to rethink how you do stuff sometimes, Trevor, you're not a young man anymore,' Darren said.

'Hey, less of the old, I can still kick your arse!' Trevor laughed.

'That may be, but first you'll need to sort your daughter out, because the way she is at the moment she can kick all our arses,' Darren said.

'Shit, is she here?' Trevor asked, looking around.

'She's outside with Andy. Are the other two secure at the back?'

'Of course they are,' Amir replied, his mask now off, 'isn't anyone going to mention how cool I was, knocking these two down? My aim was spot on,' he added.

'That was impressive, Amir, thank you,' Trevor said.

'Did you see it, bro? Hey, wait a minute, what happened to you?' Amir asked, having noticed his brother holding his left arm protectively.

'Just a ricochet, went straight through. I just need a clean and some stitches, that's all,' Mo said, his face pale from the pain.

'You're a crap liar, you know that? Trev, he needs to go to the doc,' Amir said.

'Agreed, take him to Andy and Kendra and go with them,' Trevor said.

'Come on, old boy,' Amir said to his brother, 'let's get you sorted out,' he added, putting his arm around Mo's waist and leading him gently towards the door.

'What are we gonna do with this lot?' Darren asked.

'If we involve the police, things could get very messy here, we'd have a lot of explaining to do. This is a crime scene, and they'll want to go over it with a fine-toothed comb. I think we'll have to swallow our pride and send these gentlemen somewhere where they can't do any more damage,' Trevor replied.

'Like where?' Darren asked.

'It's time to use the container again.'

20

DOCTOR TO THE RESCUE

'He's lucky I didn't go in there myself,' Kendra said as they drove away from the scene.

'Don't worry about it, K, it's probably best you deal with it when you're not so angry, don't you think?' Andy said.

'Whatever,' she muttered.

'Anyway, we have other priorities at the moment, let's get poor Mo to the doc and we can sort the rest out later,' he said, referring to the doctor the team had used in the past to avoid hospitals and therefore questions by police.

'I know, you don't need to remind me,' she said, still angry.

'How are you doing back there, gents?' Andy shouted.

'Well, he hasn't wet himself yet, so I think we're good, for now,' Amir replied.

'Seriously? No sympathy at all?' Mo said.

'Nope. I bet you'll be telling everyone what a hero you are, getting shot like that. You're such a drama queen.'

'Idiot.'

Andy looked over at Kendra and saw she was smiling at the exchange, her anger fading.

'Kendra, go easy on your dad. Remember, this is incredibly personal and painful for him, and he did it to protect you, no other reason.'

'I know that, Andy, I'm just frustrated that he doesn't even think to discuss it with me first,' she said.

'And what would you have done if he had?'

Kendra paused.

'I hate it when you're such a smart arse. You know, you're not always right,' she said.

'I beg to differ, but...'

'Don't go there, Andy, you've won this one, just don't rub it in.' She narrowed her eyes in mock anger.

'Okay, I'm done,' he said, raising one arm off the wheel in surrender.

'Good, now let's get Mo sorted out, shall we?'

THE SIX ATTACKERS were checked to ensure they were secure, and all belongings extracted from their pockets and their tactical gear removed. All electronic gear was switched off and placed in Faraday bags to avoid detection, once all the phones were accessed with facial recognition and then programmed for easy access later. Andy insisted on this with all such incidents; the data that was retrieved from phones was invaluable.

Three men were bundled into the rear of each SUV, which were then driven to the factory, with Darren following while Trevor and Jimmy stayed behind to clear up the mess at the club.

It took thirty minutes for the convoy to get to the factory, where the attackers, now awake, were taken to cubicles and handcuffed to posts before the zip ties were cut, whereby they were subsequently warned of the consequences of attempting escape or talking to their colleagues. Abramovich laughed and reached out threateningly, which led to Darren tasering him for five seconds with thirty-thousand volts. It was enough to bring him to his knees again.

He shook his head to clear it, looking up at Darren.

'I will kill you for that,' he said.

'Wow, that's a big old vein popping in your forehead there, mate. Are you angry?' Darren said.

'I will rip your throat out and feed your body to the dogs,' Abramovich continued. 'When we are bailed, which we will be very soon, I will come after you all.'

'You can go ahead and try, but you'll find it very difficult to do anything, where you're going. And what makes you think you'll be bailed? The police won't be doing anything, me ol' mucker,' Darren replied, locking the door behind him.

Abramovich was initially confused before it dawned on him that even in the progressive, law-abiding United Kingdom, there were people who worked outside of the law to get things done.

He slumped back and leaned against the wall of his prison, knowing that what was ahead was likely much worse.

THE CONTAINER, now fully stocked for a seventeen-day journey by sea, was picked up by Trevor's associate from Tilbury docks, Bruno, who had facilitated several similar journeys in the past for the team. His connections in the most dangerous and remote locations made him perfect for the illegal transport and he was paid very well for his effort.

It would be a deeply uncomfortable journey for the six gunmen. In addition to the minimal provisions they had, and the basic facilities provided for waste—namely plastic carrier bags and empty bottles, Darren had seen fit for the food to be drugged with sleeping pills so that they would remain subdued throughout the trip, making it easy for whoever opened the container to deal with them.

'Where are you sending us?' Abramovich asked, before the doors were locked and the container driven away.

'Oh, I don't want to spoil the surprise, old boy. I'm sure you'll love it there, they speak the same language as you,' Darren teased.

THE DOCTOR CLEANED Mo's injury, treated it, and then stitched up both the entry and exit wounds.

'You're very lucky, young man,' the doctor said, 'you would have been in big trouble had the bullet hit a bone.'

'I wouldn't call being hit by a bullet lucky, doc, but I get your point, thank you,' Mo replied, grimacing as the bandage was tied off.

'He's such a wuss, isn't he, doc? It's barely a scratch, you won't be able to see a scar after a couple of months,' Amir said.

'Don't start, bro, just get me out of here so I can get a pizza. I'm starving,' Mo said.

'If the doc is happy for us to leave then we can, Kendra and Andy are waiting outside,' Amir replied.

'You can go,' the doctor said, 'tell Trevor I'll send my usual invoice.'

'Will do, doc, and thanks again,' Mo said, grabbing a sweet from the jar on the side table as they left.

'I'm surprised you didn't take one,' he said.

'What makes you think I didn't?' Amir said, showing him a pocketful of the same sweets.

'I can't take you anywhere, can I?' Mo said, shaking his head.

AFTER DROPPING Mo and Amir off home, Andy and Kendra returned to the factory where her car was parked.

'Phew. That was a day and a half, wasn't it?' Andy said as he drove.

'It was, for sure,' she replied.

'You seem distant, everything okay? Is it about your dad?' he asked.

'No, sorry, that's rude of me. No, I was thinking about the scammers and what we're doing. Is it enough, do you think?'

'I think so. On top of what we're doing with their house and flats, we'll also be sending the evidence to the police, remember? Once they get hold of them, they'll be doing some serious time, mainly due to the amount of money involved and how many victims they've screwed over. The courts will not take pity on them, that's for sure.'

'Good, I hope they rot in jail for what they've done,' she said. 'I'll speak with Rick about it tomorrow so we make sure to include everything the investigators will need to take it further.'

'Good idea. You can update him on what's been happening this past couple of days, too, which is a lot. It's a shame we couldn't get the police involved with the attackers,' Andy said.

'The problem is, if we did that, they'd identify the venue and my dad, which would lead to more questions and a lot of scrutiny so we couldn't take that chance. Khan and that MP are a different story, that's national news and they both need to pay a very public price for what they've done,' Kendra added.

'Yeah, but won't they both implicate your dad anyway?' Andy said.

'Maybe, but that will be easier to deal with, there won't be any bodies to answer questions about, or anything to do with the boxing clubs being attacked again. Those two are directly implicated in the death of my mum and that's why Dad is rightly involved. He'll know how to deal with them, don't worry,' she replied.

'Fair enough. Looks like your dad is still here,' Andy said as they pulled into the car park at the factory.

'Good, we can have a proper catch-up now, can't we?'

'Want me in there with you?' he asked.

'No; thank you, but I need to deal with this on my own. I'll speak to you tomorrow,' she said.

'Remember, put yourself in his shoes before you go in there angry, okay?'

'I will, and thanks, Andy,' she said, gently putting her hand on his, before leaving the van and walking away.

'She won't listen to a word I said,' he said out loud. 'Good luck, Trevor.'

TREVOR WAS SITTING in the canteen alone when Kendra walked in and sat down opposite.

'I've sent everyone home, I guessed you'd want a chat in private,' he said. 'Fancy a coffee?'

'Please,' she said.

Trevor got up and turned the machine on, inserting a pod of Kendra's favourite coffee and waiting for it to filter through.

'Here you go,' he said, passing her the freshly brewed cup and sitting back down.

'I'm angry with you, Dad; you know that, don't you?'

'I do, and I'm sorry that you're angry. I thought things would be easy to sort out without involving too many people.'

'Don't you see that what you did was incredibly dangerous? Don't you see that it was incredibly insulting to the whole team? We're in this together, whatever the circumstances, so you going off on your own to sort things out goes against everything the team is about. It's very hurtful to me and frustrating to the others,' she said.

'I know that, darling, and I'm sorry. It's just that all this business has brought up a lot of emotions that have been burning through me, and I just didn't want you to see that,' he replied.

'But it was okay for the twins? You were okay to put them in danger but nobody else?'

'I get what you're saying. I wanted to do it by myself but those two are stubborn and wouldn't let me. Would you believe they threatened to tell you if I didn't let them help me?' He laughed.

'That's because they know what I'm like. Consider yourself lucky, old man, but if you ever pull a stunt like that again I will be more than furious. Promise me you'll involve us in anything that comes up, however dangerous, or I'll have to seriously reconsider what we're doing,' she insisted.

Trevor nodded. Seeing the effect on his daughter was tough to take but deep down he knew she was right. His daughter could more than take care of herself and he needed to trust her to do that, whatever the danger.

'I promise, love, and I'm sorry for not entrusting you with my plans. It won't happen again,' he said.

He reached out and took her hand, holding it tightly.

'Those bastards will pay dearly for what they did, Kendra, but we'll do it together... all of us, just like it should be,' he said.

21

TRIADS REVENGE

Rick Watts was already in his office the following morning when Kendra arrived early for work.

'I thought I'd find you here early,' she said. 'You okay for a quick catch-up before things get hectic around here?'

'Good, I've been feeling a little left out recently,' he said, 'so what's been going on?'

'Actually, quite a lot,' she said, 'the explosion at the office block in central London yesterday, that was my dad's old pals the Yardies; the Hackney posse, to be more accurate. Someone, not mentioning any names, told them that their mate Marvin Freeman had been nicked and that three associates-now-turned-witnesses were ganging up against him and were being protected in that office block.'

'What? They blew up a building to get to the witnesses?'

'Yep. None of them were there, it was just a way of damaging Steven Khan's operations, which I'm guessing it did.'

'So, the Yardies have turned to terrorist activities now, have they?' Rick asked.

'They have a lot to lose, Rick. Their legitimate businesses are worth millions now, let alone whatever other skulduggery they're still involved in. If Freeman goes down, they won't be happy, as he's their hero, the man who made them the success they are today. Plus, I wouldn't rule out the chances of Freeman turning against them for a more lenient sentence,' she said.

'That was a hell of a strong message to send, for sure. What's the plan moving forward with them?'

We're sending all the evidence we have on Khan and the MP, Stanwick, to the police and the press, but we have nothing on Freeman other than what Robyn Hunt confirmed, that she witnessed him killing my mum. We can't use that evidence, unfortunately, because that puts me in the shit. Got any thoughts moving forward?' she asked.

'I have, but you may not like it,' Rick said.

'Okay, we can discuss that later. What's going on with the scammers?' she asked.

'I drove to Crossbey's house yesterday to see how the builders are getting on,' he said, a smirk on his face. 'They're in for a nasty surprise when they get back, the place is a bomb site at the moment and the materials have turned up. That extension and out-house is going to be as garish as anything I've ever seen.' He laughed.

'That's great. By the time they come back from Australia it'll be done. What about the evidence against them, both the happy couple and Kim Morgan?'

'Andy's sent everything over that we need. When we're ready it'll be sent to the fraud squad, who'll lap this sort of thing up,' Rick replied.

'What do you reckon they'll get? Fraud conviction sentences were always a mystery to me.'

'Because of the number of vulnerable victims and the amount of money stolen, in the millions, the sentence should be seven to ten years, all being well. The evidence we've gathered is pretty damning to them all,' he said.

'Great, so we're almost ready to go with that, then, right?'

'Yep, we are. Once you give me the go-ahead, I'll arrange for everything to be sent anonymously to the relevant units and the press, just say the word,' Rick said, patting a large pile of folders on his desk.

'Let me speak with Dad and Andy before we go any further, I want to make sure we've taken everything that we can,' Kendra said. 'In the meantime, is there much happening here?'

'There's been a spate of robberies in the south of the borough by a nasty group of college kids who've come in from a neighbouring borough and are targeting other college kids for their phones and lunch money, so I have the team taking statements and grabbing CCTV footage where they can. We're not overloaded, if that's what you're asking,' Rick said.

'No, I was just hoping to go and speak with Jim Adair from the NCA who's about to release Freeman back into the wild. Are you okay with me going?' she asked.

'Sure, if anyone asks, I'll tell them I sent you to liaise with Jim about potential collaborations. Off you go.'

'Thanks, Rick. I'll call you if anything changes,' she said, leaving with her customary wave.

On the way down, she called Jim Adair.

'How's it going, Jim?' she asked, 'what time are you planning on releasing Freeman? I'm asking so that I can be there, if that's okay with you?'

'I'm on my way over there now. I'm about to call his solicitor and let him know, in case he wants to be there, which will buy us a little time,' Jim replied.

'Okay, I'm on my way, but it'll take me a good hour and a half,' she said, looking at her watch.

'Don't worry, I'll schedule the time for, say, ten o'clock? Will you be here by then?'

'Yeah, I should be. I'll call if I'm running late. I really appreciate this, Jim,' she said.

'No problem, Kendra, see you soon.'

I want to see your face when you leave, you murderous bastard, she thought as she drove away from the station.

'Good morning, Sarge,' Jim said to the custody officer, someone he did not recognise. 'Detective Sergeant James Adair from the NCA. I'm here to sort out the bail for Marvin Freeman, I called his brief who said he'd be here for ten o'clock.'

'Okay,' the sergeant said, looking at his watch and making the customary note on the record. He read from the screen for a minute before turning to Jim. 'It says here you're supposed to be charging him this morning?'

'Unfortunately, our witness changed her mind, Sarge, so we need to bail him to come back in a couple of months when we have sufficient evidence. She was key, sadly, so we need to start afresh,' Jim replied.

'Okay, are the CPS aware?' the sergeant asked.

'Not yet, the information has only just come to light late

last night, so I was going to call them this morning. Shouldn't be an issue, should it?'

'You know how funny they get, Detective Sergeant Adair, I'd go and see to that pronto before his solicitor turns up, just in case.'

'No problem, I'll go and do that now,' Jim said, leaving the suite. As he took his phone out to call the CPS officer dealing with the case, it rang. It was Kendra.

'I'm fifteen minutes away, will I be too late? It's five to ten,' she said, her voice slightly raised.

'Don't worry, his solicitor will be here for ten, by the time we've sorted out the paperwork it'll be at least a quarter past. Just wait outside the main entrance and I'll bring them out,' Jim said.

'Okay, thanks, Jim. See you soon.'

Jim made the call to the CPS and was back in the custody suite at precisely ten o'clock to see Freeman's solicitor, Brian Hampton.

'Good timing, Detective Sergeant, I've just sent the gaoler to bring Mister Freeman,' the custody sergeant said.

'Thanks, Sarge. Morning, Mister Hampton,' Jim said.

'And to you, Detective Sergeant Adair. I take it you've come to your senses?' Hampton asked smugly.

'I don't know about that quite yet, sir. We still have other enquiries we can make that may provide the evidence we need to charge Mister Freeman. Watch this space,' he said.

Hampton laughed.

'Come on, you're just fishing now, aren't you? Haven't you harassed my client enough?'

'Actually, no, I haven't,' Jim replied glibly, 'and talk of the devil, here he comes,' he added as the gaoler escorted Freeman to the bench.

'About bloody time, too,' Freeman spat, 'it's bloody freezing in that cell, don't you lot pay your electric bills here?'

'You know how much that costs nowadays, we have to be careful with our spending, don't we?' Jim said, 'but don't worry, you'll be back in your nice, warm, comfortable home soon enough, Mister Freeman.'

'Damn right I will be. What's happened? Decided you were full of bullshit?'

'Sadly, no. We're bailing you to come back in two months while we investigate new evidence that has come to light. We'll be having this dance again soon, don't you worry,' Jim said, grinning at the dishevelled Freeman.

'Let's get on with this, shall we?' the custody sergeant said. 'Mister Freeman, as you've just heard, you'll be bailed to a later date whilst those investigations are carried out. Here are your belongings,' he added, putting the evidence bag on the counter, containing everything that Freeman had had on his person when he had been brought in.

'Get me the hell out of here,' Freeman said, grabbing the bag and ripping it open. He put his belt on and his wallet in his back pocket, before picking up his phone. He was surprised to see that he had eighteen missed calls and almost as many voice and text messages. 'Looks like I was missed,' he said with a grin, unlocking the phone. His expression changed quickly to one of confusion when he saw that most of the calls were from Calvin and Banjo, who hadn't contacted him for some time.

'Is everything okay, Mister Freeman?' Hampton asked.

'Give me a minute,' he said, listening to the first voice message. He looked terrified as he clicked on to the next one. After listening, he went into the text messages, almost in a panic.

'Blimey, Freeman, did your missus leave you for the postman, or something?' Jim said.

'We have to go,' Freeman said, walking away from the counter.

'One minute sir, you need to sign for your possessions before you go, and also for the return date,' the custody sergeant said. 'You can't leave until you sign.'

'Shit,' Freeman said, walking back, 'give me a damned pen.'

'There's no need for bad manners, Mister Freeman, this is a process we cannot rush, however inconvenient it clearly is for you,' the custody sergeant said, handing him a pen and placing the documents in front of him.

Jim glanced at his phone, which had just vibrated.

'I'm outside,' the message from Kendra said.

KENDRA'S EYES were glued to the door, waiting to see Freeman for the first time, waiting to see what emotions would rise to the surface. She had thought about this scenario many times, especially lately, and had visions of losing control, lashing out at him, becoming crazed in her quest for justice, hence the nerves coursing through her as she waited for them to exit.

Her heart pounded as she saw Jim Adair lead the two men out. Freeman, a good foot taller than his grey-suited solicitor, put his mobile phone up to his ear and started talking animatedly as they closed the distance to Kendra. Taking a deep breath, she stepped forward and waited, blocking their path, watching Freeman, who was distracted on his phone.

'What the hell did you do, Calvin? Damn it, how many times have I told you about doing things like this without talking to me first, you damned fool? Yeah, I know you're in charge there now, but don't you ever forget who...'

The trio stopped a couple of yards short of the woman who stood blocking their path, grim-faced and staring intently at Freeman.

'... let me call you back, this place is full of crazy people,' Freeman said, ending the call. 'Who the hell is this woman?'

'I just wanted to see you one time, before you go to hell,' Kendra told him.

'Miss, who are you?' Hampton said, stepping forward.

'Never you mind, like I said, I just wanted to see this piece of shit one time before he gets his just desserts,' Kendra said.

'Listen, miss, whoever you are...' Hampton started to say before Freeman interrupted.

'Seriously, move out of the way, woman, whoever the hell you are. You don't know who you're messing with here, so piss off, okay?'

Kendra smiled and stepped to one side, her eyes not leaving Freeman's. The trio continued along the path, passing Kendra.

'Who the hell do you think that crazy person was?' Freeman asked.

'No idea, Mister Freeman,' Hampton replied.

'I think you'll find out soon enough, old chap,' Jim said. 'I'll be leaving you here, I'm sure you can find your way to your limo. See you in court, Mister Freeman.'

'Go to hell,' Freeman replied. He turned back to see Adair walking towards Kendra, who was glaring. She waved, unsmiling, making sure he knew she was still there, a mystery he couldn't figure out.

'Are you okay?' Jim asked as he reached her.

'Yes, I actually am,' she said, 'I thought it would hit me hard, but seeing him like this has helped. I appreciate it, Jim.'

'I wish I could have charged the bastard; without a witness we don't have a hope in hell of getting him to court. You know that, don't you?' he said.

'I do. It's unfortunate, but we always thought that would be the most likely outcome. Still, we tried. We got under his skin, and I think I planted a seed in his head that will fester for a while. I like that,' she said, smiling at the thought. 'I'm gonna head off back to work, Jim. Thanks again, and I'll see you soon, okay? Apparently, we may be working on other cases with you soon?'

'Yeah, for some reason your boss likes me and recommended the liaison position. Should be fun, shouldn't it?'

'Fun? I think he's had you over, Jim.' She laughed as she walked off. 'It's interesting, but fun? You'll have to find out, won't you?'

Brian Hampton drove Freeman to his country home after leaving the police station.

'To be clear, I have to go back while they investigate other possible evidence against me, but you think it's bullshit, right?' he asked his solicitor.

'I do. The likelihood of evidence being viable after thirty-odd years is very remote. The only thing that could've caused you a problem was a witness to the crime. If that happens, then maybe they'll re-open the case, but even that is slim pickings for them, we'd tear them to shreds in court,' Hampton replied confidently.

'That's good to know. Send me your bill, you've earned it this time,' Freeman said as he stepped out of the car.

As Hampton drove off, Freeman stepped up to the front porch and tried to get in. The door was locked, which was unusual as it was always unlocked when staff were on site. He hammered on the frame.

'Sylvia, let me in, goddammit,' he shouted.

The door suddenly opened slightly, just a couple of inches.

'What the hell are you doing, Sylvia?' he said, pushing the door open.

He did not see his housemaid. Only five masked men, all carrying scaffolding poles, all dressed in black. He looked to one side and there saw the prone form of his housemaid, Sylvia, behind them, her hands and ankles tied, a pillowcase over her head. At least she was alive.

'Well, now, who the hell are you lot?' he asked, readying himself for attack.

The first blow to his leg put him on his knees. He put his arm up for protection as the blows initially rained down on his arms and torso. The first bone to snap was the radius in his left forearm as he tried to ward off the blows. He dropped his arm in agony, instinctively holding it close to his body, and lifted his right arm to protect himself, in vain. The same bone in his right arm soon snapped from the multiple blows. The strikes to his body were just as damaging and he soon struggled to breathe as several ribs were cracked. He tried to stand and give himself a chance of running for cover but realised the first blow to his leg had fractured his femur, and he collapsed to his knees again. Almost the second he landed a crushing blow devastated the exposed knee, sending him forward, face-down, to the ground.

He whimpered and begged for mercy, his voice hoarse and weak.

'P... p... please, I'll give you whatever you want, j... just don't k... kill me.'

'We want your life,' one of the men said, nodding to one of his colleagues.

It was over in seconds, and as he lay on the ground, blood streaming from multiple wounds, he groaned as he almost faded into unconsciousness. The man stepped forward and lifted his mask. The triad gangster, one of the few survivors from a purge that the team had assisted with a few months earlier when they had thwarted the triads' attempt to take over a gang and cause chaos, spat on Freeman and lifted his scaffolding pole one last time, bringing it down with full force onto his skull. The skull caved in, devastated by the vicious blow.

Freeman's eyes flickered one last time as the breath left his body. His last living thought was one of confusion.

Who the hell ...?

RICK CALLED Kendra to his office as soon as she returned.

'How are you feeling?' he asked as she sat down.

'To be honest, a lot better than I thought I would. I had visions of panicking and losing control, but actually, it felt good to stare him down. I'm gutted he got away with it but we'll come up with a plan, I'm sure.'

'Not necessary,' he said, grinning mischievously.

'What do you mean?'

'We don't need a plan, it's already been taken care of,' he replied.

'Rick, stop being so cryptic and tell me, will you?' she demanded.

'You don't have to worry about Freeman anymore. He won't be bothering anyone and he will be taken care of very soon, if he hasn't been already.'

'Just tell me, will you?'

'You know that the Yardies' historic enemies are the triads, right? They hate each other, goes back years. Well, someone, and I'm not mentioning any names... someone sent our old friends, the Ghost Dragons, who we had a hand in destroying, a message,' he said.

'Saying what?' she asked.

'Telling them that the people responsible for the attack and near destruction of their lucrative empire were the Yardies from Hackney, and in particular their real leader Marvin Freeman. The message gave them his address and also stated that he was on his way there from Kidlington,' Rick continued.

'Really? You think they'd go for that?' she asked.

'Wouldn't you? Those triads were almost wiped out, millions lost, all their men nicked bar a handful, they're bloody fuming. They've been searching for answers for months, and all of a sudden, they have some very believable ones. Like I said, it wouldn't surprise me if they haven't already sorted the bastard out.'

'And the Yardies? What about them?' she asked.

'Here, take a look for yourself. I forgot to mention, the message also listed a handful of businesses in Hackney that the Yardies own and the places they hang out. Look at this report that's just been filed in Hackney,' he said, turning his monitor for her to see.

'Multiple arson attacks on taxi businesses and car showrooms' the report said.

'Wow, they don't mess about, do they, these triads?' she said.

'No, they don't, which is why we did such a great job taking them down... or helping to take them down, anyway.'

'So, let me get this straight. Freeman and the Yardies have been taken out in one fell swoop, and not by us? That's kind of genius, Rick, no comebacks to us at all and the bastards all sorted,' she said, nodding appreciatively.

'Well, not quite. We may have destroyed the Yardies' businesses but they're still at large. I contacted an old mate of mine, he a detective sergeant on the surveillance teams, Terry Franklin, and he's putting a docket together on them as a long-term project. They'll be followed and scrutinised carefully, so it'll only be a matter of time before they drop the ball and Terry can take care of the rest.'

'That's kind of perfect, Rick, great job,' she said. 'I knew it was a good idea to bring you on board!'

'That's always good to hear. Now, get out there and do some work, Detective, there's no slouching on my team, remember?'

22

EVIDENCE

The team met at the factory the following day.

'Good to see you're still with us, Mo,' Trevor said, nodding at the twin whose arm was bandaged and in a sling.

'I've been telling everyone that I took a bullet for you, Trev, so I'm here to keep up appearances, you know, show how brave I am and all that.'

'Like I said before, he's a drama queen,' Amir said, to much laughter.

'Regardless,' said Trevor, 'we're all very grateful that you're okay and thank you for your extreme bravery.'

'Thank you, oh glorious leader,' Mo said, taking a bow.

'Moving on,' Trevor said, laughing, 'we thought it was important to have a catch-up today as the last few weeks have been somewhat odd and not what we're used to. Addressing a crime after thirty years wasn't easy, and we tried to do it the legal way and failed. Luckily for us, the criminals' mortal enemies stepped in and dispensed the justice that those bastards deserved, so I can say that Kendra and I can now finally put that episode to bed. So, from us both, from the bottom of our hearts, we thank you.'

'Trev, it's the least we could do,' Amir said, 'we're a team, remember?'

'Yeah, that's a lesson my daughter drove home recently, which I realise is absolutely correct. We're more than just any old team, what we are doing is making a difference. That doesn't mean you don't deserve a huge pat on the back, though, because you most certainly do,' he said.

'Hear, hear,' Kendra said.

'Enough of the emotional stuff, let's move on to the other dastardly villains we've been dealing with. Charmaine, where are we with the shitbag scammers?' Trevor asked.

'I checked Crossbey's house yesterday and the work is coming along well, so they have some exciting developments to come back to. Stav asked to pass on his thanks for the two cars and also for the two SUVs you sent yesterday, he's a happy bunny. Kim Morgan has started contacting potential victims again but has been majorly distracted by Jimmy who is calling regularly and who has taken her out a few times to keep her busy. She's made a couple of half-hearted attempts to call victims during the love fest, but whenever she does, Andy quickly lets us know and Jimmy steps in and does his thing. It's worked so far, but for how long, we don't know,' Charmaine said.

'Honestly, it's the worst job I've ever had to do, guys, please don't keep me doing this, she's a slimy snake and I can't stand her,' Jimmy pleaded.

'Sorry, Jimmy, and thank you for your perseverance with this. We've put the evidence together for both Crossley and Morgan and they're being delivered to the relevant people tomorrow, so it won't be long before she's off the streets,' Kendra said.

'Thanks,' he replied.

'What about their finances? Andy?' Trevor asked, turning to the former detective.

'We have taken almost every penny of Crossbey and his husband's savings. His belongings will be sold as soon as we can, and all the proceeds will be added to the victims' fund as discussed. I have a feeling a lot more will be added when they're arrested as the criminal injuries' compensation scheme will be going after him for his house and any other assets that they can sell to compensate the victims. Kim Morgan is likely to suffer the same fate with her flat in London. The flat in Dubai is a different matter, she hasn't paid it off yet so we're intercepting her emails and negotiating a quick sale at a discount so we can add that to the pot when it's sold,' Andy said.

'So, all that's left for us to do is deal with Steven Khan and Nelson Stanwick, the MP. We're close to finishing their evidence dockets too, and they'll be going to the relevant authorities along with the press. The aim is to destroy Khan's credibility and along with it his entire business, which will be affected very badly indeed when the press get their teeth into what he's been doing all these years,' Kendra said.

'What's left to do then, Kendra?' Charmaine asked.

'Not a lot, really. I believe you have some decorating to sort out with the new showroom, don't you? Speak to Andy afterwards as he has some funds for you to spend. You too, Amir,' she said, referring to the new building that was almost complete.

'Woo hoo, doughnuts all round!' Amir shouted.

'Not for doughnuts, Amir, but seeing as you have all been

so great, I'll treat you to a nice selection later,' Trevor said, to a round of applause.

The team dispersed, leaving Kendra, Trevor, and Andy alone to discuss the next steps.

'I have to say, Rick certainly didn't mess about, did he?' Trevor said.

'Yeah, that was some move, pitting them all against each other like that. We should do more of that in the future, I think, let them sort each other out!' Andy laughed.

'We'd be out of a job if we did that, Andy,' Kendra said.

'Never, there's too many nasty shits left for us to take down,' Andy said, 'we'll be busy for years.'

'I'm in agreement with Andy here, love. Too many criminals and not enough police,' Trevor added.

'I guess we'd best finish this lot up and crack on with the next one then, eh?' Kendra said.

'Amen to that,' Trevor replied.

A POLICE VAN and an unmarked car were waiting for Crossbey when he and his husband Dilman Hussey arrived back home after their month-long trip to Australia.

'What's this all about?' Crossbey demanded as he stepped out of the cab. 'Aren't things bad enough after that horrid journey home; in economy class, I might add?'

'Mister Andrew Crossbey? My name is Detective Sergeant Shane McManus and I'm here to arrest you for conspiracy to commit fraud by false representation and money laundering under the Proceeds of Crimes Act. You do not have to say anything, but it may harm your defence if you do not mention when questioned something which you later rely on in court. Anything you do say may be given in evidence. Do you understand?'

'What the hell is this all about?' Crossbey spluttered. The journey home was turning into his worst nightmare.

'Your response has been noted, sir,' McManus said. 'Mister Dilman Hussey, you are under arrest for money laundering, whereby you knowingly suspected money laundering was taking place at your place of business. You do not have to say anything, but it may harm your defence if you do not mention when questioned something which you later rely on in court. Anything you do say may be given in evidence. Do you understand?' McManus continued.

'Andrew, what's going on? Do something, will you?' Hussey said, pushing his husband ahead of him.

'Will someone please tell me what the hell is happening? Crossbey asked again. 'Can we at least go into our home? I'm desperate for the toilet.'

'You can drop your luggage off and use the toilet, yes, but then you'll be coming with us to the station in Brentwood where you'll be interviewed,' McManus said. 'If you have a solicitor, I suggest you call them and let them know where you'll be.'

'Dilman, did you do something stupid with the restaurant again?' Crossbey asked as he turned the key and opened their front door.

'No, I bloody well didn't, and I resent that...' was as far as Hussey got when he saw what was inside the house, or rather, what wasn't.

'Where the hell is everything?' Crossbey screamed, 'we've been burgled!'

Dilman shrieked from the next room.

'What is it?' Crossbey asked, rushing to his husband.

'What is it, sir?' McManus asked, bemused. He turned to see what they were staring at, what had horrified them so much.

'Is... is... that mauve? Is it, Dilman? Is it mauve?' Crossbey whimpered.

Dilman slumped to the floor.

'It's mauve, Andrew. Mauve steel and fake grey brickwork. It's a monstrosity, it looks like a pub from the nineteen-seventies,' Hussey said.

'What the hell happened here? This isn't what we ordered; how could this have happened?' Crossbey said.

'Oh god, look at the stable!' Dilman shouted, pointing to the monstrosity in their garden. 'What have they done?'

Crossbey walked to the window, the missing contents of his home completely forgotten, and looked at the green-and-orange building they had commissioned and paid for. It was supposed to be in line with the seventeenth-century manor house, to complement the aesthetics and incorporate the design elements of that century. Instead, the stable block looked like a square, brutalist block with no windows, no aesthetic design, nothing remotely like their manor house, which was a listed building.

'What have they done?' Crossbey whispered in disbelief. When it dawned on him that he had paid for the work to be done, an extortionate amount due to the delicate nature of seventeenth-century design, he slumped to the floor in total shock.

'Andrew? Andrew? Andrew!'

His husband's voice faded as he fell sideways into unconsciousness, overwhelmed.

Some days later, Crossbey was charged with conspiracy to commit fraud by false representation under the Fraud Act of

2006 along with conspiracy to conceal or transfer criminal property, the victims' money from the scam, namely money laundering. Dilman Hussey was charged with aiding and abetting his husband, conspiracy to conceal or transfer criminal property, whereby he had knowingly laundered money through his business when he had known where it had come from.

There was worse to come. Much worse.

KIM MORGAN TURNED up at work as usual, determined to get back on track with the calls she had been lax with recently. She smiled at the memory of she and Jimmy spending another pleasant dinner together at her favourite Thai restaurant, a smile which turned to a grimace, of sorts, when she remembered that he had once more put off coming into her bedroom again and finally becoming intimate.

What is wrong with that man? she thought, *is he just shy? Or is it not working properly?*

As she walked into reception, she saw two strangers waiting: a man and a woman, both wearing dark suits, and both officious-looking. She then noticed the two uniformed police officers standing to one side, watching her carefully. One of them was carrying a holdall.

'Kim Morgan?' the woman asked.

'Yes, who's asking?' she replied.

The woman showed Kim her police warrant card.

'My name is Detective Sergeant Monroe, and this is my colleague, Detective Constable Frank Espinosa. We're here to arrest you for conspiracy to commit fraud by false representation and conspiracy to conceal or transfer criminal property, namely the funds illegally appropriated from dozens of scammed victims. You do not have to say anything, but it may harm your defence if you do not mention when questioned something which you later rely on in court. Anything you do say may be given in evidence. Do you understand?'

'W... w... what? What's happened?' Kim asked, dropping her Gucci bag to the floor, stunned.

'Is that your reply to caution, Miss Morgan?' Monroe asked.

'Yes... I mean no, I mean, I don't know what to do,' Kim spluttered.

'Don't worry about that, we'll explain it all to you down at the station. In the meantime, please turn around while my colleague handcuffs you. I'm going to search you, so do you have anything sharp or anything illegal on your person or in your handbag?'

'N... n... no.'

'That's good,' Monroe said, patting her down. Content that Kim was telling the truth, she then checked her handbag and removed the two mobile phones. 'What's the code to unlock these?'

'W... what? Oh, five-five, six-six, seven-seven, on b... b... both.'

'Thank you. Show us to your office, we need to conduct a search there also,' Monroe continued, passing the phones to one of the officers. 'Make a note of the PIN numbers, please.'

Monroe and the officers conducted the search of Kim Morgan's office, while she watched in tears from a chair, taking away her laptops and external hard drives, all of which went into evidence bags from the holdall that one of the officers had been carrying. Thirty minutes later they escorted her down to the waiting van, where she was taken to Limehouse police station custody suite and processed. She remained in a confused daze for several hours until her solicitor arrived, and she was taken for interview.

As with Crossbey and Hussey, there was a lot worse to come for Kim Morgan.

THE POLICE WERE WAITING for Steven Khan when he arrived at his office. His staff watched as he was arrested for various offences, including conspiracy to commit murder—by assisting Marvin Freeman with the murder of Amy March, corruption under the Bribery Act—whereby evidence revealed that Khan had paid off a number of prominent officials; conspiracy to conceal or transfer criminal property—namely money laundering and the use of Yardie resources to fund his burgeoning empire; offences against the person—namely threats to kill Trevor—and a significant breach of the Official Secrets Act,whereby he passed on top secret information to the Yardies while employed by MI5.

When he was removed from his partially repaired office block, the press were waiting in their droves, much to Khan's shock. The news over the next few days would show one particular image of Khan being dragged away by the police in handcuffs, with an expression of rage, his eyes bulging, droplets of saliva running from his mouth, like a crazed madman wanting to attack the people in front of him. The press went to great lengths to replicate the exact words he screamed when that image was taken:

'Don't you know who I am? I'll kill you all for this!'

Nelson Stanwick MP considered himself a lucky man compared to Steven Khan, what with the frightening images and news published about him. As a result of Trevor's evidence, Stanwick had resigned as a member of parliament with immediate effect. He was arrested for suspicion of misuse of public funds and suspicion of conspiracy to commit fraud, as a result of funds gained from the proceeds of crime, but the charges were difficult to prove. His now disgraced father was responsible for the more serious offences, suggesting that despite Nelson knowing exactly where the money had come from, it was not possible to prove it. Additionally, his willingness to give evidence against Steven Khan worked in his favour and so his case was dealt with quietly, with no prison sentence and no public knowledge of the full circumstances.

When it became transparent that he was no longer in office, the official comment was that Nelson Stanwick was temporarily unfit to hold public office and had resigned as a result. No more information was given, implying that he had suffered an illness or a breakdown, and he was soon forgotten. Whatever funds were left in the account that his father had set up were seized and added to the government coffers. He neither appealed this, nor did he complain in any way.

He was a very lucky man.

EPILOGUE

Odessa, Ukraine

The container was lowered onto the dock from the ship and dragged to one side by the crane operator.

'Okay, let's open her up. Remember, we're expecting people inside, so be cautious, everyone,' the captain ordered in Ukrainian.

One of the dozen soldiers sent to deal with the mysterious container moved forward and cut the padlock with a set of heavy bolt-croppers. He then pulled one of the doors open, stepping back immediately and covering his nose from the stench within.

'Koval, get the other door!' the captain barked.

With both doors open, the captain could see the miserable figures inside, all six slumped against the sides of the container, covering their eyes from the blinding light.

'Kovalenko, they're secured with chains to the container, go with Koval and cut them free,' the captain said.

The six men were freed and brought out onto the dock, still affected by the blinding light they hadn't seen for weeks.

'So, six more mercenary mouths to feed, eh?' the captain said, shaking his head. 'You will get the very best soup that Ukraine can offer, you filthy animals. Take them away.'

As the men were taken into custody, the captain looked once more at the note that had been attached to the container for the attention of the Ukraine military.

'These men are mercenaries sent to infiltrate your country. Their leader is a Russian ex-special forces operative, be cautious of that one in particular. Slava Ukraini!'

'Don't worry, my friend, I will take very good care of that one myself,' the captain muttered as he followed his squad.

Southwark Crown Court, London – Andrew Crossbey and Dilman Hussey

Andrew Crossbey was found guilty of conspiracy to commit fraud by false representation and conspiracy to conceal/transfer criminal property, for which he was sentenced to nine years' imprisonment. His husband, Dilman Hussey, was found also guilty and sentenced to three years. Their house, valued at two million pounds, was seized by the courts to be sold. The builders had had to destroy and rebuild the extension and stable block at his home as a result of the local council taking umbrage at the monstrosities. After all bills and fines were paid, the remaining funds were seized by the criminal injuries compensation scheme to compensate many of the victims. That and the additional funds in the victims' fund set up by the team and handled anonymously by a third-party legal firm went a great deal to reimbursing the victims.

'He won't be doing that again in a hurry,' Trevor said when the sentence was announced.

Southwark Crown Court, London – Kim Morgan

Kim Morgan was tried at the same court but on a different date. She was found guilty of similar offences to Crossbey and imprisoned for seven years, reduced to five because of the evidence she had given against him.

Adam, her son, was taken into care by social services and given into the custody of his father, who had provided more than enough evidence to suggest that Kim Morgan had made significant attempts to unjustly keep Adam from him. He was easily able to prove that he could care for his son and was given custody whilst Adam's mother was on remand waiting for the court case. The documentation giving full custody came soon afterwards.

Whilst waiting for the court case, her solicitor visited and confirmed that her flat in London was seized and would be sold to go towards the criminal injuries compensation scheme fund.

'By the way, I had someone contact me anonymously,' the solicitor said, 'and they mentioned something about a flat in Dubai that's just been sold at twenty percent less than you paid for it. It didn't make much sense, to be honest. Know anything about that?'

Kim slumped back in her chair and looked up at the ceiling, knowing that she had now lost everything, including the one thing she had hoped would be waiting for her when she was released.

'Just my hopes and dreams going up in flames, that's all,' she whispered.

Central Criminal Court, ***London***

At the Old Bailey, Steven Khan's case made the news all over the world, with multinational companies, global agencies, celebrities and even foreign governments all distancing themselves from the man who had been portrayed as a wealthy, powerful and influential businessman.

The case went on for more than a month and exposed Khan's operations in every possible and available detail. He was found guilty of numerous offences, including conspiracy to commit murder; fraud; offences against the persons—namely threats to kill, offences under the Bribery Act that covered a multitude of corruption-related offences and exposed dozens of high-profile officials; and also a significant breach of the Official Secrets Act, whereby he passed top secret information to the Yardies when employed by MI5 as a trusted government agent.

He was eventually sentenced to life imprisonment and all assets were seized under the Proceeds of Crime Act when it was verified that his entire multi-billion-pound empire was based on the resources funded by an international drug- and arms-smuggling gang. The scandal sent shockwaves across the world as other influential businesses and individuals were named by witnesses as having benefitted in similar fashion.

Such was the scandal that a movie was made based on

the actions of Steven Khan, with a provision made that he was never to benefit from it, and that any funds that would ordinarily have been paid to him would instead be added to the criminal injuries compensation fund.

Khan's empire collapsed within weeks, with partners and clients deserting it in droves, with the government eventually taking control and handing the company and its assets over to administrators.

Romford, Essex

'Kendra! Hello, darling, so lovely to see you again,' Martha Giddings exclaimed when she opened her door.

Kendra stepped forward and gave her a hug.

'Hello, Nana, how have you been?'

'We've been good, my love. Come in, come in, I'll make you some dinner,' Martha insisted.

'I have a little surprise for you, Nana, I hope it's alright?' Kendra said.

'You know how much I love surprises, darling. What is it?' Martha clapped her hands together.

Kendra looked to the left and nodded. Trevor stepped into Martha's view, holding a huge bunch of flowers.

'He spent half an hour picking those, Nana, I've never seen him so nervous.'

Martha put her hands to her mouth in surprise, before beckoning her son to come forward.

'Trevor, my darling, come here, son,' she said, her eyes moist and ready to gush.

'Hello, Mum,' Trevor said, his eyes in a similar state.

Kendra was already crying quietly, the emotions as strong as anything she'd ever experienced. Martha and Trevor held onto each other, not wanting to let go, the silence interspersed with the occasional sob, the flowers hanging from his hand that also gripped his mother's back.

'What's going on out here?' Clive said as he walked into the hallway from the lounge.

'Hello, Pops,' Kendra said.

'Are you crying, girl? What's wrong? And who's got my wife in a bear hug, is that your new boyfriend or something?' Clive said, as he approached them.

The hugging pair finally separated, and Clive could see that his wife was hugging their son, and they were both in tears.

'He's come home, Clive, our boy has come home,' Martha whispered.

'Hello, Dad,' Trevor said, wiping away a tear.

Clive lunged forward and grabbed his son in a bear hug, pulling him in tight.

'Let me take those,' Martha said, taking the flowers from Trevor's hand as he hugged his father. Kendra and Martha looked on, holding each other, tearful, as the men sobbed uncontrollably. Finally, Clive stepped back, releasing his son, wiping the tears from his face.

'Welcome home, son.'

THE END

'Born to Kill'

Book 7 of the ***'Summary Justice'*** series
with DC Kendra March.

https://mybook.to/Born-To-Kill

Or read on...

BOOK 7 PREVIEW

As the crowd grew in numbers they also grew in confidence. They surged through the streets of central London, chanting slogans directed at the government's perceived failures, other countries foreign policies, other religions that didn't sit right with their own beliefs, anti-government policies such as gender issues in schools, and just about everything that they demanded be fixed to appease them. They even demanded that certain comedians be beheaded for their jokes that impacted their own moral compasses.

By late afternoon there were tens of thousands of them, from all over the country, from varying communities disaffected by life in general, all wanting to voice their concerns and all angry at a government and a country that they believed was failing them, and for some, insulting them and their beliefs. Unbeknown to anyone, a small, sinister group wormed its way through the crowd, looking for those with prominent voices, looking for those they could agitate into doing more than just shout and scream at the unseen enemy.

This small group had a plan, and this was the perfect place and the perfect time to carry it out.

As dusk came, the agitators started directing and cajoling their new-found friends, pointing at buildings of supposed enemies, at expensive flash cars that were parked close by. At first, they threw the odd tin can or plastic bottle, denting the odd parked car and staining shop windows with fruit juice. The accompanying police escort did nothing, other than keeping them within the metal barriers that had been erected in anticipation of the demonstration. One of the agitators then picked up one of the barriers, disengaging it easily from the others and throwing it at one of the shop windows, cracking the large, expensive pane of glass. This elicited a roar of approval from the crowd that was gaining in conviction and getting angrier by the minute.

The police started to take notice, especially that they were severely outnumbered and not at all expecting any serious violence... or prepared for it. Still, they did nothing, electing to wait in the hope that it was a one-off, that it was, indeed, a peaceful demonstration as so vehemently claimed by the organisers. They were wrong... very badly wrong. Within just a couple of minutes the crowd surged to the sides and started taking the barriers apart, throwing them at shops, at the defenceless police escort and at parked vehicles. Within ten minutes cars were on fire and the area was now deemed an exclusion zone, with riot police called in to deal with the escalating violence.

Thirteen police officers were badly hurt before the riot police and dog handlers arrived. Mounted police joined them soon after, charging at the crowd to disperse them, whilst expertly and simultaneously guiding them to the smaller side streets where they could more easily be contained and where units from the riot squads were waiting. The violence lasted just forty minutes but lasting damage to property and persons was done, including one department store looted and set on fire... certainly enough violence to feature on news channels both domestic and foreign. Seventeen demonstrators were arrested, including several that had been influenced by the agitators.

That small, sinister group of agitators that had played such a significant part in the violence split up when it started, got rid of clothing that could identify them very quickly, and made their separate ways back to East London where they laughed and congratulated each other when they watched their efforts on the news. It had been so very easy.

'Tomorrow, you know what to do. Do it in the open and in front of witnesses, and remember to shout the words you've been practising,' said their enigmatic leader as he nodded gratefully to his subordinates.

Loud cheers followed before he quietened them with his hand gestures.

'After tomorrow, nobody will think of crossing us again... ever.'

Chapter 1

'I have to say, they've done a grand job,' Andy said, as he looked on admirably at the new building that now stood proudly behind the factory, its newly fabricated panels gleaming in the sun.

The 'factory', which was the name given by the team to their headquarters, had been bought with Albanian gang money and was situated on a large plot of land near Tilbury Docks by the river Thames. The team headquarters housed a legitimate security business, *Sherwood Solutions*, where members of the team, particularly the younger members, learnt their trades and helped build what was becoming a successful business. To that end, the front of the building was professionally laid out for the business, with a reception and staff to greet visitors and guide them to meeting rooms to discuss security solutions and products.

The back end of the factory was a different animal altogether. That was where the reinforced 'rooms' were, or temporary holding cells, for want of a better term, which would house the criminal 'guests' until they were moved elsewhere, sometimes thousands of miles away... or *disposed*, for want of a better word. Like the trash that they were.

There were also rooms to train and to store the modern and effective equipment the team had acquired over the past couple of years, some of it illegal and some of it borderline, to aid their cause.

The cause was simple, dispense justice to criminals who would typically get away with their crimes in the current climate. Where the laws of the land were ineffective or out of date and where the police were effectively handcuffed, hamstrung, and frustrated by their now diluted powers, a legacy of poor government decisions going back decades. The team had done so, effectively, and successfully, ridding the streets of London of some very nasty individuals, with a by-product bonus of 'acquiring' their wealth that would later fund their venture, somewhat illegal by the laws of the land, but hugely effective and satisfying morally... and ironic to boot. There were many occasions where the team laughed at the irony of the criminals funding their own downfalls.

The resulting success and fortune had led to the team building the new structure behind the factory that would house a ground floor state-of-the-art showroom for the modern security equipment and professional security services, including research and development, run by Charmaine, and an equally impressive training centre upstairs that would be run by Amir, who came up with the idea of the one-stop shop.

The building had only taken a few months, thanks mainly to the prefabricated nature of the framework and outer shell, allowing it to be erected in very little time. Then came the internal insulation, fittings and decorating before the equipment was brought in to complete the two-story project. Andy Pike nodded in admiration as the gleaming new construction shone in the bright sunlight.

'It's a good job you're a bit of an expert at stealing money from the criminals, otherwise none of this would be possible,' Trevor said, patting him on the back and referring to Andy's outstanding hacking abilities.

'Yeah, good job, handsome,' Kendra added, winking at him as he blushed.

'Well, now that it's done it'll be interesting to see how Charmaine and Amir get on with it, seeing as you've given them a free rein,' Andy said.

'They'll be fine, and if you recall I asked Mo to oversee the whole thing, just in case,' Trevor smiled.

'Are we gonna give it a name? We can't call them both *the factory*, can we?' Kendra asked.

'How about *the Thunderdome*, like in the Mad Max movie?' Andy asked excitedly.

Trevor and Kendra looked at him quizzically.

'I guess that's a no, then?' he asked meekly.

'You guessed correctly,' Trevor replied.

'Why did we name the factory the way we did?' Kendra mused.

'Because that's where all the work was happening?' Andy replied.

'That's about right, it was an easy one to name. Well, why don't we apply the same logic to name this shiny new building?' she asked.

'Well, there's gonna be some training upstairs and a flash showroom downstairs, it won't be as easy, methinks,' Trevor added, scratching the back of his head.

'The gym? The office?' Andy said out loud, hoping something would stick.

'Yeah, I don't think those work in this case, it's two different scenarios,' Trevor replied.

'Let's just keep it simple then,' Kendra said, 'if we can't go with something that describes the goings-on then we just use something to describe the exterior.'

'The tin can?' Andy laughed.

'The cube,' Kendra said, nodding, 'it pretty much is that shape so why not?'

'Works for me,' Trevor nodded.

'You'll get no argument from me,' Andy replied, 'that's pretty accurate and rolls off the tongue nicely.'

'It's settled then, the cube it is. Let's go and get ready to officially open it to the team and our future guests,' Trevor said.

'I'm excited about that,' Kendra said, 'if you can get some of your old army or navy friends to take an interest, we can get some very nice contracts out of it.'

'I'm sure we can,' Trevor said, 'but let's not lose sight of what we're doing behind the scenes, eh? The legitimate business will allow us to hire a few more people and get a few more youngsters off the street, and that for me is a priority.'

'Amen to that,' Andy said, 'but getting rid of criminals should always remain our main objective.'

'And it will be, don't you worry,' Kendra smiled.

'So, how many people are coming tonight?' Andy asked, referring to the small gathering they'd invited for some canapes and soft drinks.

'With the team I think there'll be around thirty to forty in total, it should be interesting,' Trevor replied.

'We've briefed the team in advance, to make sure they don't say too much to the guests. Other than those who already know, we don't want anyone to know what we do behind the scenes, okay?' Trevor insisted.

'Agreed,' Kendra said. Andy nodded.

'I'll go and get everyone,' Trevor said, walking back to the factory.

'Let's go and be ready to greet them, handsome,' Kendra said, turning and walking towards the cube.

'Such a tease,' Andy muttered, following.

'Welcome, everyone, to Sherwood Solution's new state-of-the-art showroom and training centre,' Trevor said to the group of people gathered in the ground floor showroom. 'As you can see, we have some new equipment already installed but you can be assured there will be much more following in the weeks to come.'

There was a smattering of applause and some whoops, mainly from the team members that had mingled with the guests.

'We're affectionately calling it *the cube*, so if you hear that term from now on you know what it refers to,' Kendra added.

'As you can see, we've laid out some drinks and a nice selection of hors d'oeuvres by the side there, please help yourselves. Take all the time you need to look around, both downstairs and up, and if you have any questions, you can ask myself and Kendra, but also Charmaine or Amir, who will be running the showroom and training centre respectfully,' Trevor said.

The guests made their way to the refreshments as Trevor and Kendra nodded and shook hands to some that walked past them. Kendra could see Andy at the back, standing with detective sergeant Rick Watts, her boss at the Special Crimes Unit where she worked part-time. He was now fully engaged with the team, which enhanced the team's ability to gather intelligence that only police officers had access to.

'Nicely said, dad. You seem to have the knack of public speaking, it suits you,' Kendra teased, putting her arm through her proud father's.

'When you've given as many briefings as I have in the

past, you kinda get used to it,' he replied, referring to his secretive past as an undercover officer in the British Army.

'So, tell me again who you invited,' she asked.

'Well, one of the first person that I contacted was the First Sea Lord and Chief of Naval Staff, Admiral Sir Robert Jenkins, mainly because of his assistance in taking down the Chinese triads last year,' Trevor said.

'He's the one who's life you save about a hundred years ago, wasn't it?' she laughed.

'It wasn't quite a hundred years, daughter, but it was a few decades ago when he was just a regular navy officer posted to Northern Ireland. Anyway, he's here with a couple of other big wigs to see what we're offering as a security company.'

'What do you think they'd be interested in?' she asked.

'I'm hoping we can apply for the contract for the base security, you know, guarding the permitter, CCTV, access control, that sort of thing,' he replied.

'Are we set up to do that?' Kendra asked, recognising that Sherwood Solutions had only been a registered company for a couple of years.

'It won't be easy, but I have a plan to recruit ex-staff who are looking for jobs, and I have a friend who runs a recruitment company along those lines. Unless you have a go, you won't know, will you?' he replied.

'Fair enough. Who else did you invite?'

'Mike Romain, an ex-colleague of mine who joined around the same time as me. He ended up as a Colonel in Army Intelligence, so I worked with him a few times. He's retired now but runs a surveillance company. He recently got a contract to investigate some very large sports organisations for corruption. He'll be looking for surveillance equipment and possibly personnel,' Trevor said, 'and he's here with a couple of other directors from his company.'

'Sounds very promising. Even one of those contracts would be a huge boost,' Kendra replied.

'I'm pretty confident, knowing who to call is a big part of getting things done, isn't it?' Trevor added. 'I'm not counting my chickens just yet, but we have more than enough on offer to interest any company.'

'I agree. Getting the cube built was a great idea and will show people we mean business. I have to say, Charmain and especially Amir showed a different side of themselves, didn't they? The way they've conducted themselves through the build has been fantastic and in Amir's case, surprisingly professional,' Kendra said.

Trevor laughed.

'Yeah, he can be a clown but underneath it all he is a very shrewd young man.'

Well, let's mingle then, dad. You can introduce me to some of these big-wig friends of yours,' she said, grabbing his arm again.

'Five-five-seven are you receiving, over?' the message sounded over the radio.

'Received loud and clear, November Whisky, five-five-seven, over,' replied police constable Ray Khan.

'We've just had a call from the Menorah Jewish school in The Drive, they've had someone call with death threats. Can you deal?'

'All received, November Whisky, show me as dealing. Five-five-seven, over,' Ray replied.

He wasn't surprised to hear those threats had been

made, considering the problems yesterday and in the past where Jewish establishments had been targeted. Knowing the levels of security in place at them gave Ray confidence that providing everyone at the school remained vigilant than the risk was low. It was his job as the local community officer to attend and reassure them as such.

He parked the marked police car in Woodstock Avenue where there was plenty of parking. Exiting the car, he put on his favoured flat cap, locked the car and walked towards the school entrance in The Drive, with his clipboard in his hand.

Ray didn't take any notice of the silver BMW saloon parked just a few cars behind his, nor did he see the two men exit that car and walk towards him with purpose, as he walked to the junction. He did see a woman pushing a pram put her hand to her mouth as she watched him, and wandered what that was about. It was when she screamed that he realised something was wrong and turned to see what had frightened the woman so much.

In Ray's mind it all happened in slow motion. Two men in dark clothing, each brandishing a black handgun, almost upon him. He saw the flashes and heard the awful, astonishingly loud gunshots at the same time as the two bullets hit him... one in the chest and one in the stomach. The last thing he heard was his killers shouting.

'Allahu Akbar! Allahu Akbar! Allahu Akbar!'

He didn't have time to think or to ask the question – 'why?'

His vision went black, and he was dead before he hit the ground, the clipboard still in his hand and his beloved flat cap now lying next to his lifeless body.

The woman with the pram continued to scream, and

she was joined by two other passers-by that had witnessed the brutal assassination in broad daylight.

The killers were back in their car and away at speed before anyone could react. The registration number of the car was noted by one of the witnesses, and although it was found abandoned and on fire later that evening, there would be no incriminating evidence to indicate who was responsible.

The only clue was what the witnesses had heard, the killers shouting 'Allahu Akbar.'

The evening was almost over, and most guests had gone when a tall, middle-aged, grey-haired man approached Trevor and Kendra. He was smartly dressed in a navy-blue suit, crisp white shirt and no tie, and black shoes. Flanked by two slightly younger men, also well-dressed in suits, the man extended his hand which Trevor grasped warmly, before bringing him in for a bear hug.

'I thought you were ignoring me, you old goat,' Trevor grinned, 'you've just turned up for the free grub, haven't you? Not to see your old mate.'

'Well, if you put it like that... maybe it was to check out your flash products and services, eh?' the man replied, before turning to Kendra and taking her hand. 'You must be the delightful daughter he wouldn't stop talking about. My name is Mike... Mike Romain.'

Kendra shook Mike's hand warmly.

'I'm sorry about the stories, it's only recently that I've realised that dad talks a lot more than I ever thought.,' she replied, turning to Trevor and grinning.

'Yeah, well spare a thought for me. I had to listen to him talking non-stop for years,' Mike laughed.

'You worked together in the army?' she asked.

'You could call it that, yes. We were in Army Intelligence together for a few years, mainly in Northern Ireland and a couple of other hot spots. All joking aside, he may have talked a lot, but he was bloody good at his job, we missed him badly when he upped and left,' Mike replied.

'I had to leave, Mike, it was all getting a bit boring, wasn't it? You lot didn't want us to have fun anymore,' Trevor laughed.

'You should have seen just how boring it was when I got promoted, mate. I spent years regretting it and missing that fun that you mentioned,' Mike replied, remembering their adventures from a time long past. 'Where are my manners? These two fine gentlemen are my fellow directors, Brandon Finch and Haydn Brown. Gents, this is my old mucker from the army that I told you about, the slippery one.'

They all laughed and shook hands.

'Thank you for such an inspiring introduction, Mike. Moving on quickly, we're glad that you're here today, we've been excited to get the place open so we can show you what we can do. Seen anything that appeals to you?' Trevor asked.

'Some things, yes,' Brandon replied, 'there was some nice surveillance kit that your geek was showing us earlier, especially the miniature stuff. Where do you source it all?'

'Well, that geek that you mentioned can sniff that stuff out before it's even released. He's very well connected and knowledgeable so it gives us a nice edge over the competition, which as a new company we need,' Kendra said.

'It was impressive,' mike said, I think we can work together on a couple of projects for sure, Trevor. How are you fixed for operatives? We're always looking for talented people who can mingle unnoticed.'

'Without boasting too much, we have a fine young team that can get into any place without attracting any attention. They've honed those skills over the last couple of years and we've had some excellent results. What are you thinking?' Trevor asked, concerned that he may lose some of his team.

'Don't worry, I promise I won't poach your people. I'm thinking more that we can hire your team when we're short, that sort of thing,' Mike replied.

'Or vice versa?'

'Absolutely, scratching each other's back is a no brainer for me, don't you think?' Mike said.

'Let's talk again soon, Mike, it seems we have a few options worthy of a chat, don't you think?' asked Trevor.

'Definitely, Trev. It was great seeing you again buddy,' Mike replied, giving Trevor a parting hug. 'Good to meet you also, Kendra, finally!'

Handshakes were exchanged and mike and his team departed, leaving Trevor and Kendra to look around. There were a handful of the team still loitering, talking in small groups or cleaning up.

'I'd say that was a big success, wouldn't you?' Kendra asked.

'It's not over yet, sweetheart, I have someone waiting to speak with us privately. Sir Robert is waiting for us in the meeting room over at the factory, he wants to discuss a huge business opportunity.'

'It's good to see you again, Trevor. Nice set up you have here,' Sir Robert said, shaking Trevor's hand warmly. 'This is Captain Richard Tremayne and Commander Valerie Upton, who are here on behalf of the Admiralty procurement department. I persuaded them... gently, that it would be a good idea to come and speak with you.'

'That's very kind, thank you, sir. Welcome, to you both,' Trevor said, shaking hands with the others. 'This is my daughter, Kendra, a serving police detective with the Met.'

'It's good to meet you all,' Kendra said, shaking their hands in turn.

'I'm guessing you're here about the perimeter security at bases. Unfortunately, we don't have all the equipment installed yet, but you'll be very pleased with what we'll be able to offer,' Trevor said. 'In terms of staff, that depends on what your requirements are, but I have every confidence that we can fulfil them.'

'Actually, that's not why we're here, Trevor. Yes, there is a contract coming up for the bases, but we're more interested in speaking with you regarding some... how do you say... unofficial arrangements?' the First Sea Lord replied.

'Um, not sure what to say here. What do you mean by unofficial arrangements?' Trevor asked, confused, and caught somewhat by surprise.

'It's a rather delicate matter that we should sit down and discuss in private,' Sir Robert replied. 'Is there somewhere we can sit and talk?'

'We have a canteen area upstairs,' Kendra said, beckoning them towards the stairs.

They made their way to the first floor, after Kendra had spoken briefly with Charmaine to explain they'd be in a private meeting upstairs, and if she could take over downstairs and see everyone off. Trevor made some hot drinks, and they were soon all sat around the table waiting on Sir Robert to explain why he was there.

'About four months ago we heard rumours that someone was stealing weapons from a navy base somewhere in the south and selling them to drug gangs in London. We did some inventory checks and found everything to be in order, nothing missing, and dismissed the rumours out of hand. About a month later we were contacted by a detective from Brixton, in south London, about an SA80 A2 self-loading rifle had been seized during a house search for a multiple murder suspect who had shot and killed two people during a drive-by shooting in the borough. The detective told us that the serial number had been scratched off but recovered by forensics, and it was one of ours. It was the weapon used to kill those people. This led to a second more thorough inventory check which resulted in a somewhat disturbing discovery,' Sir Robert said.

'I'm afraid to ask,' Trevor replied.

'It's actually a lot worse that what you think. When we opened the boxes at Stonehouse Barracks, we found that the new SA80s had somehow been replaced with old stock and the boxes resealed to make it look like nothing was amiss.'

'What? How was that possible?' Trevor asked.

'There's more. It turns out that the old stock was actually weaponry that had been handed in during a firearms amnesty in London recently and had been earmarked for destruction,' Sir Robert replied.

'Wait, you're saying that someone stole weapons from the Met and then stole newer weapons from Three Brigade Commando and replaced them with the old crap without anyone knowing?' Kendra asked.

'That's the sum of it, yes,' Sir Robert replied.

'Do you have any suspects?' Trevor asked.

'Only one, colour sergeant Reg Malone, the armourer at the time we believe the switch was made.'

'Is he in custody?' Kendra asked.

'Nope. He went AWOL and hasn't been seen since.'

'Bloody hell, that's a hell of a scenario, sir,' Trevor said, shaking his head in disbelief.

'How many weapons were taken, Sir Robert?' Kendra asked.

'One hundred SA80s,' he replied.

'Wow, that's a lot of serious weaponry,' she said, 'got any ideas as to whether they are all on the streets now?'

'I don't think so, hence me coming here. We think a handful were sold and the rest are being stored somewhere in London, but we've come up short. Think your team can help us?' Sir Robert asked, smiling at his old friend.

'We can certainly try,' Trevor said, 'as long as you're okay with us using unofficial methods.'

'Oh, don't worry about that, this operation will be entirely off the books, and you'll be paid by a shell company that can't be traced back to us,' Sir Robert said, winking.

'We'll be paid for it too, eh? That's a nice, unexpected result, I guess it was worth sending you that invite,' Trevor laughed.

'Don't think I've forgotten about the upcoming security contract, either. If you can prove that you can do a good job for us, then there's a good chance that can come your way also. Commander Upton will send you the official documentation for that.'

'I'll just need your contact details, sir, and I can get that to you tomorrow, first thing,' Upton said.

'Can we have all the information you have to hand about the guns?' Kendra asked.

'Of course, Captain Tremayne will liaise with you and stay in touch moving forward, I hope that doesn't cause any issues? I don't want him treading on your toes at all.'

'I'm sure we can manage. Here's my card, please send everything and I'll update you regularly as to any progress,' Kendra said, handing Tremayne her Sherwood Solution business card.

'Yes, ma'am, I look forward to working with you,' Tremayne replied.

The visitors left soon after, leaving Trevor and Kendra alone in the now-deserted showroom.

'That took a weird turn, didn't it?' she said.

'It certainly did, a very *interesting* turn too,' Trevor replied.

ACKNOWLEDGMENTS

My ongoing thanks to you, the reader, for continuing on this amazing and fulfilling journey with me. I hope that you are still enjoying these books as much as I am writing them and especially in developing the characters within.

I'd like to thank fellow author and ex-cop Mark Romain for his expert recollection and knowledge relating to murder investigations from the past. I highly recommend his DCI Tyler series, you won't get much more accurate detail than what you'll read in that series!

Linda Nagle has done her usual fabulous work as editor and I must also give huge thanks go to my partner, Alison, for her help with the cover for this book and for her ongoing support.

Finally, a few words for my loved ones without who I would not be able to continue this journey, thank you for the love and support that drives me to put the words down each and every day.

Thank you, to you all.
TH

You can reach me at: theo@theoharris.co.uk

ABOUT THE AUTHOR

Theo Harris is an emerging author of crime action novels. He was born in London, raised in London, and became a cop in London.

Having served as a police officer in the Metropolitan Police service for thirty years, he witnessed and experienced the underbelly of a capital city that you are never supposed to see.

Theo was a specialist officer for twenty-seven of the thirty years and went on to work in departments that dealt with serious crimes of all types. His experience, knowledge and connections within the organisation have helped him with his storytelling, with a style of writing that readers can associate with.

Theo has many stories to tell, starting with the 'Summary Justice' series featuring DC Kendra March, and will follow with many more innovative, interesting, and fast-paced stories for many years to come.

For more information about upcoming books please visit theoharris.co.uk.

Printed in Great Britain
by Amazon

46506040R00165